"Hello, this is Jasmine." Soft Mozart music played in her ear. "Hello?" Jasmine looked at Chloe, hiking her eyebrows and one palm. The music faded. "Listen, I can hear you breathing. Who is this, and what do you want?"

Chloe skewed her head and frowned.

"You." A deep voice replied. "I want all of you, Jasmine. And it's only a matter of time before I'll have you all to myself. Then I'll make you mine—forever."

The seductive tone with a hint of a southern drawl sent tentacles of fear crawling up Jasmine's spine. Her arms fell limp at her sides.

The phone clamored to the floor.

Had RodeoCowboy found her like he said he had? Or was some other nut playing sick tricks on her?

She struggled to draw air into her collapsed lungs. Through a daze of slow motion she watched Chloe pick up the phone.

"Who is this?" her sister demanded. "Hello. Hello." Chloe's voice sounded hollow and distant.

The room rotated and Jasmine swayed with it.

White spots danced in the darkness of her gaze.

Her body thumped against the floor.

And then nothing.

If only she had listened...

Forewarned

From New York Times Bestselling author

Debra Ullrick

ISBN-13: 978-0615976754
ISBN-10: 0615976751

Published by:
Sweet Impressions Publishing – 2nd edition

Front Cover Design: Lynnette Bonner
Cover image ©BigStock-1245609

Library of Congress Cataloging-in-Publication Data is
available upon request.

*Publisher's Note: This is a work of fiction. Names, places,
characters, and incidents either are the product of the author's
imagination or are used fictitiously, and any resemblance to
actual persons, living or dead, events, or locales is entirely
coincidental.*

Printed in the United States of America.

I dedicate this book to You, Father God.

Thank You for loving us enough to warn us when we're about to do something that will harm us or others. May we learn to take heed to those times when You do. Thank You for sending the Holy Spirit to teach us and to guide us into all truth and for the gift of salvation through Your precious Son, Jesus.

I love You, Lord.

A special thanks to my dearest and most treasured friend,
Staci Stallings.

Each moment I have with you is a gift that I value and treasure.

You are one amazing person, my friend.

Thank you for always being there for me, for teaching me the craft of writing, and for your numerous hours of endless editing. But more importantly, thank you for teaching me how to live my life to the fullest by putting God first, by listening to the Holy Spirit's guidance, and by trusting Him to take care of things.

I love you dearly.

Your forever friend,

Deb-a-reb-Deb (*smiling*)

CHAPTER ONE

PEEPING TOM STRIKES AGAIN

For the fifth time in the last two weeks, police received a report about a Peeping Tom in the Steamboat Springs area. Tuesday evening, a frightened local Colorado woman called 911 when she spotted a man wearing a ski mask peeking through her window. The man allegedly broke into her home and forced her out the back door. When her screams aroused the neighbor's dog, the canine jumped the fence and latched onto the Peeping Tom's leg. The victim broke free and ran off. The alleged perpetrator is described as ...

To think that some crazy man was loose in Steamboat Springs made her body quake worse than the ice-cold weather did.

Lord, comfort that poor woman. And please help the police find that weirdo, and soon.

"That's creepy." Jasmine Moore tossed the newspaper article onto a nearby end table but missed. She turned and faced her sister Chloe. "I can't believe you drove all the way out here in this blizzard just to show me that."

"Do you know who that woman was?" Chloe asked, shifting her Louis Vuitton purse from her hand to underneath her arm.

"No. Why?"

"It's Trista Davenport."

"So. Who's Trista Davenport?"

"Trista is one of my regular customers. She bought the Stensons' place."

A sick feeling barreled over Jasmine. The Stensons' place was just a little over a mile from her house.

Chloe unzipped her fur-lined parka and removed her angora scarf. "It's not safe for you out here. Come stay with me until this guy is caught." It wasn't a question. It was an order.

Dear, Lord, not again. "You're joking, right?"

"No, I'm not. You shouldn't be alone out here all by yourself."

"I'll be fine. Besides, I can't come live with you every time something bad happens." In the past, she'd let Chloe talk her into that very thing. But not this time. She might be lonely, and she might be scared, but she didn't want to be dependent on her sisters or anyone else for the rest of her life. She wanted a life in spite of her handicaps, and she was bound and determined to do whatever it took to get one.

"Okay. Then I'm staying with you. I'll go get my things and be right back."

Good grief. Would the woman ever treat her like an adult instead of a child? "Listen, Chlo, I appreciate the offer. But I'll be just fine."

Chloe crossed her arms over her chest. "I'm *not* taking no for an answer."

Jasmine swallowed the anger welling up inside her. Just who did Chloe think she was anyway? Her mother? Even her mother and father didn't treat her like this. How dare Chloe try to bully her again. "You'll just have to." She glanced at the clock on the wall.

Chloe's line of vision followed hers. She swung her scarf around her neck and zipped up her parka. With her hand on the doorknob, she looked back at Jasmine. "I have to go, but this discussion is *not* over." She flipped her hood onto her head and outside she went.

Jasmine raced after her and slung the door open. Flakes of snow and freezing cold rushed inside, but she refused to let them distract her. "Yes, it is," she yelled above the howling wind, but her sister kept right on walking. Jasmine closed the door and swiped the offensive white stuff off her arms and shoulders and hurried to the fireplace where she massaged heat into her hands.

Her focus snagged on the newspaper. She picked it up and turned her back to the fireplace. While rereading the article, the lights in her house flickered.

Jasmine flung the paper aside, grabbed the long-handled lighter off the mantle, and scrambled through her house, lighting every candle and oil lamp she could find in case the electricity went out. Tonight she wanted as much light as possible. Much as she hated to admit it, the article, along with knowing how close the Peeping Tom had been sent her spine into a spasm of a million dancing spiders.

If only Jack were here.

No! She had to stop depending on him. When she moved, there would be no one to depend on but herself, which was exactly what she wanted. Make that needed, so she could prove not only to herself but everyone else that she was more than capable of taking care of herself. As long as she lived here, they, meaning Chloe, Shanell, and Jack wouldn't let her.

God, please help me do whatever it takes to gain my independence back.

The rattling of her living room windows along with the wind howling through the cracks made the hair on the back of her neck and arms rise.

Outside, branches from a large broken tree limb scraped across the glass pane like long fingernails or like someone trying to claw their way in. "Why didn't I move that stupid branch earlier while it was still light outside?" Jazz asked the ceiling. The sound of her own voice helped ease her fear somewhat, but it did nothing to erase the clawing on her windows. Maybe she should go move it now, so she could eradicate the creepiness it sent through her.

She dreaded going outside. Not only because of the bitter cold, but because her mind kept conjuring up the article about the Peeping Tom in her neighborhood.

As she made her way to the door, each scrape of the branch on the glass grated on her skittish nerves.

A vision of an unknown man's face peeking in her window popped into her mind when she leaned over to put on her boots.

The loud ringing of her telephone made Jasmine spring up like a Jack-in-the-Box. She patted her chest, trying to calm its erratic beating.

Another ring.

She hurried to the phone, snatched it up, and pressed it against her ear. "Jack!"

"Nope. It's me. Hi, sis!"

Jasmine pressed her back against the wall. Disappointment visited her like the unwanted blanket of snow covering her yard. Not because it was her sister calling, but because it wasn't Jack. After taking a deep breath to calm herself, she added a perkiness to her voice she didn't feel. "Hey, Shanell. What's up?"

"Not much. I just called to check up on you."

Jasmine sighed inwardly. First Chloe and now Shanell. Since her accident, she couldn't remember when the last time was they called just to say hi and chat.

"What are you doing?"

Oh nothing much—just having a little panic attack over the idea of some Peeping Tom running around the neighborhood. That's all. But she wouldn't dare tell Shanell that. Or Shanell would tell Chloe, and then Chloe would pack her bags and move in with her. Again. She might be lonely, and she might be scared, and she might be desperate, but not desperate enough to have Miss Take-Charge-Chloe move in with her again. "Nothing."

"Is Jack coming over?"

"I doubt it. I haven't talked to him much lately."

"Wow. That's a shocker. You two are practically glued at the hip. I keep waiting for you to announce your engagement."

"What? Are you nuts?" Jasmine shook her head and stared at the ceiling. "Marrying Jack would be like marrying—."

"—I know, I know. Your brother. I just don't get you."

"You should. You know I've never been interested in Jack that way, and that I'd never marry anyone who lives within five hundred miles of a snowflake." The pain in her wrist, toes, and joints reminded her daily of that fact. With each passing winter the pain increased. "Give me warm sunshine and rain any day."

"Hey, speaking of rain... did you know that 'Singin' in the Rain' is playing at church tonight? You want to go with the four of us?"

And be a fifth wheel? No, thank you. Jasmine pulled back the curtain and glanced at the thermometer. "Are you nuts? It's 20 degrees outside and blowing snow like crazy." She let the curtain drop and snatched up her Farmer's Almanac chart. She quickly factored in the twenty degrees, along with the forty-miles per hour winds. That made the wind chill factor about twenty-one below zero. She tossed the chart aside. "Only a snowman would be caught outside on a night like this. And the last time I checked, I wasn't made of snow."

"It was just a thought, Jazz."

"I know. I'm sorry. But you know what the cold does to me and how much I hate it."

"Yeah, but I also know how much you love that silly movie. Especially the part—"

"—where Gene Kelly taps in the rain puddles. I so envy him. All we ever get here is snow, snow, and more snow. Could you see me out there in my Llama fur boots tap dancing in the snow? I'd be on my backside in two seconds flat."

"No. That's more like something *I* would do."

"That's for sure." Jasmine laughed, enjoying the calming reprieve. "Well, I'm hoping I won't have to put up with this weather too much longer." Or with everyone's shielding her and treating her like a fragile child. She didn't need coddling. She just needed to move. Grandma Moore had convinced her of that fact. Since her dad's parents had moved to a warmer climate, Grandma Moore's pain had greatly diminished and her active lifestyle had returned. Someday soon, Jasmine's would too. "I keep praying Granddad will hurry and make up his mind about selling me his cabin."

"What are you going to do if he doesn't?"

"I don't know. As long as I can remember, I've dreamt of living at that place. And when Granddad told me he was thinking about selling me the lake house, I felt like God was answering my prayers about owning it and moving someplace warm. I'm having a hard time getting my greeting card orders finished. So, if he doesn't make up his mind soon, I'll have to find someplace else that's warm year around." The idea of giving up her life-long dream hurt worse than the pain in her body. "Stupid frostbite anyway."

"I feel so bad for you, Jazz."

"There's no need for you to feel bad. I've got a few ideas rolling around in my head. I'll figure out something."

"Don't make any rash decisions. You need to weigh out your options and…"

Jasmine tuned her sister out. She'd heard the same lecture a million times. Didn't the three of them think she had a brain? It was rare for her to make a hasty decision because her analytical mind rationalized things to death.

"Promise me you'll pray before you do anything. And I hate to cut our conversation short again, but Chloe just got here. Before she has a tizzy fit about being late for the show, I'd better go. Ouch! Jazz, Chloe's pinching me."

Normally Jasmine would have laughed at their antics, but she was still upset with Chloe. "Well, I know how Chloe hates being late, so tell Miss Punctual goodbye for me."

"I'll tell her goodbye, but I'm *not* telling her what you called her."

"You? Not tell? That'll be a first, Miss Blabbermouth."

"Meanie. I don't *always* blab."

Jasmine faked a cough.

"Well, not on purpose anyway. Okay, I gotta run. Talk to you later, tater. Love you."

"Love you too." Jasmine disconnected the call, and the fear returned, drifting through the emptiness of her house like a ghost.

The low mourning wail of the wind wasn't helping matters either. Even eyeing the glass etching of a lone wolf howling at the moon on her kitchen cabinet gave her the willies.

"This is ridiculous." She stormed over to her loveseat and flopped down. "I can and will overcome this fear. After all, 'I can do all things through Christ who strengthens me.' And 'God hasn't given me a spirit of fear, but of power and love and a sound mind.'"

Quoting scripture helped, but she still needed to find something to keep her mind off of the spine-chilling noises and loneliness. Speaking of loneliness, she wondered how Miss Schamburg was doing this evening. A quick glance at the clock and she decided to give Filomena a call. She picked up the phone and dialed the older woman's number.

"Hello."

"Hi, Miss Schamburg."

"Jasmine. What a pleasant surprise. It's so nice to hear from you, sweetheart."

"I wanted to call and check up on my favorite lady."

"You'd better not let Katharina hear you say that. She thinks she's your favorite." Her hoot and strong German accent brought a smile to Jasmine's face.

"Well, then I'll just have to rephrase my comment. How is *one* of my favorite ladies doing this evening?" Jasmine asked through a stroke of humor.

"Better now that you called. How are you doing? How's the wrist feeling? Are your joints doing any better? What about your toes? Is the cold bothering them this evening?"

"Thank you for asking, but I didn't call to talk about me. I want to know how *you're* doing."

"That's so sweet of you, sugar. I was just sitting here staring at the four walls, wishing someone would call. I know Katharina's only been gone three days, but I miss her already."

"When will Mrs. Ethelstein be back?"

"I'm not sure. She wants to stay with my niece until she knows Chrissy is well enough to be left on her own. I don't know how long that will be." Sadness drifted through Filomena's voice.

Poor little thing. Jasmine knew how hard this must be for the older woman. Sixteen years ago, when Mrs. Ethelstein's husband passed away, she had moved in with Filomena, and the two women had been inseparable ever since. Having her sister gone for who knew how long had to be hard on Miss Schamburg. Well, Jasmine would do what she could to make the woman's time less lonely. "How is Chrissy feeling?"

"Not too good. The chemotherapy is making her pretty sick. But the good news is the doctors are pretty confident they got all the cancer."

"Oh how wonderful. I'm so glad to hear that."

"I was too. Well, precious, I hate to cut this short, but I'm ready to go take a long, hot bath and go to bed now. Thank you for calling and making this old woman's day."

"The pleasure was all mine. Now don't you forget what I told you earlier. If you need anything, you holler, okay?"

"I will. Thank you, dear. And thanks for the cookies and brownies. I've already had three brownies and two cookies. But don't tell Katharina. She thinks I need to watch my weight. Which I am. I've been watching it grow for years." Again she cackled. "Nite, sweetie."

The line went dead. Jasmine shut off her phone and smiled. Even though the sweet woman never talked but a few minutes each time, it meant a lot to Jasmine to cheer up the former neighbor who had been so dear to her since her childhood.

Jasmine missed those days. Days when she was treated like an equal instead of a cripple. Warm climate would soon change all that.

Until then, she needed something to occupy her time. She refused to sit around feeling sorry for herself.

She could bake more cookies. A task that had become impossible for her until she'd purchased her new KitchenAid electric mixer. Best money she'd ever spent.

Without it, she wouldn't have been able to bake the ten dozen cookies and two huge pans of brownies she'd taken the abused women's shelter earlier this afternoon.

No. Baking cookies was out because, wanting to beat the storm home, she forgot to buy butter and sugar to replace her depleted supply.

An interior decorating magazine caught her eye. No. She'd read it and the others at least ten times each.

Watch TV? No. Nothing good on tonight. She'd already looked at the guide earlier.

Work on her greeting cards? That might work. But she needed to down a pain pill first—something she hated doing.

After taking the prescribed medicine, and allowing time for the pain in her wrist to ease, she went into her art studio and got to work.

Without warning, sharp pain shot through her wrist. Her hand jerked and a line of paint streaked across the almost finished greeting card, ruining it. Several tries later, she had no choice but to put it aside. For now anyway. A few ruined cards wouldn't stop her from doing what she loved and what God had called her to do. She'd get back to them when the pain subsided.

Determined to find something else to pass the monotonous minutes away, her open laptop computer caught her eye. Now was as good time as any to try out that instant message thingy her friend Lori had told her about. Conversing with people from all over the world would at least be something new and different, and new and different were definitely in short supply. And if pain shot through her wrist, nothing would get ruined if her hand jerked.

Jasmine hurried and fixed herself a cup of hot apple cider and placed her drink on the end table before settling herself onto the loveseat and pulling her laptop onto her legs.

Other than checking her website for orders and visiting a couple of Christian chat rooms, Jasmine wasn't quite sure how to go about working the instant chat messenger. She double-clicked on the ICM icon and played around with several tabs until she finally figured out how to use the thing.

Studiously, she chose her preferences.

Single.

Christian.

Male or female-30 to 35.

The first nickname to appear was Seriousman: 33, single with four-year-old, looking for a wife and mother.

Jasmine shook her head and wrinkled her nose. *Um... uh-uh.* She wasn't ready to be a mother. Next, she clicked.

Skibum: good-looking, intelligent, loves to ski.

Oh brother. No way would she consider someone who called himself 'good-looking.' Having been born and raised in Steamboat Springs—ski resort extraordinaire—she'd heard enough dreaded ski stories to last her a life time, thank you very much. She clicked Next again.

Mamasboy.

Next.

Thehunkster: Single. 35, looking for a good time. No serious people even attempt to contact me.

What a loser. But an honest one, she admitted, chuckling.

Next.

This was a lot harder than she thought it would be. But she wasn't about to give up. She clicked several more male and female names.

Never taking her eyes off the computer screen, she reached for her cider. Sweet apples mingled with cinnamon tantalized her taste buds. She took several sips and set her cup down.

Twenty-eight names later, her chances of meeting some new friends online looked pretty slim. Perhaps this wasn't such a good idea after all. None appeared interesting or shared like interests with her, but the thought of giving up didn't sound too appealing either. She poised her fingers above the keypad and decided to give it one more try.

Simonrapport: I enjoy meeting new friends from all

over the world. Clean chat only. Hobbies include: reading, writing poetry, visiting museums, artistic designs, and taking long walks along the beach.

The beach? Sounds like my kind of man. Well, that was if she were looking for a man. Which she wasn't. She clicked the information tab next to his nickname. A screen popped up, revealing more intriguing details about him.

Her cat jumped on the loveseat and wedged her way in between Jasmine and her laptop. "Not now, Bougé." She picked up her Manx and moved her off to the side. After circling several times, Bougé curled on top of the blanket next to Jasmine's thigh.

"Listen to this, baby." She darted a glance at her cat and then the screen." Here's a thirty-year-old Christian guy. He's a computer analyst, and he lives in Anaheim, California."

She again glanced at her feline companion who showed no interest whatsoever in what she was saying. Jasmine turned back to the list. Her interest spiked with each piece of information.

While she never intended to meet with anyone from online in person, the idea of knowing someone from someplace where it didn't snow eight months out of the year appealed to her. Then, as usual, the analytical side of her kicked in. *What if he turns out to be a nice guy? Then what? Why would you even want to befriend someone like that if you never plan on meeting them? Where's the logic in that?*

Well, there might not be any logic in it, but the idea of conversing with someone to help fill the void in her life clinched her decision to continue.

Well, here goes nothing. Or something. She pressed the message tab and typed her message in the box, then re-read her note.

Hello, I read in your information that you are a Christian. So am I. I too enjoy meeting new friends from

all over the world. One of my favorite pastimes is reading.
Especially the classics. I'm also artistic, and I love going
to cultural museums. Let's talk. Message me, Jazzy.

When she raised her hand to click on Send a strange pit settled into her stomach.

Again her annoying analytical voice reared its ugly head. Was the uneasiness due to the fact that she was about to talk to a total stranger online or because she was about to do something different and exciting?

She gnawed at her thumbnail, her own questions tumbling around in her brain.

How many times had she talked herself out of doing something fun and exciting because she might get hurt? Too many to count. And playing it safe had gotten her nothing but boredom and isolation. Both of which bored her even more.

Besides, how could she possibly get hurt by just talking to someone on the Internet? Especially if she never planned to meet them in person?

Pushing all of the annoying thoughts away, she clicked Send.

Jasmine rocked back and forth, waiting to see if he'd respond. With each second that ticked by, she rocked harder and became more anxious. She needed some comfort food.

Chocolate came to mind.

She snatched a Dove chocolate from the candy dish, peeled off the wrapper, and popped it into her mouth. She pressed the square morsel against the roof of her mouth and closed her eyes as the creamy milk chocolate melted and slid down her throat.

Without taking her eyes off the monitor, Jasmine grabbed another piece of chocolate and devoured it. And then another.

Minutes later, the blue bar on the message screen flashed, bringing with it the feeling of a million buzzing hornets swarming around her stomach.

She didn't give it much thought because chocolate did that to her sometimes.

With one click of the touchpad, Simonrapport's message stared back at her.

And a warm hello back at you from the sunny state of California. It's always fascinating meeting fellow believers. By the way, your nickname is intriguing. It gives me a smidgen-of-a-hint about you. I'm looking forward to getting to know you better and to find out if you really are Jazzy. HA HA. How did you come up with that nickname?

Her fingers couldn't fly over the keys fast enough as she typed her reply.

A very dear friend gave me the nickname years ago when he picked me up for my high school prom. He said I looked pretty Jazzy. And the name stuck. So, tell me, how did you come up with your nickname?

With her attention glued to the screen, she tapped out a staccato beat with her fingertips, waiting for his response.

Tap-tap-tap-tap-tap... tap—tap. She jumped at the sound of Jack's familiar shave-and-a-hair-cut knock at her front door.

Drawing in a steadying breath, she hollered. "Be right there."

"Okay." Jack hollered back.

"Sorry, baby, I've gotta get up." Unable to keep the smile from her face, she massaged the back of her cat's head, and moved her off to the side. Bougé shot her an annoyed how-dare-you-bother-me look.

She moved her laptop and slid out from under the blanket before she slipped her feet into her purple fuzzy slippers and hustled to the front door.

Unlatching the dead bolt, passage lock and the heavy-duty security chain that Jack had insisted she needed to be safe living so far away from town, she turned the knob and swung it open. Bitter cold air swirled inside and wrapped its icy fingers around her. "Brrrr." She shivered and rubbed her arms.

Jack grinned. "Bet you didn't expect to see me."

"Jackson Warren! Are you crazy? It's freezing out there. Quick, get in here." She pinched the sleeve of his coat and tugged him inside. His large frame filled her entryway, barely giving her enough room to move.

Another chill shook her body, and she couldn't get the door shut fast enough.

"Does this mean you're glad to see me?" His hazel eyes twinkled with humor.

Jasmine quirked her mouth and planted her gaze on the ceiling. "Why me, Lord?" She sighed like a drama queen and then shot Jack a 'just-kidding' grin. Having missed her best friend something fierce, she fought the urge to grab him and hug him like she did her favorite childhood teddy bear.

Jack returned her smile. "Oh, you know you love me. Besides, what would you do without me?"

He really didn't want her to answer that, did he?

Jack held up his hand as if he'd read her mind. "Don't answer that."

She punched his arm even though she knew he couldn't feel it through his heavy parka. "I thought you were working, like every other night for the past two months. Whatever possessed you to be out in this biting cold?" She allowed a 'you idiot' tone to fill her voice as she squeezed her way around him in the narrow entryway.

"Well, I figured with this being a Friday night and colder than dry ice outside, you might want to play a game." He held up his leather Backgammon case. "And." He reached inside his bulging pocket and pulled out a brown paper bag, raising it to her eye level. "What would a cold night be without hot chocolate and marshmallow crème?"

Jasmine stood on her tiptoes, peeked inside the sack, and sighed with a contented smile. She tilted her head and looked up at him. "How did you know I ran out?"

"I didn't. I just know you."

Sometimes it was downright scary just how well he did know her. Jasmine watched as he scanned her face. His dashing smile lit up his whole countenance. And his straight, sparkling white teeth reminded her of crystallized ice glistening across the snow. She really had missed him lately. And there was no doubt she would miss him when she left town. But leave she must.

"You seem a million miles away. You okay?"

"What? No." She blinked. "Yes. I mean. I'm fine."

"Um huh." He chuckled. "Whatever you say." He hung his hat and coat on the hooks.

"Sorry. I'm kind of distracted tonight."

"No kidding. You weren't busy or anything, were you?" He peered over her into the living room.

She glanced at her open laptop. "Um...not really."

"What's with all the candles and oil lamps? Did your electricity go out?"

"No. The lights flickered earlier and I wanted to be ready in case it did." That wasn't the whole truth, but she didn't want to tell him about the Peeping Tom article and how frightened it had made her. He worried about her way too much the way it was and she didn't want to add to his worry.

Jack situated the game and paper bag on the edge of wooden bench-seat in the entryway and sat next to them, then tugged the strings on his boots. He looked like a little boy with his blond hair sticking out in several places.

How many times had she seen him like that? The battle she constantly struggled with reared its ugly head again. Even though Jack tended to coddle her way too much, every time she thought about moving away from him, her heart pinched a little harder.

Jack stood and looked at her. "How's your wrist?"

"Fine." As if to prove her point, she pivoted it. The pain pill she'd taken earlier would remain her secret. He already worried about her getting addicted to them even though she rarely took one.

"The cold's not aggravating it?" His hiked brow revealed his skepticism.

Nothing got past him. He knew her too well. "It's fine." She hoped her smile reassured him.

"Whatever." He slipped past her. His familiar woodsy cologne, mixed with fresh, crisp mountain air, lingered in his wake. "Tell you what. You go finish what you were doing, and I'll make us some hot chocolate."

"Sounds great. I'll be just a minute."

Jack headed into the kitchen.

On the way to the loveseat, Jasmine snatched up the news article and buried it under a pile of magazines before settling herself and picking up her laptop. The blue bar on the ICM flashed like a neon sign. She glanced over her shoulder at Jack, standing at the center island, removing the beverage and marshmallow crème from the bag. She swiveled her focus and blazed through Simonrapport's message.

After you get to know me better, then you'll see how I got my nickname. By the way, while waiting for your reply, I looked under your personal notes, but you don't have anything listed. You are female, I hope. I'm curious. How old are you? Sorry to ask, but sometimes teenage girls message me pretending to be adults. Eventually they slip, and I find out their age. Now, I ask up front. Yes, I know you could lie to me and tell me anything, but I have this strange peace about you.

She peered over her shoulder again and caught a glimpse of the logo on the back of Jack's jeans as he reached inside the cupboard and pulled out two cups.

As fast as she could, she typed her response so she wouldn't have to explain to Jack why she was chatting with a total stranger.

I pray I never run into the kind of deception that you have. I just downloaded this ICM last night. You're the first person I contacted. The only interaction I've had with people on the net is through my business web site or in Christian chat rooms. As to your experience online, I can only imagine how you must have felt. Well, I can assure you, I am twenty-six years old, and I loathe deception of any kind. Listen, I'm sorry, but I need to run. A friend of mine just came over. Will you be online later? I'd really like to chat with you. BTW I'm definitely a female.

When she placed the arrow on the Send tab, an unnerving feeling fluttered in her spirit. She chose to ignore it and instead she clicked the Send button.

Another quick over-the-shoulder glance. This time Jack was busy placing mugs in the microwave, so she delayed shutting down the computer a moment to see if there'd be a last reply before she had to go.

When the musical note chimed, Jasmine chided herself for not turning down the sound. The thought of Jack hearing the tone increased the jitteriness in her body. Seeing Jack was still busy, she relaxed. Her eyes flew over Simonrapport's reply.

I'm sorry, too. I was looking forward to chatting with you. I'll be online for a few hours. I have some work to finish. So, if you're still up, message me. By the way... where are you from?

The hair on the back of Jasmine's neck stood at attention.

"What are you doing?"

Jasmine sucked in a sharp breath, and her body jerked.

Oh, great. How was she going to explain this one?

CHAPTER TWO

"You scared me half to death, Jack. Don't ever sneak up on me like that again."

"Don't you know how dangerous it can be talking to strangers on the Internet?" The sharpness in his voice and his stony expression infuriated her.

She opened her mouth to retaliate, but the look of concern shadowing his hazel eyes stopped her. It bothered her to see Jack worrying about her yet again. She would love nothing more than to put his mind at ease by telling him that she wouldn't talk to any strangers on the net, but she couldn't. Isolation and loneliness had taken its toll on her until she feared she would go crazy if something didn't change soon. Meeting Simonrapport, although only briefly, had helped.

But Jack wouldn't understand that. So, it'd be best if she just changed the subject. "Did you find everything you need to make our hot chocolate?" She cringed at the sound of her nauseatingly sweet voice. Judging from the look on Jack's face, it didn't bode any better with him either. The man knew his way around her kitchen almost better than she did. Still she hoped her question would distract him.

He crossed his arms over his broad chest and stared hard at her. "Oh no. You're not changing the subject. Not this time."

The timer dinged on the microwave.

"The hot chocolate's ready." She flashed him a sassy smile in hopes of lightening the mood.

"It can wait." Jack leaned over her shoulder and zoned in on her laptop. "Whatever possessed you to start writing to guys online? That's crazy, Jasmine. You're just asking for trouble."

That did it. She'd had enough of being told what she should or should not do. Plopping her laptop down, she lunged off the loveseat and whirled around. "Listen here, Jackson." She pointed her finger at him. "I don't owe you or anyone else an explanation for what I do or don't do. I'm not stupid, so don't treat me like I am." Her eyes followed him as he walked around the loveseat and stood next to her. "And if Chloe or Shanell sent you over here to check up on me then you can just—" She let the sentence dangle between them and glanced at the door.

Jack followed her glance, then looked back at her. "I never meant to make you feel like you had to answer to me for what you do, and I don't think you're stupid. I'm just concerned. That's all. And neither Chloe or Shanell had anything to do with my coming here. I just wanted to spend time with you. I'd been so busy lately, I thought maybe you missed me as much as I missed you." He glanced at her laptop. "But obviously I was wrong." He turned and strode toward the door.

A lump filled Jasmine's throat as she watched him walk away. She could kick herself. She never meant to hurt his feelings.

Jack stopped and looked her square in the eyes. "Be careful, Jazz. There are all kinds of nuts out there. I can't bear the thought of you getting hurt. I lo—" His gaze dropped from hers. "Forget it."

The tenderness in his voice and face were her undoing. She rushed to his side and clutched his arm. "Jack, wait. I shouldn't have lashed out at you like that. I know you meant well." *But don't you see that sometimes you and my sisters make me feel like a helpless, reprimanded child? What happened to the days when we were all equal?*

She moved in front of him and gripped both of his

upper arms. His rock-solid muscles bulged under her fingers. She couldn't count the number of times his strong arms had offered her comfort. Now they just felt hard and distant. "Jack, please look at me."

A moment that seemed to drag forever passed before he slid his hurt-filled eyes toward hers. The black and yellow flannel shirt he wore brought out the brown specks in his hazel eyes.

"I'm sorry, I overreacted. Please forgive me?" Jasmine nibbled on her bottom lip. She'd never been cruel or snapped at Jack before. In fact, except for the one lone fight, they'd been inseparable ever since Jack had rescued her from Gill Hammerstein, the fourth grade bully. She looked up at him, remembering how safe she'd felt in his presence since that day. "I know I have a funny way of showing it, but I've missed you too."

Not knowing what else to say or do, Jasmine stared at the floor. She released her grip on his arms and started flicking her thumbnail against her teeth.

Jack drew her hand away from her mouth. With his other hand, he cupped her chin and tilted it up. Embarrassed by her outburst, she kept her eyes downcast.

"Look, your words stung, but you're right. It isn't any of my business. I shouldn't have read your note. I'm sorry. I didn't mean to be so hotheaded. But when I saw that he'd asked you where you lived, a sick feeling came over me. Especially after hearing on the news a couple of weeks ago about how some psycho met this lady in a chat room and coaxed her into telling him where she lived." He paused, pulling his hand through his hair. "They still haven't found her."

With one look, the apologies dissolved between them. He drew her into a tight embrace and pressed her head against his broad chest. At five-foot-eight inches, she felt small against his six-foot-four inch frame. Jack had a way of comforting her like no other.

"I just don't want you getting hurt," he whispered against her hair.

"I know, Jack, and I appreciate it. You're the best friend any woman could ever have." She stepped out of his arms and with a quick jerk of her head motioned for him to follow her. "C'mon. We don't want to waste good hot chocolate, do we? Besides, I want to show you something that will put your mind at ease."

Leading him into the kitchen, she opened the microwave, removed the hot chocolate, added a huge dollop of marshmallow crème in each cup, and handed one to Jack.

They both took a sip.

When Jack lowered his mug, Jasmine giggled. "A marshmallow crème mustache doesn't become you, Jack-o." She reached over and swiped her thumb across the sticky goo on his upper lip. The feel of Jack's soft, firm lips flushed her insides with a strange kind of warmth. A sensation so foreign to her she didn't know how to process the whole thing.

And if that wasn't bizarre enough, she wondered what it would be like to feel his lips on hers.

His tongue raked over the spot she had just touched, and something about the way he did it caused her lungs to stop moving.

What was happening to her?

Her eyes inched upward until they collided with his.

Jack studied her face, searching, probing, until finally settling near her mouth.

In that second, Lori's limp body lying on the floor flashed through Jasmine's mind. The devastating tragedy that had befallen her friend after she'd crossed the line of friendship over into romance slapped Jasmine back to reality.

Kissing Jack was *not* an option. Ever.

"Excuse me. I have to wash my fingers." Jasmine

darted to the sink and rinsed her hand.

Another gust of howling wind filled the silence.

Broken branches grated against her windows and her spine.

Her attention flew toward the hair-raising sound.

She clutched her hot chocolate tighter, barely avoiding a near spill.

"What was that?" Jack asked.

"Tree branches scraping my window."

Jack set his hot chocolate on the end table, slipped into his boots and coat, and disappeared into the darkness before she had a chance to stop him.

Again, she beat herself up for not taking care of the branch earlier. If she had, then Jack wouldn't be out there in the nasty blizzard — in the dark.

Oh no. Jasmine set her drink next to his, rushed to the window and pulled the curtain back, hoping the light from inside would add to the dim solitary streetlamp.

Seeing his silhouette in her window, the words Peeping Tom flashed through her mind, along with a millisecond of fear, but she refused to entertain either one of them. She'd had enough of that earlier.

The wind danced with Jack's hair as he dragged the branch away from the window and vanished around the corner.

She dropped the curtain and hurried to the door, slinging it open. The wind and snow rushed in as if it were on a vengeful mission to invade her space.

"Brrr." He rubbed his ungloved hands together and stepped inside. "That wind is like ice."

"Tell me about it." Jasmine pushed the door shut and helped Jack shed his coat before hanging it up.

He lowered his tall frame onto the bench and removed his snow-packed boots.

"Thank you, Jack. I don't know what I'd do without you." Like sleet in the wind, her words whipped back at her, stinging her soul with their truth. The thought of being without him terrified her. But then again, so did staying. She had to leave. She just had to. Like Lori, her very sanity depended on it.

Wanting to escape the turmoil going on inside her, she stepped over to the end table and picked up the two purple mugs of hot chocolate.

When she handed Jack his, the memory of wiping the marshmallow crème from his lip and thoughts of kissing him breezed through her thoughts. *Oh no you don't, Jazz. Don't even go there again. Once was weird enough.*

"Come on." She jerked her head once toward the loveseat.

Careful not to spill her drink, she scurried away. She set the mug on the coffee table, gathered Bougé up along with the blanket, and settled her onto the white sofa before sitting down and hoisting the computer onto her lap. She patted the spot beside her.

Jack's muscular legs were now at eye level. And his snug jeans did nothing to hide their strength. The man really did have a nice physique. *Don't even go there, Jazz. Remember Lori's warnings and the price she paid.* Jasmine yanked her attention elsewhere while he set his drink next to hers and lowered his tall frame onto the seat. His broad shoulders took up a large amount of space. He stretched his long legs in front of him and tugged his neatly pressed jeans over his stocking clad feet. She laid her hand on the side of her face and shook her head, grinning.

During the winter Jack always wore thick red socks with white toes. They reminded her of the old-fashioned Christmas movies where those type of stockings hung from fireplace hearths with large-headed nails.

"What did you want to show me?" Jack moved closer to her.

That familiar outdoorsy scent eased its way up her

nostrils again. Only this time, she found the aroma relaxing and surprisingly intoxicating. *Good grief!* She gave her head a mental shake to rid her mind of the disturbing notion, then looked Jack square in the eye. "I know you're concerned about me talking to people on the Internet. But I want to assure you that I will never do what that missing lady did. I'll never give out any personal information. And, I'll *never* tell anyone my real name. I go by the nickname Jazzy." She shot a quick glance Jack's direction.

His eyes dimmed and his brows furrowed.

Before he could say anything, Jasmine hastened forward. "I don't have any personal information in my profile." Concentrating on the screen, she clicked the information tab. "See."

Jack leaned closer, his head now mere inches from hers.

"I didn't put my age, gender, where I live or anything. I left them all blank. So, you see," she smiled, feeling proud of herself. "I'm perfectly safe." That niggling feeling resurfaced. The analytical part was beginning to wonder if there really was more to it than the chocolate buzz. But she'd ponder that later. Right now, she didn't want Jack to see her uncertainty, so she diverted her attention toward the dwindling fire and away from him.

"Look at me." He hooked her chin and turned her toward him. His eyes burrowed through her. "I know you think it's safe because you didn't put down any personal information. But there are people who know how to find people. Besides, when you downloaded this messenger, you had to fill out a form and—"

"—It said that the information was private, and that it would not be sold or given out." Once again, she hoped to reassure him. Or perhaps she was trying to reassure herself? She wasn't sure. But one thing she was certain of, she hated analyzing everything to death. Just once she'd like to do something without having to go through the whole thing in her mind or with every person who wanted every single detail of every single thing she did.

"Jasmine, there are other ways."

She transferred her attention back to Jack and his compressed lips.

"Here, let me show you." He motioned to her laptop and drew up his knees. She placed her computer on his lap.

He threw the instant chat screen down to the start bar and brought up a web browser page. In a popular search engine he typed Jackson Neil Warren and hit enter. In a matter of seconds his name popped up.

Jasmine refused to allow her shock to show. She peered closer. "What's that?" She pointed to a little icon beside his name.

"I'll show you." Jack double-clicked on it.

A map with precise directions to Jack's remote home stared back at her. She cupped her hand over her mouth and gawked at the screen. "I—I never knew that was there. How…? Is—is my name there too?"

Jack typed Jasmine Rose Moore and clicked on *search*.

In bold, black letters, her name popped up several times, including her website addy, the name of her greeting card business—Creations By Jazz, and each online group she belonged to.

Knowing her website contained her business phone number, her throat tightened. *Quit overreacting, girl. Who would ever look there?* She tried to beat back the fear, but the fear clung to her.

Jasmine sensed Jack's intense stare, but she refused to look at him. "How do they get all this information?" She struggled to keep her voice from quavering.

"I don't know. I'm no computer expert. But they

have their ways."

Her eyes trailed down the list. Puzzled, she looked at Jack. "Wait. How come I don't have a map icon next to my name?"

"I went in and removed it, okay?" His voice held no apology. He stood and placed the laptop next to Jasmine. "I know how easy it is to find people on the Internet, and I didn't want any weirdo finding you."

She looked up at him as the puzzle pieces fell into place. "You just told me there were several ways they could find you and that you were no computer expert. How did you know people could be found that easily to begin with?"

"Dave at The Computer Tech store. We got to talking about computers, and he mentioned people were complaining about their personal information being plastered all over the Internet, including the map icon next to their names. I asked if it could be deleted, and he showed me how. So, I went in and removed the map from your name." He sat on his heels in front of her and laid his hand on her arm. "Listen, Jazz. Computer savvy people have ways of finding out things. Think about it. You hear a lot on the news about how young women get involved with some guy on the Internet, and then they end up—" He raked his hand through his thick blond hair.

Jasmine knew that gesture well. He only did it when something really bothered him.

"What kind of people use those chat things any way?" He tossed out. "Probably all kinds of psychotic freaks."

"Thanks. So, now you're saying I'm a freak because *I* use an instant chat messenger?" She stood and rested her hand on his arm. "Listen, Jack."

His muscle twitched under her hand.

"I know you're worried about me, and I thank you for that. But I have no intention of ever meeting anyone I talk to on the Internet. Besides, you typed in my full name. No one knows my real name. They only have my nickname. And Lori's been doing this for quite some time, and she hasn't run into any danger."

"Yet," Jack scoffed.

Jasmine stifled a frustrated sigh. Convinced Jack was just being over protective again, to prove her point, she sat down, picked up her laptop, and typed in 'Jazzy'.

Pages and pages came up. Anything from chairs to videos to books. "See."

Jack squatted next to her.

She turned her laptop so he could see it and pointed to the screen before clicking on several pages. "There's nothing connecting my nickname to me or my website or anything else. So, I'm perfectly safe. So, there's really nothing for you to worry about. Millions of people go online and chat. Anyway, Internet catastrophes on the news are few and far between. More people get hurt just going to the grocery store, or to their job, or to school. And there are no guarantees in this life. Except for Christ. And He's big enough to protect me."

"He also gives us wisdom, and expects us to use it."

"I know that, Jack. I'm not stupid. I appreciate your concern, but I'll be careful and use discretion. I refuse to live in fear of what might happen." She strode over to her living room window. "I don't want to talk about this anymore."

From the corner of her eye she saw Jack adding logs onto the hot coals in her fireplace. Jasmine pulled back the curtain and stared at the swirling snow and blank nothingness that had become her life.

Jack's warm hands covered her shoulders. She leaned back against him as she had so many times during their friendship. Heat emanated from his body, spreading warmth into hers. If only Steamboat Springs wasn't so bitterly cold, then she wouldn't have to leave her dearest friend. *That's not true, and you know it, Jazz. The snowy weather isn't the only reason you need to leave.*

Ever since she'd gotten lost hiking three years ago, and had spent two nights alone with a broken wrist and minimal food and water, Jack and her sisters had taken it upon themselves to watch over her. To protect her—even to the point of suffocating her. She hated feeling needy, had always prided herself on her independence, but her wilderness experience had stripped that from her too.

An ache deep inside of her resurfaced.

Lord, I can't stand the person I've become since my accident. I miss the old Jasmine. I miss me, Lord. It seems like all I think about now is myself, and my situation, and what I'm going through. But, I don't know how to push past the pain in my feet and hands. I've tried, Lord. But I keep failing. Please heal my body and my mind. Help me to be what You want me to be. Help me to let go of this negativity and self-pity. I can't do it alone, Lord. I need You.

"Jazz." Jack's soft voice penetrated her thoughts. "Why do you feel the need to talk to strangers online?"

So, it's back to that again.

Jack's expression saddened her. He didn't understand and had no clue how hard she worked to try and turn her situation around. And how could he understand? He was fully functional and had a satisfying life.

"I don't feel the *need* to talk to strangers online, Jack." Jasmine slipped from his embrace and crossed her arms. "I just wanted to find something fun to do while being cooped up inside all winter. When I called Lori the other day, she said she was having a blast on the Internet. That she'd met some terrific Christians using an instant chat messenger. It sounded fun, so I found one and downloaded it."

Those nagging feelings flapped around her again. Tired of dealing with them, she swatted them away like she would a pesky mosquito.

"But you don't need to do that. Chloe and Shanell are here for you, and so am I."

"Not lately." When he started to say something she held up her hand to silence him. "It's okay, Jack. I understand and know that you've all been super busy. I also know that I can't depend on you three to keep me occupied all the time. You guys have your own lives. Besides, let's face it. Someday you'll find a wonderful Christian woman and get married, and where will that leave me?" The second the words left her mouth, a sick feeling came over her. She hugged her stomach. Her best friend married? Could she bear it?

CHAPTER THREE

Jasmine's words hit Jack like a sucker punch. Marry another woman? Never! He needed air. And he needed it now. "I have to go."

"What?" Jasmine blinked. "Why? Are you okay?"

No, I'm not okay, he wanted to yell. Instead, he turned, jerked on his coat, boots and cap and yanked the door open. "I'll talk to you later." Without looking back, he strode to his truck, struggling each step of the slippery way.

Guilt plagued him for leaving the way he had, but it was imperative that he get away and think before he said or did something he would regret later. Like taking her in his arms and kissing her like she'd never been kissed before and telling her how much he loved her and how he wanted her to be his wife and that there wasn't anything he wouldn't do for her. That he would sell everything he owned and move anywhere she wanted if she only gave him the slightest hint of a future together. But after her last comment, the chances of them ever getting married melted like the first snow of winter.

Not only that, there weren't enough beads on an abacus to count the number of times he'd heard her say, 'You're the best friend a girl could ever have.' And nothing in her eyes or body language indicated anything more than friendship toward him.

Except for that brief moment when she wiped the crème off his lips, and stared at his mouth, looking as if she wanted to kiss him. But he was wrong. He discovered that fact when he made the mistake of looking at her lips. That's when she bolted to the sink like a scared bird. The last thing he wanted to do was frighten her away.

Seeing what his high school buddy had gone through years ago was enough to stop Jack from doing anything foolish. Jack could still see Stan sitting on a bleacher in the gymnasium after a homecoming dance, shoulders hunched, rubbing his hands, and saying, "Oh man, I blew it big time."

"What do you mean?" Jack had asked, following Stan's line of vision. The only thing he noticed was Beth exiting the gym with her boyfriend Ron.

"You know how I was dating Sandy?"

"Was?" He looked back at Stan. "Did you two break up?"

"Yeah, but that's not what's bugging me."

"I don't get it."

"You know how Sandy's sister Beth and I were really close. How Beth came to me anytime she needed advice about some guy, or needed protection, or help with her drawings, and just her life in general. That girl shared everything with me. And I loved it. She made me feel needed." Stan ran his hands through his hair before sitting up straight.

"Three months ago, I went to pick up Sandy for our regular Saturday night date, only she wasn't there. She'd stood me up. And left Beth to tell me. I was so mad I decided to get even with her by asking Beth out."

"You didn't."

"I did. Beth was uncomfortable with the idea, but I talked her into it anyway. We went the movies, and I ended up kissing her."

"You kissed her?"

"Yeah, I know. It was stupid. That's not even the half of it. We even went on a few more dates after that, until she told me she couldn't go out with me anymore because every time she kissed me, she felt like she was kissing her brother."

"Ouch."

"Ouch is right. The worst part about this whole thing, she's so uncomfortable around me now that she completely avoids me. Man that hurts. I knew better, and now I'm paying for my stupidity. I've lost the most special friend I've ever had." Stan shook his head. "I'd give anything to have things back to the way they were. I should have never compromised our friendship. I'd rather have her as a friend than not at all. I miss her big time."

It took years for Stan to get over losing Beth's friendship. Jack never wanted to feel the kind of pain Stan had.

"What am I going to do, Lord? I always hoped there was a chance for us. But now she thinks I'm going to marry someone else. Is that what she wants me to do?" The thought just about killed him.

Poor visibility due to the thick swirling snowflakes made it difficult to see the road, and a good foot of white powder covered the asphalt. His 4X4 slid and came within inches of hitting a post. Jack corrected his truck's trajectory and steered back onto the road.

He had to stop thinking about Jasmine and keep his focus on looking for snow banks, guardrails, fences, and any other markings that would help keep his vehicle on the highway. At the rate he was going, it would take thirty minutes or more to get home.

After a tense six miles of hazardous conditions and several near misses, he finally pulled up to his log home, drove inside the garage, and killed the engine.

No matter how hard he tried, Jack couldn't shake the uneasiness bedding down inside him. For the twentieth time he glanced at the clock on his bedroom nightstand, 2:15 a.m. Only five minutes later than the last time he checked. "Come on antacids, do your thing." Worrying about Jasmine had caused his ulcer to flare up again.

He tried to roll over, but because he had tossed and turned so much his blankets wrapped around his legs, cocooning him.

He unraveled himself from his covers and placed his hands under his head and stared at the ceiling. "Lord, every time I think about her talking with that Simon what's-his-name, I get a huge pit in my gut. Along with increased heartburn," he added with a wry chuckle. He pressed his hand against the dull ache in his abdomen and continued. "Send Your angels, Lord, to watch over Jasmine and to keep her safe."

Knowing nothing else could be done right now, he fluffed his pillow and closed his eyes hoping to get at least a few hours of sleep before his morning meeting with Monroe.

"Help me, Jack! Help me!"

"Where are you, Jasmine?"

"Over here. Please hurry, Jack. Don't let him hurt me."

Jack stumbled his way through the dense fog. "I can't find you, Jasmine. Tell me where you are."

"Jack! Hurry! He's coming back!" Jasmine's piercing scream filled the inky darkness.

Jack searched frantically for her—plowing through the tree branches like a banshee.

Panic rioted within him.

His stomach burned as if someone held a lit blowtorch in it.

"He's got a gun, Jack! He's going to kill me!" The horrendous fear in her voice tore at Jack's heart and his mind.

"Where is she? Help me find her, Lord."

"If I can't have you," a man snarled, "no one will." His venomous tone sent chills of dread racing up and down Jack's spine.

Earsplitting gunfire shattered the darkness.

Jack's heart slammed against his ribs.

Sinister laughter swirled around him, mocking him, tormenting him, until he thought he would go mad.

"You're too late, Jaaaa...." Jasmine's faint voice echoed in his ears.

Silence.

"Noooooo!" An agonizing moan ripped from the very depths of Jack's soul.

He bolted upright.

Sweat dripped down his face.

Damp clothes clung to his drenched body.

His eyes darted about the dark room, and his breathing came in rapid gasps.

His stomach burned like a raging forest fire.

Jack snapped on the bedside lamp and fell against the headboard, relieved the dream was a nightmare and not real.

Moments later, he stood on shaky legs and staggered toward the bathroom. He opened the bottle of liquid antacid and downed a big swig.

His haggard refection in the mirror stared back at him. Dark circles bagged under his eyes and sweat-matted hair clung to his scalp.

He turned on the cold water. Cupping his hands, he splashed his face, and patted it dry, wishing he could blot the memory of his nightmare away as easily as he had the water from his face.

He rolled his head in a slow circle and arched his shoulders. After putting on some dry clothes, he ambled his way back to his log-framed bed where he flopped onto the mattress and glanced at the clock. "Oh man. It's only a little after three." In two hours it would be time to get up.

Each time his eyes drifted shut, his mind replayed the bad dream. Knowing sleep would elude him until he figured out a way to stop Jasmine from making a colossal mistake, he headed downstairs to fix a pot of decaf coffee, wishing his gut could handle caffeine. He could sure use some about now. But drinking caffeine would only exacerbate the ulcer pain.

While the dark brew dripped, he toasted a bagel, smeared strawberry cream cheese on it, and let Willbee, his only roommate, out of his kennel. The Golden Retriever yawned and stretched, then dropped onto his side. "I know. This isn't part of our normal routine." The dog's eyes glanced at Jack and then closed.

Jack grabbed his favorite mug from the cupboard. Jasmine had special-ordered the silver insulated cup bearing his company's logo. The logo she'd designed. When she'd given the mug to him the first day he'd opened for business, her face beamed with pride. "A special gift for a special guy. I'm so proud of you, Jack." Her lingering hug had stimulated his senses.

That day, her wispy, short brown hair was styled to perfection, and the shine in her blue-green eyes had driven him wild. Thinking about how her body felt next to his, and her soft-looking lips…. Jack gave himself a mental shake. He needed to stop tormenting himself. It was all a fantasy. None of it was real. He had to quit thinking about Jasmine in such an intimate way.

But not thinking about her was like not breathing.

Daily, he prayed for the adventurous, fun-loving, carefree, full-of-life Jasmine to be restored to her former self. Before her accident nothing had stopped her from doing the things she loved. Like planting a variety of vegetables to give to those who couldn't afford them. Or growing fresh flowers and taking them to elderly women who loved flowers but were no longer able to grow them for themselves.

Once again, Jack wished he could solve all her problems and protect her from every bad thing life threw her way.

That old feeling of helplessness resurfaced like a dead fish, and he needed to get his mind free from the stench of it.

He poured himself a cup of steaming coffee, picked up his bagel, and headed toward the living room.

Seated in his brown leather recliner, he sunk his teeth into his bagel and glanced around the living room.

Because he'd built this home with Jasmine in mind, he had her pick out the furniture and the décor. His attention fell on the three-piece sectional leather couch. Several leopard, red fox, and coyote imitation fur throw pillows lined the back of the sofa. In the middle of the log coffee table sat two carved wooden candlesticks with white artificial rabbit fur under each one. Jasmine had placed tan rabbit fur under each lamp that sat on the matching end tables.

Jack's line of vision landed on the angora rug in front of the fireplace. He imagined himself lying there with Jasmine in his arms, a wedding ring sparkling on her finger. He closed his eyes and could almost feel her soft lips under his and her womanly curves pressing against him as they clung to each other until the wee hours of the morning. Inhaling a deep breath, he forced the intimate image from his mind, knowing if he let his thoughts wander too far in that direction a cold shower would be in order.

Jack finished the bagel, drank several long gulps of his coffee, and eased himself up from the chair. On the way to the kitchen, the abrupt way he'd left Jasmine's the night before kicked him in the gut. *I hope she's okay.*

The message she received from that guy online flashed through Jack's mind in jerky movements like an old home-reel movie, haunting him. *Where do you live? Where do you live? Looking forward to getting to know you better. Where do you live?* Jack slammed his fist on the counter.

Willbee jumped up, trotted over to him, and pushed his wet nose into the palm of Jack's hand. "Sorry, boy. I didn't mean to scare you." He ruffled the dog's fur. "Hey, I'd better get you something to eat. I don't know where the time went, but I gotta leave here in forty minutes, and I haven't even showered yet."

After last night's snowfall, he hoped the skiers and snowmobilers paid heed to the avalanche warnings and stayed away from the high country and off limit areas. Otherwise Routt County's Search and Rescue team would be giving him a call. As a certified member of that special team, so far he and his dog Willbee had worked one avalanche, several lost cross country skier and snowmobile incidents, and even a missing child. All victims were rescued—and all the stories had a happy ending thanks to Willbee and his specialized training.

He squatted down in front of his pet. Willbee lapped his tongue at him, but the dog knew better than to lick Jack's face—something Jack couldn't stand. After a quick hug, Jack stood. "Okay, boy, I gotta shower. Eat up." He set the bowl on the floor and hurried up the winding staircase he'd designed because Jasmine loved them.

Doubts of Jasmine ever becoming his wife and sharing his home bombarded his thoughts. Sometimes it made him angry, other times it made him sad. Most of the time sad. The times it had made him angry were the times he wished he didn't love her like he did. Loving someone who didn't love you back was just too painful. Pain or no pain though, he'd hang in there until he was absolutely certain there was no future for them. The thought of living without her caused a stabbing pain through his heart.

"Lord, if for some reason Jasmine will never belong to me, then please take this desire to marry her out of my heart. I can't live like this." He swallowed the pain those words resurrected.

Be still and know that I am God. Delight yourself in

the Lord, and He'll give you the desires of your heart.

God's promise eased his heartache, but he still had to deal with the frustration her words of marrying another evoked in him. Now that feat was going to take some doing.

He stepped into the shower. The hot, pulsating water beat some of the tension out of his body, but not out of his mind. He scrubbed his body and face with soap.

The telephone rang.

His eyes darted open. Soap trailed into them, causing his eyes to burn like crazy.

The phone rang again.

Who would be calling this early in the morning?

He quickly rinsed his eyes, but they still stung. With his body still soapy, he turned off the water, grabbed a towel, and snatched up the receiver.

CHAPTER FOUR

"Come on, Jack, pick up the phone," Jasmine barked into the receiver.

"Hello?"

"Jack? Why do you sound so out of breath? Did I get you at a bad time?"

"I was in the middle of a shower."

Heat rose to her cheeks. "Oh. Um... do I need to let you go?"

"Are you okay?" His gruff voice held a hint of impatience.

"Yeah, I'm fine. Look, why don't you finish taking your shower, and then call me back?"

"I'll call you as soon as I get a chance." This time, the impatience came through loud and clear. "I gotta go. I've got soap in my eyes, and I'm dripping all over the carpet."

"Oh. Okay. Bye." The droning dial tone in her ear made her feel empty inside. She wanted to blame Jack's reaction on the fact that he was in the middle of a shower and had gotten soap in his eyes, but she knew that wasn't the case at all. He was still upset with her. She slunk into a chair, and her arms hung as limp as a wet noodle over its white pillowy sides.

Movement outside her picture window caught her attention. Five head of deer crossed her yard and headed up into the trees. Morning sunlight streamed through the aspen and pine branches, making the deer appear broken and distorted. It reminded her of the House of Mirrors she and Jack had gone to at one of Denver's amusement parks.

Jack.

Every memory seemed to include him.

She couldn't wait to hear from him again. His abrupt departure last night plagued her until her stomach churned with nausea.

Jasmine yawned wide and long. Her eyelids felt heavy from a lack of sleep. She had tossed and turned most of the night as her parting words to Jack played through her mind. *Someday you'll find a nice Christian woman and get married.*

The thought of not spending time with Jack, and the idea of him married to some strange woman... Well, she couldn't even think about that. It was too painful.

Something inside her had changed when she wiped the marshmallow from his lips. For the first time since she'd known him, she saw him as something other than just a friend. She saw him as a man. And that frightened the bajeebies out of her.

The telephone rang. Jasmine bolted upright and snatched up the receiver.

"It's me." Jack's tone was as flat as week-old snow on the roadway.

Not knowing what to say, she popped out the first thing that came to mind. "I'm so glad you called." Her voice came out shy and timid. "I was just thinking about you."

"What about me?"

"Oh. Um... " Clearing her throat, she scuffed the toe of her slipper on the Oriental rug and chewed on her thumbnail. She tried to get the words to come, but they weren't cooperating.

"Jazz, quit chewing your nail and talk to me."

"How did you know what I was doing?" She stretched her neck like a goose chasing a predator. Looking at the ceiling, she followed it all away around the living room. Sometimes she wondered if he had a hidden camera planted in her house.

"I just know you," Jack said, and thankfully his tone had softened. "Now tell me what you were thinking about."

"I already told you. I was thinking about you."

"You were?" Was it just her imagination, or did he sound pleased?

"Yes. Why wouldn't I be? We've been friends for a long time. Anyway, that's not why I wanted you to call me back. I called earlier because I wanted to apologize to you. I obviously said or did something last night that upset you, and I'm sorry." She had no clue what it was, or she'd try to make it right somehow if she could. "I don't want anything I said or did to ruin our friendship." She drew her knees to her chest and hugged them. "Please, forgive me, Jack."

Silence.

"Jack?"

"I already forgave you last night. Listen, I'm gonna be late for a meeting. I have to go. I'll call you later. Bye."

Jasmine pulled the receiver away from her ear and stared at the device. Jack hadn't even given her a chance to say goodbye.

If he'd truly forgiven her, then why did he sound so distant?

Emptiness settled in on her like a weighty mist.

What she needed now was a reprieve from the emotional onslaught brought on by Jack's indifference toward her. Her laptop caught her eye.

Once seated on her loveseat, she grabbed her laptop and pressed the power button. The familiar Windows chime jingled while it booted up. When it finally finished loading, she clicked her ICM icon.

"Yessss!" Fist clenched, she jerked her arm once toward her chest. The yellow happy face glowing next to

Simonrapport's nickname indicated he was online.

Good morning. How are you? I'm surprised to see you on here this early. She clicked Send.

Well, good morning to you too, Jazzy. I'm doing great though I hardly slept a wink. I've never enjoyed a conversation as much as I did ours last night. I'm online this early because I have some work to catch up on. But since I'm the boss, I can do what I want. And what I want right now is to converse with you. That is, if you have time. Why are you on here so early?

Jasmine typed her response.

I, too, enjoyed last night. I still can't believe we talked until two this morning. The reason I'm on here so early is because I'm an early riser, and... I must admit, I hoped to find you online. I am the owner of my company also. And I, too, choose my own hours. What is it you do? And, yes, I have time for a chat.

She hit Send.

Since you're being so honest, I will too. <grin> I hoped to find you online also. I'm a computer analyst. What do you do? If that's too personal, just tell me. I don't want you to give out any information that you're not comfortable sharing.

She tapped her teeth with her index finger, wondering if it would be okay to tell him. Surely, if she didn't give the name of her business it would be safe.

The second she settled her fingers on the keyboard, apprehension flooded her gut. "Not again," she growled.

She wasn't going to take the time to analyze it until she remembered the unpleasant encounter she'd had with RodeoCowboy last night. About forty-five minutes into their online conversation, RodeoCowboy, a Dan Hobbs from Texas, got flat out nasty with her because she wouldn't divulge her real name, where she lived, and what she did for a living.

Even now the memory of RodeoCowboy saying he'd

already discovered her whereabouts made her shiver.

She reflected on Jack's words about people having ways of tracking a person. At first, she thought he was just saying that to keep her from talking to strangers on the Internet. But now she was beginning to wonder if Jack was right.

About some people anyway.

After all, not everyone on the Internet was dangerous or out to find her. Last night, she'd met JesusFreak32. A thirty-two-year old youth pastor from an on fire church down in Golden, Colorado. And KiwiAuthor4Christ. A very nice gentleman from New Zealand who loved the Lord and wrote non-fiction Christian books. Both had sent her an instant chat message, and both had spent the whole time talking about Jesus and what He was doing in their lives. Not once did either of them ask where she lived or for any personal information.

Other than RodeoCowboy, who had been demanding and a real horse's behind, everyone else she'd talked to online, women and men alike, had been nothing but kind and considerate. The same with Simonrapport. Just like now. How sweet of him to make a point of saying he didn't want her to articulate anything that made her uncomfortable.

His thoughtfulness brought a smile to her face.

Without giving her stomach another thought, she typed out her reply.

I create greeting cards. My sister sells them and my oil paintings in her store here in town. So, tell me... is it warm there? If it is, please give me details, and don't leave out a single thing. I live where it snows seven months out of the year, and I detest the cold. Well, hate is more like it. I've tried and tried to talk myself into loving it here, but being stuck inside all winter long makes being here almost unbearable.

She sent her message, and raked her thumbnail with

her teeth, trying to ignore her jittery stomach. Maybe a cup of hot chocolate would calm it. Jasmine chuckled at the oxymoron. Chocolate to calm her? Um, no. Usually it had the opposite effect on her. But hey, it sounded good, so she deposited her computer off to the side and darted into the kitchen where she quickly made a cup of the chocolaty brew and topped it off with a generous dollop of marshmallow crème.

A half-moon image of marshmallow crème above Jack's upper lip popped into her mind. His lips reminded her of Collin Firth's, who played the hunky Mr. Darcy in Pride & Prejudice. The man she'd dreamt about kissing her ever since the first time she watched that show. Only now, it was Jack's lips she imagined covering hers gently, tenderly, passionately.

Passionately?

It was if someone splashed a pitcher of ice water on her, yanking her out of the ludicrous daydream and back into reality.

Whatever was happening to her concerning Jack was making her crazy and driving her to distraction.

She had to stop it. Never, ever would she allow anything more than friendship between them. She had seen firsthand what happened when life-long best friends become romantic. And it wasn't a pretty picture. Lori and Steve's devastating situation was enough to convince her of that fact. She couldn't bear it if her and Jack's relationship ended up like theirs.

Jack's friendship was too important to her. At least she hoped they were still friends.

Oh, Jack. Please call me. I can't stand the thought of you mad at me.

Jasmine sauntered toward her loveseat and placed her laptop on her legs. Without her usual exuberance, she read Simonrapport's message.

Why are you stuck inside all winter? Why don't you

move? After all, you said you were your own boss. Can't you ship your drawings to your sister? Because you sound so sad, I hesitate to tell you what the weather is like here.

Don't let that stop you, she quickly typed and sent it. *I want to hear all about it.*

Are you sure?

I'm sure.

Very well then. I'm sitting in my bay window sipping my favorite beverage hot chocolate with marshmallow crème on top, and staring at an amazing blue sky dotted with only a few jagged clouds. The heat from the sun is magnifying through the glass pane, warming my house. By noon it will be like a sauna in here, but right now the temperature is a cool sixty-nine degrees.

Jasmine sighed. Envy rippled through every fiber of her being. Sixty-nine degrees. In her dreams.

Thank you for that lovely description. I'm so jealous. Someday soon I hope to move where it's warm all year round. By the way, my favorite drink is hot chocolate with marshmallow crème too.

Click.

Another thing we have in common. <grin> You know, Jazzy, you could always move here. We never get snow. You said you design greeting cards. I'm curious, do you draw each card and then have prints made, or is each one an original?

"Ah, that's so sweet. He's actually interested in what I do," she spoke to the empty room.

I sell the copies and keep the originals. There are times when I get requests to paint a card for a client, and that person will buy the original and the copyrights to guarantee that they are the only one to have that certain design. As for moving there, I have my heart set on someplace else. I just pray everything works out. I almost have enough money saved to make my dream a reality.

Click.

That's so kewl about your cards. I'm impressed. Too bad you have your heart set on someplace else. It would be nice to have you here. I meant to ask you earlier, where are you that it's so cold?

Jasmine's stomach squirmed at his question. This time, she wouldn't ignore it. No matter how much she liked him, she would not tell him where she lived.

Let's just say, where I live feels like Iceland. *smiling* I'm sorry I can't be more specific, but when I downloaded this messenger, I decided I would never divulge any personal information that would give away my whereabouts. I hope you understand.

Send.

She nibbled on her lip, wondering if he would continue talking with her. Then came the familiar chime.

No problem. I certainly understand. You can never be too careful these days. Especially a single woman living alone. At least I assume you live alone. You've never mentioned anyone else living with you anyway. <grin> Do you share your home with a roommate?

Her forehead crinkled, and her stomach churned. She wouldn't answer that question either. No matter how sweet it was of him to ask.

Listen, I haven't had breakfast yet, and I'm famished. Will you be online later?

Send.

Yes, I will. I'm online most of the time. And, now that you've mentioned hunger... hehe. I think I'll run to McDonalds and grab a Sausage McMuffin and a potato cake. I know, I know, it's not very nutritious, but hey, what can I say, I love Mickey D's food. Besides, I get tired of eating my own cooking. Not that I'm a bad cook, it's just that I prefer McDonalds every now and again. Well, enjoy your breakfast. I look forward to conversing with you again. It's been a real pleasure. I hope your day is filled with the warm sunshine you seem to crave. I

*would be more than glad to share mine with you. <grin>
Bye, Jazzy.*

Jasmine chuckled. A man after her own heart. She loved Mickey D's food too. Jack never wanted to eat there, so she only went when he wasn't around, which wasn't much—until lately.

Jack.

She glanced at the phone, wondering if and when he'd call, then back at her screen.

Too bad one couldn't bottle up sunshine. I'd have you send several gallons my way. I love Mickey D's! In fact if it weren't so cold, I'd get a Sausage McMuffin and potato cake myself. Of course if I did, I'd have to spend an extra twenty minutes on my treadmill. *smiling* But it would be worth it. Okay, well, I'm going now. I'll contact you later. Feel free to message me anytime. Have a wonderful day. Bye.

Send.

Jasmine shut down her computer. She hadn't experienced this kind of warmth for a long time, and it had nothing to do with the fact that the thermostat was set on ninety. Simonrapport intrigued her like no other man she'd ever known. Okay. If she was honest with herself, Jack was the most dynamic man she knew, but he was her best friend and nothing more. And after their brief conversation this morning, she wondered if even their friendship was in danger. Until she found out, the wait would be as grueling as traipsing through knee-deep snow.

When Jasmine stood, the photo of her sitting on her favorite dapple-gray gelding Mr. Dapper snagged her attention. Six summers in a row, she and Jack had ridden several of the trails nestled in the Colorado Rocky Mountains around Steamboat Springs. Memories of warm sunshine, leafy trees, felled pine cones, bright fuchsia wildflowers, purple columbines, white and yellow daisies, and lush green meadows pranced through her mind. She could almost smell the mixture of sagebrush, sweet clover, pine, horseflesh, and leather.

She ran her fingers over the glass, tracing the outline of the cherished horse.

One day she had asked Mrs. McGuire, the horse's owner, if she could buy him, but the aging woman wouldn't part with Mr. Dapper. Not that Jasmine blamed her. She wouldn't want to part with him either. Owning Mr. Dapper just wasn't meant to be.

She set the picture down and headed into the kitchen to find something to eat. She opened the fridge and scanned its contents. Bacon and eggs sounded good, and so did a bagel with strawberry cream cheese. Jack's favorite. Jasmine quickly pushed any thoughts of Jack from her mind.

How about some Yogurt? No.

Leftover pizza. No.

McDonalds. Yeah.

She closed the door, walked over to the window, and pulled back the curtain. Using the cuff of her sleeve, she scrubbed off the thick frost.

Eighteen below zero.

So much for treating herself to McDonalds.

I hate winters. That's all there is to it.

Back to the fridge she strode. The bottles in the door rattled when she yanked the door open. She snatched up the bacon and eggs and plopped them on the stove. The sound of eggshells cracking irritated her even further. She opened the carton to discover three of them bore the tell-tale jagged lines.

"Temper, temper, Jazz," she admonished herself. Leaning her hip against the counter, she shook her head in frustration, feeling like a Popsicle—stuck inside the freezer until summer. She groaned. Cold weather always seemed to bring out the worst in her.

She pushed herself away from the counter and grabbed a small bowl. Maybe she could salvage those eggs. One by one, she carefully removed the broken ones and dumped them in the dish. Eggshell particles swam amongst the yellow mass. She tried plucking them out, but they slithered away from her fingers. With each attempt, her ire rose.

Several agitating minutes later, she tossed the runny eggs down the drain, shoved the ingredients back into the fridge, and huffed her way up the stairs and into her bedroom.

Thermal underwear and jeans now clothed her body. She grabbed the first turtleneck she came to and stuffed herself into the warmest sweater she owned.

One hard yank on her sock drawer, and it headed toward the floor with her fingers still curled around the handle. "Stupid thing," she growled, dropping the drawer. She snatched up a pair of heavy wool socks and yanked them on.

Boy did she need an attitude adjustment.

But right now she was too angry to get one.

She tromped over to the bathroom and looked in the mirror.

Short brown hair stuck straight out in all directions, reminding her of the guy on the movie Home Alone 2 when he grabbed the sink faucet and got electrocuted. She ran a brush through her hair, washed her face, brushed her teeth, and fled downstairs.

Jasmine stuffed herself into her outer winter garments.

The phone rang.

"Not now." She trotted to the phone and snatched up the receiver. "Hello."

Silence.

"Hello, is anyone there?" Jasmine pressed the phone closer to her ear and listened carefully. She could hear someone breathing. "Speak now, or I'm hanging up." The dial tone droned in her ear. "I don't have time for this." She slammed the receiver down, shoved her driver's license into the back pocket of her jeans, grabbed her keys off the mahogany dumbwaiter, and braced herself for the assault of cold when she opened the door.

The bitter wind plunged needles of ice into her exposed cheeks, making them sting like crazy.

"I hate this!" She stormed toward her car. Each step she took her feet slipped and slid on the ice.

The next thing she knew, she found herself flailing backward. Her hands and backside thudded against the pavement. Jabs of pain shot through her. She clutched her wrist as tears sprang to her eyes. Within seconds, anger overrode any pain she was feeling.

Three feet from the driver's side door, Jasmine aimed her key at her SUV and pushed the unlock button.

Days like this she wished she would have taken Jack up on his offer to build her a garage. But she didn't want to take advantage of his kindness, so she'd told him no. And now, the inevitable ten minutes of arduous window scraping awaited her.

She reached for the door handle, but never made contact with it because her feet flew out from under her again.

Her head slammed against the concrete.

Pain shot through her skull.

A glimpse of blue sky.

Then nothingness.

CHAPTER FIVE

"Jasmine!" Jack rammed his pickup into neutral and hopped out. His truck started inching down her driveway, heading toward a hefty blue spruce. "Oh, man." He got his pickup stopped and set the emergency brake. Slamming the door shut behind him, he slipped and slid his way to where Jasmine lay on the icy pavement.

He dropped to one knee beside her. Tearing off one of his leather gloves, he stuck his forefinger under her scarf and checked for a pulse. "Thank you, Lord." He blew out a long breath, removed his coat, and gently tucked it around her.

"Come on, sweetie, wake up. Talk to me."

Nothing.

"Jasmine? Can you hear me?" He wanted to pull her into his arms, but he'd had enough medical training to know not to move her. He jerked his cell phone from his pocket and punched 911.

"This is Jackson Warren. I need an ambulance right away." He gave them Jasmine's name and address. "She's obviously fallen. I don't know how long ago. Please, hurry." He disconnected the call knowing he should have stayed on the line, but right now he only cared about Jasmine.

The numbness in his fingers started to tingle, so he shoved his glove back on, and then hurried to his pickup where he grabbed a couple of heavy wool blankets from the back seat. He doubled them and tucked them around her.

He called his client. "Monroe, this is Jack. Listen, an emergency came up. I'm not going to be able to meet this morning."

With his eyes glued on Jasmine, he listened as his friend blurted out his great news.

"Congratulations," Jack said in a rush. "Listen, tell Cheryl I'll be praying for her and your new son. I gotta go. I'll call you later." He pressed End and shoved the phone in his pocket.

His eyes caressed Jasmine's face. He envied Monroe because he had a wife who loved him, a healthy four-year-old son, and now a newborn baby boy as of four-thirty this morning.

Someday Jack hoped to win Jasmine's heart and have a whole passel of kids with her. The woman he'd loved forever.

"Jazz. C'mon, baby. It's Jack. Open your eyes." He touched her bright-red cheek with the back of his fingers.

Her head shifted from side to side.

Jack leaned over her. "Jasmine. Sweetheart, can you hear me?"

Without opening her eyes, barely above a whisper, she asked, "Is that you, Simonrapport?"

Jack yanked his hand back as if a hot iron had scorched him. His gut twisted. He couldn't believe what he'd just heard. She used to cry out his name when she needed help, and now she called for a total stranger? Mercifully, the shrill wail of the siren eradicated his turbulent thoughts.

The ambulance pulled up and stopped. Two people jumped out and grabbed equipment from an outside compartment. They hurried toward Jasmine and knelt next to her. One fired questions at Jack while they both worked on her.

"What's her name?"

"Jasmine."

"How old is she?"

"Twenty-six."

"Does she have any medical history of diabetes?"

"No." Jack tried to focus on the rapid-fire questioning but found it difficult as the reality of the situation hit him. His ulcer flared up making the burning sensation almost unbearable. But that pain was nothing compared to the spikes of pain driving into his heart.

One of the technicians handed him his coat.

He slipped it on, aware of the faint fragrance of Jasmine-scented perfume.

"How did she fall?"

"I don't know. I'm assuming she fell on the ice. I just talked to her on the phone forty-five minutes ago, and she was fine."

The female attendant called Jasmine's name and kept asking her questions. No reply.

Jack felt helpless standing there watching. "Is there anything I can do?"

The female attendant darted a glance at him and smiled. "You already did by covering her with those blankets."

They placed an oxygen mask on her face and administered air. Jack knew because of the extreme cold they had to move fast, and that they would do most of their work inside the ambulance on the way to the hospital.

The EMT driver backed the vehicle into the driveway and got out. The male attendant leaning over Jasmine hollered to the driver. "Richard, grab a C-collar and a backboard."

With the C-collar in place, they had her on the gurney within seconds and wheeled her into the ambulance.

"Which hospital you taking her to?" Jack asked.

"Yampa Valley Medical," the driver answered, then slid behind the wheel.

"I'll notify her family," Jack informed one of the attendants before the man stepped inside and closed the door.

They took off, sirens blaring.

On the way to his truck, his cell phone rang. "This is Jack."

"Jack. I'm so glad you answered. Is Jasmine okay?" The quiver in Chloe's voice was a dead giveaway that she knew something was wrong.

It never ceased to amaze Jack that the triplets seemed to sense when one or the other were hurt or in trouble. Especially Chloe. He climbed into the warm cab of his truck.

"Listen, I'm glad you called. Jasmine—"

"She's been hurt, right." It was a statement not a question.

"The ambulance just left. They're taking her to Yampa Valley."

"What happened?"

"She slipped and fell." Jack ran the stop sign at the end of her lane and swerved to avoid hitting an oncoming car. He knew better than to talk on his cell while driving. Breaking the law and getting hurt himself wasn't going to help Jasmine. "Look. I can't talk now. Call your parents and Shanell, okay? I'll meet you at the hospital. Bye." He ended his call and tossed his cell phone onto the seat.

Jamming his pickup into fourth gear, he drove to the hospital as fast and as safely as he could on the snow packed roads.

Jack pulled up just as the ambulance attendants wheeled Jasmine into the hospital emergency room entrance. He swung his truck into a nearby parking space and sprinted inside. The instant the automatic doors slid open, the antiseptic smell permeated his nostrils.

He followed the paramedics until a nurse stopped him. "I'm sorry, Sir, but you can't go in there." She sent him a sympathetic look. "Are you her husband?"

Only in my dreams. "No, she's not married. I'm her

friend." That one word 'friend' irritated him like a giant pebble in his shoe.

"Could I get some information from you then?" For the first time, he noticed she held a clipboard and pen.

"Sure."

After answering all the questions he could, he went to the empty waiting room, shed his coat and hat, and sat down.

Minutes ticked by at the speed of less than one mile per hour.

Alone in the waiting room, he placed his elbows on his knees and bowed his head. "Father, please let Jasmine be okay. Heal whatever is wrong with her. Help me be patient. You know how much I love her. I pray that someday she'll love me back."

"You silly man. Of course she loves you."

Jack's gaze shot upward. He hadn't heard anyone come in. He rose on unsteady legs.

Chloe stood in front of him holding the blankets he'd covered Jasmine with. She was the spitting image of Jasmine with her blue-green eyes and brown hair. But the resemblance ended there. Ninety percent of the time Chloe dressed and carried herself like an aristocrat. Today she wore an expensive white ski parka trimmed with fur around the hood, cuffs, and hem, her matching fur-trimmed gloves, gray wool slacks, and fur-lined boots, and had on the same pricey designer fragrance she always used.

Jack preferred Jasmine's perfume—the one she'd been named after—and her wholesome down to earth style of dress, which consisted mostly of casual blue jeans, flannel shirts, and the llama hair boots he'd bought her one year for Christmas. Chloe wouldn't be caught dead in anything like that.

He took the blankets from her and put them with his coat.

Chloe removed her white fur-lined gloves and folded them into her purse before lowering herself onto the chair with the grace of a queen.

Jack sat next to her.

"I keep telling you that Jasmine loves you. She just doesn't know she loves you."

They'd had this same conversation for over two years. Chloe tried reassuring him time and again that Jasmine really did love him. She said triplets know and sense these things. He wished he could sense it too.

Jasmine's sweet face popped in his mind like it often did. Over the years, he'd memorized every detail of her face, down to the smattering of freckles across her nose. Sixteen to be exact.

"Jack, did you hear a word I just said?"

"Sorry. I was thinking about Jasmine."

"So, what else is new?" For a split second her eyes twinkled then turned serious. "I answered your question. Mother and Daddy are with her now. They sent me out here so you wouldn't be alone. Shanell didn't have anyone to cover for her, so she asked me to keep her informed and said she'd be praying." She smiled that same sweet smile as Jasmine's.

It was amazing how three women could look identical and yet be so different. Chloe was all business and no-nonsense, Shanell was bubbly, outgoing and a bit klutzy, and Jasmine was a combination of the two.

It saddened him to think how the last couple of years he hadn't seen much of Jasmine's bubbly side. With each new winter season, she seemed more depressed—and more determined to leave. Jack dreaded the idea of her moving away. All he could do now was keep working on his plans to keep her in his life.

He twisted his wrist and looked at his watch. Only forty minutes had passed since he'd sat down in this room, but it seemed like hours. Isolation and loneliness invaded his being. Was this how Jasmine felt most of the time? If it was, his heart broke for her. *Lord, is there something I can do to help Jasmine so she doesn't feel so lonely? I know I haven't spent much time with her lately. But, I've been so busy.*

A couple of ladies, followed by a small group of teenage boys barreled into the waiting room. They all started talking at once. Jack watched the middle-aged receptionist and admired her ability to remain calm and proficient in a seemingly chaotic situation.

"I wonder how Jasmine's doing?" he asked without looking at Chloe.

"I don't know. Mother went in with her while Dad finished giving the nurse her insurance information and medical history. They were going to wheel her down for a CAT scan of her head. I pray they don't find any bleeding. The doctor's concerned because she goes in and out of consciousness."

He could still see Jasmine's still form lying on the cold pavement. He squeezed his eyes shut to blot out the memory. *God, please let her be okay.*

"Jack?"

"Yeah." He looked at Chloe and inwardly groaned. When she raised a single eyebrow and bit one side of her lower lip that meant something was coming that he wasn't going to like or that he didn't want to hear. He braced himself and swallowed hard as the burning pain from his ulcer intensified. He removed three mint-flavored antacids from the roll and popped them into his mouth.

"Your ulcer bothering you?"

"A little," he spoke around the mouthful of chalky pills. "But don't worry about me, I'll be fine." He put the roll back into his pocket. "What did you want to ask me?"

Chloe stood and strode over to the other side of the now empty waiting room. Right above her hung a ski collage picture. Although it was an excellent piece of artwork, in his opinion Jasmine's paintings far exceeded it. Chloe faced him. Resting her arm against her stomach, she tapped her fingers on her lip.

He pushed himself up, and in three long strides he stood in front of her. Placing his hands on her shoulders he coaxed her to look at him. Her eyes searched his.

"Something's bothering you. Tell me what it is. Does it have anything to do with Jasmine's fall?"

"No, that's not it. It's… it's just that she kept saying something each time she came to."

"Chloe, just tell me." His gut was killing him, and he had no patience to play fifty questions. After all that happened the night before between him and Jasmine, and then finding her hurt this morning, he didn't need any more surprises. Whatever Chloe had to say, he just wanted her to spit it out.

Chloe drew in a deep breath. "Who's Simonrapport?"

Chapter Six

After a night in the hospital, Jasmine and her sister pulled into her driveway. While she loved her white two-story house with the wraparound porch and blue-lavender shutters, it was just that — a house — someplace to live until she could move to her granddad's in Louisiana or someplace else warm.

The two of them stepped out of the SUV and onto the icy pavement.

"Why don't you get some Ice Melt and put it on your driveway?" Chloe asked while steadying Jasmine as they made their way toward her porch.

"It doesn't do any good. You know how hard it is to keep up with it here. It's a never-ending job. Besides, Jack usually takes care of it. He was going to spread some before he went home the other night but he left—" Thank goodness she stopped herself from blurting out why he'd left in such a hurry. She did *not* want to discuss that evening with Chloe.

They made their way up the steps.

Chloe put the key in the first lock and turned it. "You think you have enough locks? We'll freeze to death before I get them all undone."

"Blame it on Jack. He's the one who installed so many."

Chloe stepped aside and motioned for Jasmine to go in first. When she stepped inside, warmth encapsulated her. Bougé sat in the narrow entryway, meowing and staring up at her.

She leaned over to pet her cat. Sharp pain shot through her head. "Sorry, baby. I can't pick you up right now."

"Jasmine! It's cold out here. What's the holdup?" Chloe boomed from behind her.

"Sorry. Bougé's in the way, and you know how stubborn she can be."

"Well, it's freezing out here. Move that stupid cat out of the way for pity sake, and don't let that little brat anywhere near me." She nudged Jasmine forward.

"Watch it! You almost made me step on her."

"I'm surprised you, of all people, have to be told to move out of the way when it's this cold. You normally bolt for the house and have the door slammed shut within seconds. Now granted, I know you aren't in any shape with your head injury and all, but really, move it, Sis."

Jasmine nudged Bougé out of the way and stepped further inside.

"Sit there. I'll take your boots off," Chloe ordered.

"Yes, Miss Mother Hen."

Chloe's forehead wrinkled. She shed her outer garments and hung them on the coat rack. With two dainty tugs, she removed Jasmine's shaggy-haired llama boots and set them aside.

Jasmine headed to the sofa and sat down. She pulled the purple fleece blanket off the back of the couch and snuggled into its softness.

Bougé jumped on her lap and pressed her nose against Jasmine's. Her whiskers tickled Jasmine's face. "Did you miss me, baby?" she crooned, stroking the cat's rabbit-soft fur. Bougé licked her whiskers and made an umm noise deep in her throat.

"Oh, baby. I'm so sorry. I bet you're famished." She moved Bougé out of the way and flung the blanket aside.

"Oh no you don't." Chloe tossed the coverlet back over her, never taking her eyes off of Bougé. "Just tell me what you need, and I'll get it. And don't even think about arguing with me."

She hadn't planned on arguing with her because she knew she wouldn't win anyway. She never did. Besides, Chloe was going to do what Chloe wanted to do, and no one or anything would stop her. Like now. While Jasmine was grateful for Chloe's help, it perturbed her that she had no say in her sister's coming to stay with her, and that Chloe ordered her about as if she were some two-year-old instead of a twenty-six-year-old woman. "Chloe, who's minding the shop today while you're playing nurse?"

"Don't you worry about my store. It's in good hands. And besides, I assured the doctors I would stay with you."

"I can't let you do that. This is your busy season. I'll be fine on my own." Sharp pain sliced across the back of her head. She hoped Chloe didn't see her wince. Jasmine could handle the pain in her back and shoulders from being jarred when she fell, but the pain in her head, now that she wasn't so sure about. But she'd rather deal with it than with Chloe.

With her intense focus glued on the cat, Chloe placed her cool hand on Jasmine's arm. "Listen, Sis. You're more important to me than my store. I know your head's hurting, so let me get you some pain meds and a glass of water, and anything else you might need."

Guilt pressed in on Jasmine over her stinky attitude. Chloe might be bossy and overbearing at times, but she would help anyone, anytime, anywhere.

"You know, Jazz. I knew something was wrong yesterday." She turned and headed toward the kitchen. But not before Jasmine saw how much this whole thing was affecting her. She felt ashamed of herself knowing Chloe really did care.

God, help me not to be such a brat. Chloe means well. Teach me to be gracious and to accept her help with gratitude.

Chloe looked back at her. "I get so scared when I know that my baby sister is hurting."

"Baby sister? You're only nineteen minutes older than me."

"That still makes me older." She wrinkled her prissy nose at Jasmine.

Jasmine stuck out her tongue at her. They both giggled.

"Would you do me a favor? Bougé doesn't have any food in her dish. Would you mind feeding her?" Jasmine hated asking, but stooping over made her head pound as if it were going to explode.

The color siphoned from Chloe's face.

"I'm sorry. I shouldn't have asked. I'll do it." She started to rise.

Chloe held up her hand and squared her shoulders. "No, no, I can do this. But only if you don't let *her*," she pointed at Bougé, "anywhere near me. I've seen her in action when you feed her, and it isn't a pretty sight. Why you love that ornery cat is beyond me." She raised her chin and swallowed hard. "Where do you keep her food?"

"In the pantry. There are cans of Fancy Feast on the bottom shelf and a bag of Science Diet in a big square container underneath. Just dump a can in the blue dish, and fill the red one with the dry stuff. Water goes in the yellow."

Chloe took a deep breath. "Okay."

"Chloe?"

"Yes."

"Thank you."

Chloe shook her forefinger at her. "Don't you ever say that I don't love or care about you." She quirked her lip and pointed at Bougé. "I mean it."

"I won't." Jasmine reached for the cat. Her pet's loud motor vibrated against her chest. "And would you please feed her before getting me the meds?" Jasmine hated asking for help. But, as much as she hated to admit it even to herself, she needed it today. In fact, her head writhed with so much pain, she wouldn't even fret about being babied.

"Okay, but just hold that overgrown fur ball and don't let her go until I have her food and water taken care of. I don't want her rubbing against me or biting me."

"She's never bitten you or scratched you. You're perfectly safe, Chlo. I promise."

Chloe mumbled something as she picked up the red cat dish and headed toward the pantry.

Hearing the dry food being dumped into her dish, Bougé squirmed, trying to get free, but Jasmine held her tighter.

"Sorry, baby. You have to wait, she's almost done."

Her sister pulled the tab on the canned food.

Bougé wiggled harder.

Chloe finished getting everything ready before stepping into the living room. "Okay you can let her go now."

Bougé sprung from her lap and bolted toward her food like she'd been shot in the bottom with rock salt.

Chloe shrieked and slammed her back against the wall. Her movement reminded Jasmine of an old Tom and Jerry cartoon. Her sibling, 'Miss Priss', dressed in her black angora sweater, gray wool pants with her shoulder length hair curled to perfection, and looking every bit the proper lady, stood flattened against the wall, her face devoid of color. Chloe stepped sideways, moving as far away from the kitchen entry as possible, before bolting down the hallway and out of sight.

Poor Chlo. Jasmine couldn't blame her sister for acting the way she did. When Chloe was little, a stray mama cat had viciously attacked her when she'd touched her kittens. It took several stitches to sew up the deep tears. And, truth be known, Bougé had been known to bite unwelcome strangers before.

Knowing her sister's deep-seated fear of cats, her

willingness to take care of Bougé made Jasmine's heart overflow with love. Her chest rose and fell with more guilt. Even though her siblings and Jack were overly protective of her and sometimes smothered her until she wanted to scream, when she moved, she would miss her family something fierce—and Jack too.

Jack.

Why hadn't she heard from him? Usually when she was hurt, he was the first one there and never left her side. Was he still that upset with her? That thought brought more pain than the concussion.

"Chlo?"

"Just a second, Jazz," Chloe hollered from the bathroom. "I'm getting you a drink."

Chloe strode over to her, handed her a glass of water and two prescription pain killers. She sat in the white chair opposite of Jasmine and kept glancing toward the kitchen. No doubt making sure that Bougé was still eating.

"Did Jack come to see me while I was in the hospital?"

Chloe looked at her and opened her mouth to answer but the telephone rang. She snatched it up. "Hello." After a long pause, she repeated, "Hello?" Another pause. Chloe's brows linked together. She pulled the phone away and stared at it before hanging up.

"Who was that?"

"I don't know. All I heard was heavy breathing, and...."

"And what?"

"Well, it sounded like a man whispering, but I couldn't make out what he was saying."

Jasmine recognized the look of concern on her sister's face.

"Jazz, do you get weird calls often?"

"No." Jasmine shook her head. Big mistake. The

movement caused it to throb harder. She decided to close her eyes and sleep, dismissing the call as a wrong number until she remembered a similar call the morning she'd fallen. Was someone playing tricks on her? She made a mental note to get caller ID and soon.

Chloe's last words to Jack at the hospital echoed through his brain.

"Who's Simonrapport?"

Talk about a kick in the gut. Until Jasmine's dad walked into the room, he debated on just how much he should tell Chloe.

His gut instinct told him he needed to clue her in and take her into his confidence. Between the two of them, they could formulate a plan to keep Jasmine safe.

He leaned back in his office chair and threaded his fingers through his hair. His mind replayed the horror stories he'd heard about women and the Internet. Well, he refused to let Jasmine become one of those statistics. He'd do everything in his power to keep that from happening. With that thought in mind, Jack picked up the phone and punched in Stan's number.

"Hey, Jack. How are ya, buddy?"

"I'm okay. It's Jasmine I'm worried about. Listen." He leaned forward. Picking up a lead holder drafting pencil, he rapped it on his desk. "I need you to do something for me. I need you to check on a Simonrapport from California." After he gave Stan what little information he had about him, he thanked God for his private investigator friend. Deep in his gut, Jack knew that Simonrapport spelled disaster... with a capital D.

CHAPTER SEVEN

Jasmine's eyes fluttered open. Still drowsy, she sniffed the air. Garlic, tomato, and sausage—Chloe's special lasagna. She rubbed her eyes and looked around until her gaze landed on Chloe, standing at her kitchen counter, slicing a cucumber.

She tossed the blanket aside and slid her feet into her favorite purple slippers, and rose. Knives of pain stabbed her head. She clutched her temples and lowered herself back onto the sofa.

"Chloe," she rasped through a throat as dry as toast.

No response.

Clearing her throat, she tried again. "Chlo."

Her sister continued to chop away at a tomato.

Jasmine groaned. Once her sister had her mind set on something, nothing distracted her.

Another assault of pain hammered through her skull.

Bougé jumped onto the sofa and rubbed her face against Jasmine's cheek. "Not now, baby," she croaked, gently pushing her cat away.

Her tailless cat trotted into the kitchen and brushed against Chloe's leg.

An earsplitting scream and a knife clamoring onto the counter echoed through the house. "Get away from me!" Chloe shrieked as she rushed into the living room with Bougé right on her heels. Chloe leapt onto the sofa. "Go away. Shoo. Shoo." She waved vehemently. "Go away!"

Bougé stopped and strutted toward the loveseat. She jumped up on it and curled into a ball. They stared at her cat and then looked at each other. Did her cat do that on purpose, knowing Jasmine needed help? Surely it had to be some kind of fluke.

In an attempt to moisten her throat, Jasmine swallowed numerous times. Her stomach growled.

Chloe stepped down from the couch in as ladylike manner as possible and straightened her clothes. "Hungry are we?" She smiled as if nothing was amiss, but her nervous giggle was a dead giveaway that she was still shaken. "Did you have a nice nap? How's your head feeling?" She darted a quick glance toward Bougé, then back at Jasmine.

"I don't even remember falling asleep. And I have a horrific headache."

Chloe glanced at her watch. "It's been over four hours. I'll bring you more meds."

"I'm sorry to be such a bother, but I'm famished and thirsty too." Cotton was the best way to describe her mouth's dryness.

Chloe waved off her concern. "You're not being a bother. I'm glad I can help."

"Thank you, Chlo." Jasmine glanced at her big picture window and did a double take at the pitch darkness outside. The quick movement made her head hurt worse. She glanced at the time: 5:55 pm. She couldn't believe she'd slept most of the afternoon.

"I know what you're thinking, but you were sleeping so well I didn't have the heart to wake you. Dinner will be ready in fifteen minutes. Can you wait that long, or would you like a banana to hold you over?" Chloe asked, tilting her head.

"I can wait." She knew dinner would be ready exactly when Chloe said it would be because her sister was always punctual.

"Can I help with anything?"

"Don't you even think about helping me. You stay put. You hear?" Chloe didn't wait for a response. She knew Jasmine would obey her orders.

Jasmine yawned and stretched.

Chloe returned with a glass of water, a few crackers, and some pills. "Here, eat these first so you don't upset your stomach." The pills hadn't bothered her earlier, but to appease her sister and her growling stomach, she sat up, sipped some soothing water, ate the crackers, tossed the pills into her mouth, and chased them down with the remaining water.

"Thank you." She handed her sister the glass.

"You're welcome." Chloe returned to the kitchen.

When Jasmine laid down on her side, she noticed her laptop on the coffee table. With Chloe busy arranging lettuce, tomato, cucumber, green pepper, and cheese into wooden salad bowls, Jasmine was tempted to boot up and write Simonrapport to let him know why she hadn't written him. But she wouldn't because her head hurt too much, and her sister would ask all kinds of questions, questions Jasmine didn't want to answer.

Her gaze traveled around her living room until it landed on the fireplace where blue, orange, and red flames danced like tickling fingers. She loved fireplaces and often dreamt of lying on an angora rug in front of a blazing fire with her husband. Jack's face popped into her mind. She batted away the absurdity of such a thought.

The doorbell rang.

"Don't you dare get up. I'll get it." Chloe snatched up a towel and wiped her hands off on the way to the door.

Jasmine watched, wondering who it was.

"Jack." Chloe sounded both surprised and happy. "Come on in. I'm so glad you decided to come."

She should have known it would be him. Almost every time she thought of him, he either called or came over. Her insides pranced at the thought of seeing him.

Chloe backed up, and Jack's familiar face came into view, but he didn't look her way.

Her excitement dissipated.

He handed Chloe a white pastry box.

"What's this?" Chloe held it up.

"I brought dessert. Chocolate Caramel Cheesecake."

"Yummy, my favorite," Jasmine whispered under her breath. Her insides puddled like melting snow on a warm spring day at his thoughtful gesture.

Jack glanced over at her, raised his cap, and threaded his fingers through his blond hair. The uncertainty on his face pinched her heart. She couldn't remember a time when he'd ever looked that way around her. Except for the other night when she'd practically told him to leave her alone. Her eyes squeezed shut at the guilt-ridden memory.

"Hi, Jack." She passed him an I'm-sorry smile, hoping to reassure him and make him more at ease.

"Hey." He rushed the word out and then looked away.

Oh, God. What have I done? Forgive me, Lord. And please, do something. I can't stand this strain between Jack and me.

A questioning frown marred Chloe's face as her gaze darted back and forth between the two of them. "I'll just take this dessert into the kitchen."

Jack took his time removing his winter outerwear. He sat on the wooden bench-seat and unlaced his boots. When he finished taking them off, he just sat there.

"Jack."

He glanced over at her. She patted the spot next to her on the sofa. Every movement hurt. "It's good to see you. Please. Come sit down."

With a stilted gait, he headed toward her.

Jasmine did *not* want this wall between them. The thing she feared the most was losing Jack's friendship and ending up like Lori and Steve. Jasmine didn't think anything would ever separate those two. Boy had she been wrong. Well, as long as she drew breath, she would do everything in her power to prevent what had happened to her friends, from happening to her and Jack. She wouldn't even allow her moving to interfere with their friendship. She planned on calling and writing him often.

When are you going to stop letting fear rule your life? Trust and accept the wonderful gift of Jack's love.

Huh? Without moving her head, her eyes shifted back and forth, wondering if anyone else had heard that.

Apparently not.

It had to be God.

What'd you mean, Lord? Of course I accept my friend's love. But the reason I'm afraid is because of the way I treated him the other night. I haven't seen him since. He didn't even visit me in the hospital. Oh, Lord. Her heart constricted. *I just pray I haven't put a permanent strain on our friendship.*

"Jasmine? Are you okay? You don't look too good."

Jasmine blinked. "What?"

"You're staring as if you're in a daze. Are you okay? Are you in pain?" A tender look of concern poured from those yellowish hazel eyes of his.

She didn't deserve him or his compassion.

No longer able to stand it, remorse for her stupidity and the emotional strain of the last couple of days crashed over her in tidal waves. She placed her face in her hands as regret pooled her eyes with tears.

In the time it took to draw a breath, Jack was sitting next to her. He wrapped his strong arms around her and tucked her head against his chest.

"What's wrong?" he whispered against her ear while rubbing her back.

Torment continued to crush every fiber of her soul. "Oh, Jack," she blurted between sobs. "Can you ever forgive me? I'm so sorry for the way I treated you." She pushed her palms against his chest and willed her eyes to show her genuine remorse.

He thumbed the tears off her cheeks and cupped her chin, "Don't cry, Jazz. It's okay. I'm sorry, too, for the way I snapped at you on the phone. I'm not used to this awkwardness between us, and I'm afraid I haven't handled this whole thing very well. That's why I came over here yesterday morning. To apologize to you. Only I never got a chance."

Jasmine blinked a number of times as her brain scrambled to process what she'd just heard.

"I'm glad I did too. Hard telling how long you would've been lying there if I hadn't."

Jasmine stared, unbelieving. Her family had failed to mention that detail to her. "I didn't know." She glanced down and plucked at the fuzzy pills on her fleece blanket. "No one told me any of this. I was so devastated because I hadn't seen or heard from you since the night you left in such a hurry that I figured you were still upset with me. That you never wanted to see me again."

The mixture of uncertainty and forlornness on Jasmine's face left Jack speechless. She thought he didn't care about her anymore, and that crushed him to the core.

He collected both of her hands between his. "There is nothing you could do or say that would make me not love you." Realizing his blunder, he quickly added. "We've been friends far too long to let something come between us. And I'm sorry no one told you anything, and that you thought I no longer cared. Now I wish I would've stayed longer at the hospital, but I left when Chloe asked—"

"When Chloe asked what?" She searched his face.

"Jack, could you come and help me, please?" Chloe hollered from the kitchen.

Relieved he didn't have to answer Jasmine's question, with a quick squeeze to her hands, he stood. "I'll be right back." He turned and strode into the kitchen.

"Thanks, Chloe. You're timing was perfect," he

whispered next to her.

"My timing? What are you talking about?" She tugged some purple mitten potholders on and reached inside the oven, pulling out a large oblong pan.

"Never mind."

She set the pan on the stove and spiked one eyebrow up at him.

Me and my big mouth. He shouldn't have said anything to her, and if he had any kind of luck at all, she'd let the subject drop. He didn't want to discuss what he and Jasmine had been talking about. Not yet anyway.

"Jack?" Both brows rose this time. When Chloe got something on her mind it was hard to keep her from prodding until she got her answer.

"Forget it." He gave her a pointed look. The same one he used to inform Chloe to stop badgering him. "What did you need my help with?"

She studied his face, looking like she wanted to ask him again, but then nodded. "Okay. I'll forget it...for now."

That woman didn't know when to give up.

"Would you get some TV trays out?" Chloe asked. "We'll eat in the living room so Jazz will be more comfortable."

Chloe turned back to the stove. Jack grabbed three wooden trays off the rack near the dining room table and scanned the room. On the table sat two blooming plants with a Get Well Soon balloon sticking out of one of them, a large box of chocolates, and three stuffed animals, but no bouquet.

He set the last tray down in front of Jasmine and asked, "Where are the flowers I sent you?"

She scrunched her shoulders. "What flowers?" Before he had a chance to open his mouth, she asked, "Can we talk later? Please?" The vulnerable look on her face reminded him of an insecure child. And Jasmine was anything but insecure.

One of the things he loved about her was the confidence she had in herself, in her artistic abilities and business savvy, and in her knack for handling any situation that life threw her way. Until lately that is. Something was bothering her, but she wouldn't tell him or anyone else what it was.

"Sure. But right now I need to finish helping Chloe." He waited until she nodded, and then he headed back into the kitchen.

"Were any flowers delivered at the hospital yesterday for Jasmine?"

"No. Why?"

"Because I ordered some, that's why. I'll be back in a second. I've gotta make a quick phone call."

After giving the flower shop a piece of his mind, it hit him why Jasmine had looked so vulnerable. Between the undelivered flowers, their last phone conversation, and not knowing he had been at the hospital, it was no wonder she thought he no longer cared about her. If she only knew how much he really did care. How much he adored her. But then again, how would she know?

When she'd mentioned about him marrying another and had cried out for Simonrapport, his own pain and wounded pride had kept him from visiting her. Shame pinched him in the gut over his childish behavior. But he'd find some way to make it up to her and prove his undying devotion.

The sight and smell of bubbling hot lasagna made his stomach growl.

Chloe giggled. "I'd better hurry. Your stomach sounds like Jasmine's."

"Even our stomachs are in sync."

"What's that supposed to mean?"

He tilted his head and looked down at her.

Chloe grinned. "Ahhhh. Never mind. Now if you two

would just get your hearts in sync." She handed him a small bowl of salad, and a dinner plate loaded with lasagna, stuffed mushrooms, and garlic bread with melted mozzarella cheese on top. "Would you please take this over to Jazz?"

Jack finished helping Chloe. After they all had their food and drinks, they bowed their heads and prayed. No one talked during dinner as they chowed down their food as though they hadn't eaten in days. Every time he looked Jasmine's way, he caught her staring at him.

Even with her rumpled hair and lack of make-up, she was the most beautiful woman he'd ever known. And the only woman he ever wanted to know.

The doorbell rang.

"I'll get it." Jack shifted his tray out of the way and strode toward the entryway.

He swung the door open. All he saw was a plastic bag and flowers until they lowered and a lady with apologetic blue eyes gazed up at him.

"I'm so sorry, Mr. Warren. My new driver forgot to deliver your flowers. If there's any way I can make it up to you, please let me know."

Knowing it was a mere oversight and one that had better never happen again, he handed her a tip and thanked her. He closed the door and headed toward Jasmine. "This is what you were supposed to get yesterday." He removed the plastic, rearranged things on the end table, and set the vase down.

Jasmine's sleepy eyes widened. "Fire-and-ice roses. My favorite." She ran her fingers over the purple vase. "I love purple."

"I know." Jack handed her the card. "Here."

As she read, he mentally recited the words he'd written.

Jasmine,
As always, I'm thinking of you, and praying for a

speedy recovery. Don't ever scare me like that again!
   All my love, Jack.

A lone tear trickled down her cheek. Jack fought the urge to take her into his arms and kiss it away.

"Thank you." She smiled.

"You're welcome." Not knowing what else to do, he sat down, forked the last bite of his lasagna into his mouth, and watched Jasmine yawn as she struggled to stay awake.

She set her fork down and looked at Chloe and him. "I'm sorry I'm so sleepy. It must be the medicine. I think I'm gonna lie down and close my eyes for a few minutes."

Chloe pushed herself up off the loveseat, but Jack motioned for her to remain seated.

He moved Jasmine's tray and waited for her to lie down before he draped a blanket over her and kissed her forehead. "Sleep well. I'll talk to you later."

"Jack."

"Yeah."

"I still want to know what Chloe asked you." With that her eyes drifted shut.

Jack stared into her sleeping face. He wanted to run his fingers down her smooth cheek and over her sweet lips. The overwhelming desire to hold her in his arms and kiss her with all the suppressed love inside him tugged at his heartstrings until he finally had to force himself to look away.

He thought about her request and what he would say to her. How could he tell her the truth about why it bothered him that she called out Simonrapport's name instead of his? He knew if he poured his heart out to her now, it would scare her, and she'd leave sooner. He refused to take that risk. Instead, he'd bide his time until God showed him when the timing was right. Meanwhile, he needed to figure out a way to avoid answering her. Their future, if any, depended on it.

CHAPTER EIGHT

Jasmine woke up with a splitting headache.

10:37 p.m.—time for more medicine.

Her focus drifted toward the loveseat where Chloe lay curled up in a ball with one foot sticking out from under the heavy comforter. Light from the television flickered across Chloe as it switched scenes from an old black and white movie. How could her sister sleep with all those flashes of light dancing across her face?

Jasmine glanced around the room hunting for the prescription bottle when her line of vision fell on her laptop. She wondered if Simonrapport was online.

She tossed aside the heavy comforter. The cold air drew a loud gasp from her lungs, so she grabbed her fleece coverlet and pulled it tight around her shoulders before sliding her feet into her purple fuzzy slippers.

Keeping her gaze frozen on Chloe, she picked up her laptop and crept into the kitchen. She hated being sneaky. But if Chloe woke up and saw what she was doing, there would be a repeat performance of the blowout she and Jack had when he discovered her talking to a stranger on the Internet. The last thing Jasmine needed or wanted was to explain herself yet again.

She shifted in her seat until she found a comfortable position, and booted up her computer.

Windows chimed. Jasmine quickly muted the speakers. When it finished booting, she brought up her instant chat messenger. Even though her head throbbed, her fingers were numb, and her wrist and body ached, seeing Simonrapport online brought a smile to her face. She'd deal with the pain after she sent a message to the man whose company had helped make her life less lonesome. A man who somehow made her feel special.

Good evening, Simonrapport.

Jasmine pressed Send, then made her way to the bathroom. Because the blanket had slipped off her shoulders when she typed, she decided to wear her soft and warm purple robe.

After downing a pain pill, she headed back to the table toting hot water, one of her favorite warm-up drinks, and a small space heater which she turned toward her chair and clicked on high.

Easing herself onto the chair, she spread the heavy coverlet over her lap, and clicked on the flashing message screen.

Hey there. I thought you'd forgotten about me. <grin> I'm glad you didn't. What have you been up to lately?

Silly man. Of course she hadn't forgotten him. She typed her message.

*Remember how we talked about McDonald's and Sausage McMuffins? Well, it sounded so good, I decided to go get one. Only I never made it. I slipped on the ice and ended up in the hospital with a concussion. Can you believe it? They kept me overnight. So, you see, I didn't forget about you. Quite the contrary, actually. *smiling**

She wanted to tell him she had thought about him often, but she didn't want to give him the wrong idea.

Her foot jiggled as she waited for his reply.

I'm so sorry to hear about your fall. I hope you're doing okay. Are you in much pain? Shouldn't you be resting? I wish I could have been there to help you. Is someone staying with you now?

What a sweetheart to be so concerned about her health.

Yes, my sister is staying with me for a couple of days. I'm still in a lot of pain, but I'll survive. I've been through worse things than this before. Thank you for your thoughtfulness, Simonrapport. She paused, then decided to go ahead and ask the question on her mind. *I know this is personal, and I hope you don't mind my asking, but I was wondering if you'd be willing to give me your first name. It feels rather strange calling you Simonrapport all the time.*

She clicked Send.

Jasmine picked up her drink and sipped it. The quiet hum from the heater filled the silence.

When he didn't reply right away, she flicked her thumbnail with her teeth, and stared at the screen. Minutes later, the monitor lit up with his answer, and she stopped bothering her nail and relaxed.

Did your sister take time off of work so she could stay with you? And, no, it's not too personal of a question. I'm a man, so I don't have to be as careful as a woman does about giving out personal information on the Internet. However, I still use caution. If you think real hard, you'll be able to figure out my real name. Take a wild guess. <grin>

How fun. Jasmine smiled at the game she was about play.

Okay, let's see. Peter? Paul? Henry. No, wait, I know—Simon? As in Simonrapport. Am I right?

While waiting for his reply, she brought up a dictionary web page and typed in *rapport*.

Definition: Relationship, especially one of mutual trust or emotional affinity. Relation marked by harmony, conformity, accord or affinity.

The nickname fit him, and he definitely harmonized with her emotions.

A flashing light on her start bar caught her eye. She downed another drink of her water and then clicked on the message.

You're good. hehe. Actually, it wasn't too hard to

figure out. Simon is correct. If you ever feel comfortable enough with me, perhaps you could tell me your first name. ONLY if you want to though. I don't want you doing anything that you're uncomfortable with.

Indecision about what to do tumbled around her mind. Surely giving him her first name only wouldn't hurt, would it? There had to be thousands of Jasmines on the Internet. Besides, he'd been nothing but kind and considerate and the man professed to be a Christian.

Do not be deceived.

Deceived?

Deceived about what?

Silence.

She had no clue what the message meant, so she went ahead and typed her post.

In answer to your earlier question, my sister is able to stay with me because she owns her own business and has a trusted employee taking care of things for her. You're right, you are a man and you don't have to be as careful, but for some strange reason, I trust you. My name is Jasmine.

The instant she clicked on Send, Jack's warning bombarded her mind, and a sinking feeling washed over her. After pondering the whole thing, she figured Jack was just being paranoid and overprotective again, at least where Simon was concerned anyway, because not every person on the Internet was bad. Numerous magazine articles were written about fulfilling Internet relationships and marriages. Besides, she wasn't looking to marry Simon or anyone else.

Jasmine's a beautiful name. Isn't that the name of a flower? How'd your mother come up with it? My mother named me after her favorite singer. Can you imagine her favorite was Paul Simon? Not that there was anything wrong with him, mind you, it's just that out of all the singers in the world, she loved him best. Good thing she didn't love Tiny Tim. I can't imagine me at six-foot two, weighing two-hundred and ten pounds, being called 'Tiny'.

Jasmine muffled a giggle.

That is too funny. Somehow the nickname Tinyrapport isn't nearly as appealing. hehehe Now, to answer your question. My mother loves perfume. So, when my identical sisters and I were born, she named each of us after one of her favorite fragrances. But she spelled Shanell differently.

Send.

You said, 'your identical sisters', as in plural. Are you a triplet?

Yes, I am. My other sister's name is Chloe. She's the one staying with me now.

Jasmine rubbed her weary eyes. The pain pill made her drowsy, but she was enjoying herself way too much to stop.

They continued talking until twelve-thirty when Simon announced he needed to go and asked if she'd be online tomorrow. She told him she would try. Although it had only been seconds since she'd shut her computer down, she missed Simon already. He was an enigma she longed to know better.

She turned the space heater off, headed to the sofa, and slid under the heavy comforter.

"What were you doing on your computer for so long?" Chloe asked.

Jasmine sucked in a sharp breath. "Chloe! You scared me half to death. I thought you were sleeping."

"I know I'm a sound sleeper, Jazz, but I've had my ear tuned to your every movement."

"Now you know why we call you Miss Mother Hen," she responded with a hint of sarcasm. Sometimes Jasmine didn't mind Chloe's doting and her nosiness, but other times it irritated her to no end.

"So, what kept you interested for so long?"

"If you must know, I was talking to a friend online."

"You have a friend online? Who is she?"

As usual, her sister ignored Jasmine's cynical response and plunged forward. Knowing Chloe, she wouldn't stop until Jasmine spilled it all out. Well, not this time. "Can we can talk later? I'm tired and I wanna go to sleep. Good night." Jasmine didn't bother hiding her irritation. She pulled the comforter under her chin and ignored Chloe's heavy drama queen sigh. It was none of her sister's business who she talked to.

If nothing is wrong with what you're doing, then why were you being so secretive?

Lord, I'm tired of explaining my every move to them, that's all. Besides, it's nobody's business what I do.

Not even Mine?

Lord, You know everything I do is Your business and that I've always included You in my daily plans and sought Your will for my life.

Except in this area.

Can we talk tomorrow, Lord? I'm tired.

Silence.

Lord?

More silence.

Well, I'm taking that as a yes.

Guilt trailed through her spirit like ants at a picnic. Jasmine knew why God didn't respond. Normally she included Him in all her plans, but lately she had tossed Him aside like a discarded book. Well, she felt abandoned too.

The more she thought about it, the angrier she became. It was wrong to be angry with God, but for the first time in her Christian walk, Jasmine didn't care. God didn't seem to be in any hurry to relieve her suffering. For five years she'd asked God to heal her, to deliver her from the isolation and loneliness that plagued her all winter like a deadly virus.

The only answer she saw to her plight now was to move some place warm. Preferably her granddad's lake house. But that was another unanswered prayer. Tired of waiting for God's timing, with or without His help she'd move someplace. Even California if she had to.

California? Where had that thought come from?

Simon lived in California.

When she'd gone online, she wasn't looking for a man, only friendship. But perhaps God had something different in mind and hadn't forgotten her after all. Could Simon be the answer to her prayers and she just wasn't seeing it? Stranger things had happened. The moment she made up her mind to get to know Simon even more, the place underneath her left ribs fluttered with giddiness, and her stomach rattled as if she'd eaten a whole box of chocolates in one sitting. What was up with that?

CHAPTER NINE

Jack stood over his stainless steel stove and flipped his sausage, cheese and egg omelet. The smell of fresh brewed coffee filled the air and called to him. Normally he drank decaf because of his stomach ulcer, but after talking to that cyber nut last night for over two hours, he needed a strong dose of caffeine.

If Jasmine knew how much interest Simonrapport had shown 'Kailee', the disguised nickname Jack had given himself, she wouldn't spend so much time with the dirt bag. As much as he'd love to tell her, he wouldn't. She'd be livid with him if she knew what he had done.

Simonrapport had been polite and sickeningly sweet. Worst of all, he was as sneaky and conniving as a poisonous snake when he tried worming personal information out of 'Kailee'. Jack wondered if he talked all flowery to other women and Jasmine like he had to him. If so, he hoped and prayed Jasmine didn't believe all of his malarkey. But knowing how trusting she was, he doubted she saw through Simonrapport's line of bull. Deep in his gut, he had a sinking feeling she might be giving advantageous information to Simonrapport without even realizing it, enabling the nut to find her.

He slammed his fist into the palm of his hand. The idea of Simonrapport sweet-talking and deceiving his Jazzy drove a spike through him that threatened to drive him crazy. He would like nothing more than to rearrange the guy's face.

The phone rang.

Hoping it was Jasmine, he turned off the burner and reached across the counter to answer it. His elbow bumped his coffee cup, tipping it over.

"Oh no," Jack groaned as the brown liquid headed toward his commercial designs. The ones he'd been up most of the night finishing. He snatched the papers right before the coffee reached them and quickly unraveled a bunch of paper towels to sop up the liquid.

He yanked the phone off the wall. One more ring and it would have gone to the answering machine. He tamped down his frustration before punching the talk button. "Hello."

"Jack. This is Chloe."

"Chloe?" He switched the phone to his other ear. "Why are you whispering? Is Jasmine okay?"

"She's fine."

"You'll have to speak up. I'm having a hard time hearing you." He turned the volume up on his phone, gathered the wad of soaked paper towels, and dumped them into the trash.

"I can't. I don't want Jasmine to hear me. She's in the shower now, so I'll make this quick. Do you remember the guy you told me about last night after Jasmine went to sleep? The one from the Internet?"

"Yes. What about him?" Jack pressed his fist into his burning gut and slunk into a dining room chair.

"Well, Jasmine was on her computer for two hours last night. When I asked what she'd been doing, she told me she'd been talking to a friend. I'm assuming it was him because she got kind of snippy when I asked. I can't quite place my finger on it, but something isn't right about this whole thing. Every time I think about it, I get this unsettling pit in my spirit."

Jack spiked his fingers through his hair. He understood exactly what Chloe was saying. He felt it too.

"I didn't get that before when Jasmine told me about being in chat rooms and stuff," Chloe continued. "But this time, I have this... I don't know... a feeling, a sense, a something. Maybe it's because Jasmine's never been so secretive before. Whatever it is, Jack, I have to admit, I'm worried."

"I know, Chlo. Every time I think about this guy, I get a major check in my spirit too. Last night," he paused, deciding just how much he wanted to reveal. Knowing he could trust her, he trudged forward. "I called Stan, who you might remember from high school."

"Yes. I remember him."

"He's a private investigator. When I told him how I felt, he suggested I disguise myself as a lonely female. I didn't much care for the idea at first because I hate deception, but I went ahead and downloaded the same chat messenger Jazz has and contacted Simonrapport. I used a fake user name, Kailee, and talked to him. I could tell the guy was choosing his words carefully the whole time we talked, and he was just a little too nice and a little too perfect." Jack picked up a lead holder and twirled it through his fingers. "Come to think of it, what time did Jasmine go online?"

"About ten-thirty or so. Why?"

"That's just about the time I finished talking with him"

"Jack, there's more. Last night when I answered Jasmine's phone, I heard someone breathing and whispering. It sounded like he said he wanted her and loved her. This morning when the phone rang, I answered it and whoever it was, hung up."

Certain this guy had already found Jasmine, Jack swallowed the panic rising in him. He had to keep his wits about him so he could think clearly. He opted to keep his suspicions to himself, not wanting to worry Chloe more than she already was. Jack jotted down a note to himself to call Stan about the phone calls.

"Do me a favor. If she gets any more calls like that, let me know, okay? And see if you can get her talking about him. Find out all you can about this guy and get back to me."

"I will."

He detected the concern in her voice. "Don't you worry, Chloe, I'll handle this."

"I know you will, Jack. Thank you. Listen, I don't hear the shower running anymore. I'll see what I can do. And, Jack?"

"Yeah?"

"Don't give up on her. I know she loves you. She's coming. I have to go. Bye." Her last five words strung together in one long syllable and then the dial tone buzzed in his ear.

He replaced it in its cradle and pinched the bridge of his nose. He needed to get his mind off the whole mess and trust God, so he sent up a quick prayer. "God, I know people make prank calls all the time, so please show me if I'm just being overly protective here and jumping to conclusions. If not, would you please help me to keep her safe?"

His stomach rumbled. He tossed the cold omelet onto a plate and stuck it in the micro. While waiting for it to nuke, he grabbed two of his favorite chocolate peanut butter cookies from the plastic container Jasmine had brought them in. That sweet woman loved to bake goodies for the abused women's shelter, the homeless shelter, Miss Schamburg, and the charity bake sale benefits. And for him. Her thoughtfulness and kindness never ceased to amaze him.

The microwave bell dinged. Jack removed his omelet and filled his coffee cup before heading to his breakfast cove. He straddled the wooden pine stool, hooking his heels on the crosspiece. After he finished off the eggs and cookies, he cupped the coffee mug in his hands, leaned his elbows on the split-log slab he'd made into a long tabletop, and stared out the window.

Jack watched in awe as the sun rose from behind the mountain. It was as if God had taken a canvas and painted streaks of pink, yellow, and orange across a blue sky. Icy glitter danced in the sunlit air. Icicles hung from the roof like intricate pieces of blown glass. Frosty shards of crystallized glass clung to the weeds and bushes. "Well done, Lord," Jack whispered reverently as he continued to peruse God's masterpiece.

Snow perched on the limbs of the aged pine trees. A thick blanket of snow, dotted with evidence of passing elk, covered the landscape.

He blew into his coffee cup and took a sip. Too bad Jasmine wasn't sitting here with him, enjoying this breathtaking scene. He could live here a happy camper the rest of his life. *Without Jasmine? Yeah right.*

Jack released a weighty sigh and closed his eyes as defeat stomped him in the chest. If only Jasmine loved him as a woman loved a man, then regardless of how much he loved this place, he'd marry her and move any where she wanted in a heartbeat. Without God's intervention, that wasn't likely to happen anytime soon. He wondered if there was anything he needed to say or do to help things along with Jasmine.

Jack glanced at his watch. He still had time before his meeting, so he picked up his Bible. It fell open to the middle of the book. Proverbs 3:5,6 seemed to leap off the page at him:

Trust in the Lord with all your heart and lean not unto your own understanding. In all your ways acknowledge Him and He will direct your paths.

"Thank You, Lord. I really needed to hear that today. Direct my steps and show me what to do, and when." Feeling some of the melancholy lift, he fed Willbee, took his shower, and left for his office.

Like a jog along the Yampa Valley River on a hot

summer day, the long, hot shower refreshed Jasmine. Ready to enjoy this new day, she descended the stairs with a light step. "Good morning, Chloe," she chirped as she entered her living room.

"Good morning, Jazz. You sure sound chipper for not sleeping very well."

Jasmine refused to let her sister's keen intuition get to her. "I feel pretty good other than a headache."

"I made you some waffles. How many would you like?"

"You don't have to wait on me. I feel fine. In fact," she glanced at the clock, "you have to be at the shop pretty soon, don't you?"

"Nope. Not today. I'm staying here with you."

"Chloe," Jasmine deposited her hands on her hips. "It's not necessary. I really do feel pretty good today. Besides, I need to get some work done and you know I can't work with someone else around."

"Well, I can go in another room so I won't disturb you, but I'm not leaving you by yourself today." The look she shot Jasmine brooked no room for argument.

"Okay, suit yourself." She shrugged and headed toward the kitchen with Chloe on her heels.

Jasmine popped a fresh strawberry into her mouth and reached for a plate.

"Oh no you don't, Jasmine Rose. I'll get that for you. Go. Sit. Down." Chloe turned her toward the living room and gave her a light shove. "Scoot."

"Yes, Mama," she tossed over her shoulder.

Chloe popped her bottom with a tea-towel.

"Hey! No fair. You have a weapon and I don't." She spun around, determined to get even.

Chloe held her hands up. "Give. Give. I surrender."

Peals of laughter rolled out of them both. It hurt her head to laugh, but she didn't care. Laughter was something she hadn't experienced very much of lately and she missed it.

"Okay go sit down now," Chloe ordered again, still chuckling. "I'll bring you some breakfast."

Jasmine grabbed a TV tray and headed to the sofa. Chloe placed a hot beverage and a plate with two waffles smothered with whipped cream and fresh sliced strawberries on the tray.

"This looks heavenly. By the way, where'd you get the strawberries?"

"Mother and Daddy brought them over yesterday when you were sleeping, and Shanell brought you the Irish Crème coffee."

"They were here?" Her eyes widened. "Why didn't you wake me?"

"You needed rest. You didn't get any in the hospital with the nurses waking you up all the time."

"It cracks me up, the nurses tell you to rest, and then they keep you awake most of the night, checking on you and giving you medicine. If you need rest, a hospital is no place to get any."

"That's for sure." Chloe giggled, then pursed her lips. "Can I ask you something?"

"Sure." Jasmine took a bite of waffle and licked the whipped cream off of her upper lip. "This tastes so good," she said around the food in her mouth. "Thank you. What did you want to ask me?" She forked another bite and started chewing.

Chloe tilted her head. "Who's Simonrapport?"

Jasmine gasped, sputtered and started hacking. Chloe took a step to help her, but Jasmine waved her away. "I... I'm fine," she rasped, tapping her chest. Then she coughed harder.

"Here, take a drink."

Jasmine grabbed the water and sipped on it until her throat cleared. "Thanks." She set the glass on the tray.

Chloe stared at her. "So, who's Simonrapport?"

"How do you know about him? Did Jack tell you?" Jasmine narrowed her eyes.

"Cool your jets, Jazz. At the emergency room you kept asking for Simonrapport. Is that some guy's name? Simon Rapport."

Jasmine tamped down a rising scream of frustration. *God, if you care about me at all get me out of here. I'm tired of answering to them and fed-up with their smothering me.*

Nonetheless, knowing Chloe wouldn't give up until she told her, Jasmine decided to give her enough information to make her satisfied. "Simonrapport is the nickname of a Christian guy I met online. The reason I probably said his name was because I was suppose to contact him when I got back from Mickey D's the other day. And," she twitched a shoulder, "I wasn't here."

"You know him well enough you'd be that concerned?" Chloe tilted her head and spiked one eyebrow.

"No, I don't," Jasmine bit back.

Chloe slipped onto the loveseat next to Jasmine. "Listen, Jazz. I just wondered. Don't go getting yourself into a dither." She smiled. "I just thought he must be someone pretty important to you for you to mention his name so often."

Just what all had she said that day? Jasmine shoved another bite of waffle into her mouth, no longer enjoying it.

"If you don't mind, I'd like to ask one more question." Chloe folded her hands in front of her.

Dread washed over her, but she nodded for Chloe to go ahead.

"How does one meet Christian males online? I might like to try it."

Again, Jasmine choked on her food. She quickly grabbed her water to wash it down.

"Y—you?" she gasped. "Miss-no-nonsense-I-have-everything-together wants to meet a guy online?" Jasmine moved the tray with her half-eaten plate of food aside before turning toward her sister. "Don't you go gettin' any flaky ideas about meeting some nut from online. It isn't safe."

Chloe raised both eyebrows this time and gave her an I-rest-my-case-look.

Jasmine groaned. Chloe had set her up. She had to figure out a way to wipe that smug look off her sister's face.

"I'm only talking to this guy to fill in the lonely hours when it's cold outside." Well, at least it started out that way anyway. But she wouldn't tell Chloe that. "I'm not stupid you know," she huffed.

You gave him your first name last night, and your sisters' too.

Her defensiveness evaporated like a wisp of smoke in the wind. *You idiot. What have you done?*

"Jazz," Chloe paused, sending her a loving look mixed with trepidation. "Pray about this Simonrapport person. You have no way of knowing if he is who he says he is, or if he's really the way he portrays himself to be. Only God does. The Holy Spirit gives us a conscience. Pay close attention to what yours is telling you about this situation." Chloe pushed herself up and gazed down at her. "You know what I don't understand?"

Jasmine shook her head.

"Why you feel the need to talk to some guy on the Internet when you have Jack."

Longing filled Chloe's eyes, but as usual, she masked it. Chloe had always been in love with Jack, but Jack didn't return Chloe's feelings. This scenario was a wheel they had all been around before.

"You know Jack and I are just friends."

Chloe cocked one brow.

Jasmine tucked the long bangs that draped across her left eye over her ear. "Trust me, there's nothing between us." *Nor will there ever be. I refuse to end up like Lori and Steve.*

It was clear Chloe wanted to argue, but the phone rang. Jasmine looked at the end table but didn't see the phone in its cradle, and it wasn't on the coffee table either.

On the third ring Chloe rushed into the kitchen and snatched the phone off the wall. "Hello. No, this isn't Jasmine. Just a minute and I'll get her."

Jasmine walked up next to her. "Who is it?" she whispered, hoping it was Jack.

Chloe covered the mouthpiece with her hand. "I don't know. I don't recognize his voice. Maybe it's a customer." She handed Jasmine the phone.

A customer? Jasmine's face puckered. They wouldn't have her private, unlisted number. They'd call her business number. "Hello, this is Jasmine." Soft Mozart music played in her ear.

"Hello." Jasmine looked at Chloe, hiking her eyebrows and one palm. The music faded. "Listen, I can hear you breathing. Who is this, and what do you want?"

Chloe skewed her head and frowned.

"You." A deep voice replied. "I want *all* of you, Jasmine. And it's only a matter of time before I'll have you all to myself. Then I'll make you mine—forever."

The seductive tone with a hint of a southern drawl sent tentacles of fear crawling up Jasmine's spine. Her arms fell limp at her sides.

The phone clamored to the floor.

Had RodeoCowboy found her like he said he had? Or was some other nut playing sick tricks on her?

She struggled to draw air into her collapsed lungs. Through a daze of slow motion she watched Chloe pick up the phone.

"Who is this?" her sister demanded. "Hello. Hello." Chloe's voice sounded hollow and distant.

The room rotated and Jasmine swayed with it.

White spots danced in the darkness of her gaze.

Her body thumped against the floor.

And then nothing.

CHAPTER TEN

Jack raised his fist.

A high-pitched scream cut through him.

He barreled into Jasmine's kitchen.

Chloe whirled, screaming.

His gaze flew to Jasmine, crumpled in a heap on the floor.

Jack dropped to one knee next to her.

He jerked his coat off and slung it aside.

"Oh, Jack, I'm so glad you're here." Chloe knelt down opposite of him, trembling.

Jack searched for a pulse and blew out a short breath when he found one. "What's going on?"

"She fainted."

"I can see that. What happened? The concussion?"

Chloe shook her head.

He frowned, then his eyes roamed over Jasmine's pale face. "Jazz, can you hear me?"

She stirred, mumbling something incoherent.

"Come on, baby. Wake up." Jack willed the adrenaline rushing through him to slow down, so he could concentrate on Jasmine's condition and Chloe's answer. "Why'd she faint?"

Chloe jerked a palm upward. "Some man called asking for Jasmine. I assumed it was a customer. When she asked, 'who is this and what do you want', she looked scared and dropped the phone. I picked it up and asked, 'Who is this?', but all I heard was a dial tone." She paused. "Jack, do you suppose it was...?" She grabbed his gaze and questioned him silently.

Jack nodded. Anger tried to grasp him, but he

punched it away. Right now he couldn't let his mind dwell on the caller. Jasmine needed all his care and attention. Placing his arms underneath Jasmine's shoulders and knees, he picked her up and carried her over to the sofa. He sat down, cradling Jasmine in his lap. "Would you go get a cool cloth, please?"

"Sure. Do you need anything else?"

Only Jasmine, but he didn't say that out loud. "No thanks."

He ran his hand over Jasmine's cheek. "Hey, Jazz. Come on. Wake up. Can you hear me?"

Chloe handed him a wet cloth.

Jack blotted Jasmine's face and settled the washcloth on her forehead.

She twisted her head from side to side. "That's cold," she muttered, slipping the washrag off of her face and letting it drop to the floor.

Her eyes shot open.

She bolted upright, clipping Jack's chin with her head.

Her gaze flew about the room.

Fright-filled eyes landed on him.

Her body trembled.

"Hey, hey, it's okay. I've got ya." To affirm what he said, he pulled her tight against him, pressed her head against his shoulder, and settled his chin on top of her head, despite the fact it still hurt from her ramming it.

A moment slipped by, then Jasmine pulled back again. Tears pooled her blue-green eyes and spilled down her face. "Oh, Jack, it was awful." She flung her arm around his neck and clutched him tight.

Jack held her and allowed her tears to soak his shirt. "You're okay, Jazz. Can you tell me what happened?"

She drew in several choppy breaths, leaned her head back and gazed up at him. "Some man said—" Her voice cracked.

He tucked her head closer into his shoulder. "Calm down, sweetie. Take your time."

She clung to him, trembling.

He kissed the top of her head. Seeing the woman he loved tormented like this made him want to hold her even closer and kiss away the memory of whatever had terrified her. Her nearness wreaked havoc on his senses— bombarding his mind and his body until his whole being ached to comfort her. Jack immediately cast down the longing sensations running through him. God's Word controlled him, not his male desires.

Pulling himself together, he motioned for Chloe to hand him some tissues, and pressed them into Jasmine's hand.

After blowing her nose, she drew in a shaky breath, pinched her eyes shut, and swallowed several times. Tears streamed down her cheeks. "It was so creepy. He sounded so seductive and frightening."

Jack rubbed his hand up and down her arm, tugging her close. He couldn't wait to find out what the man had said, but he would not be impatient. Jasmine needed time to gather herself together. As far as he was concerned, she could have forever.

She rested her head in the crook of his elbow and looked up at him. "When I asked him what he wanted—" She sniffed, her eyes dropped from his. She tugged and twisted the tissues.

"It's okay, baby. Calm down. Take your time."

She nodded, and her hair tickled his nose. She drew in a short breath. "He said he wanted *all* of me and that it would just be a matter of time before he had me all to himself."

Anger flashed through Jack, white hot and destructive. He watched her swallow several times, and her eyes seemed to plead with him to make everything go away.

"And that he'd make me *his* forever." Jasmine pressed her head against his chest and wept. "Why would someone do this?" Her lips brushed his chest. "I'm so scared, Jack. Who is he? What does he want from me?"

His heart broke seeing Jasmine so helpless and scared. Jack swallowed hard against the lump in his throat as the reality of the situation slammed into him full force.

Some nut was after his sweet Jasmine.

He wanted to find the guy and beat him to a bloody pulp—to make him pay for frightening her. He wanted to protect her from every bad thing in her life. From every bad person.

Trust Me.

His flesh and his spirit battled, until his spirit finally won. *I want to do what's right, Lord. Help me to leave this in Your hands.*

"I'm going to call the police and report this," Chloe stood.

"Good idea," Jack agreed. "Oh, by the way, I'm sorry I barged in here and scared you. But when I heard the scream, I didn't think, I just acted." He frowned. "Come to think of it, why wasn't the door locked?"

"I needed some paperwork from my car." Chloe shrugged. "I didn't see any need to lock it in broad daylight. I probably should have knowing there's a Peeping Tom running loose in the neighborhood."

"What do you mean there's a Peeping Tom running loose?"

"Haven't you been reading the papers?" Chloe continued to keep her voice down.

"I haven't had time." Jack spoke above a whisper.

"A customer of mine, Trista Davenport, lives a little over a mile from here. At the Stenson place. Anyway, she was accosted by a Peeping Tom last week, but her neighbor's dog helped her escape. From what I've heard, some of the other women weren't as fortunate.

Supposedly they started receiving phone calls and then he showed up." Chloe's eyes widened. "You don't think it was him do you?" Her attention flew to the window.

Jack didn't know anymore. Earlier he was certain Simonrapport had been behind all of this. And now...

All he knew was some psycho was frightening his Jazz. And that psycho would pay. Whoever he was.

Chloe turned her attention toward the door and pumped her foot. Fidgeting in her chair, she leaped up and scrambled to the door and locked it. She headed toward the window and started peering around, then flew into the kitchen where she snatched up the phone.

Jack's eyes drifted to Jasmine.

Jasmine leaned her head back and looked up at him.

He waited for her to move off his lap, but she didn't. Her translucent, bluish-green eyes collided with his, taking him prisoner.

After staring at each other for a whisper of time, Jack's eyes drifted toward her lips. As he pondered what it would be like to feel her sweet mouth under his, a tingling sensation teased his lips. His eyes traveled up her face. What he saw made him blink.

She looked at his mouth.

A flicker of hope ignited within him. Did she want to kiss him as much as he longed to kiss her?

She looked up at him with a shy smile. Her eyes drifted shut and her chin rose, as though she were welcoming his kiss.

Jack's blood raced through his veins as he lowered his head. His stomach leapt with excitement. Her breath, a mere whisper away, mingled with his.

"Jack, I wonder if you—"

Jack jerked his head up.

"Oh." Chloe's face reddened. She quickly averted her gaze. "Sorry."

Jasmine squirmed, then wiggled her way out of his

arms and stood unsteadily. Not looking back, she headed toward the bathroom.

Jack's eyes slammed shut. He wanted to kick himself into next week for allowing her nearness to toy with his emotions. And for leading him to do something he should never have done.

What an idiot he'd been. How could he have forgotten so quickly that she only thought of him as just a friend? What kind of friend put another friend in that awkward situation? This time, he wouldn't blame her if she sent him away for good. His stomach plummeted.

"I'm sorry, Jack. I ruined it for you, didn't I?" Chloe whispered with eyes full of remorse and sadness.

"It's okay. I had no right to—" He ran his hand through his hair. "Just forget it, okay. I should go now."

He rose and strode toward the door.

"Jack." The softness in Jasmine's tone bade him to stop.

He wasn't sure he wanted to face her right now, but he would have to eventually, so he figured he might as well get it over with. He made a quick plea to the Lord before turning around. "Yeah?"

Jasmine walked up next to him and rested her hand on his arm. "Where are you going?"

Her eyes questioned him with a mixture of sadness and fear. Seeing no sign of her being upset with him, his muscles relaxed, and he answered her. "I have to get back to work. I have several appointments today."

"Oh." Sadness shielded her face. Her hand dropped, and she nodded.

Worry for her pressed in on him. "You okay?"

"I'm fine." She raked her thumbnail over her teeth.

Jack knew that gesture well. She wasn't fine. Somehow he needed to make things right between them again. He tipped her chin up. "Listen. Why don't I order Chinese food for dinner tonight, and we can all play some

UNO?" He released her chin and glanced at Chloe. "You'll still be here, right?"

A look of understanding passed between them.

"Oh yes," she stated, matter-of-factly, then sent Jasmine a look that dared her to argue. "She's not getting rid of me that easily."

"Good. It's settled then." He turned to leave. "Why don't you call Shanell? It'll be just like old times, the four of us friends playing UNO together." Jack made a point of emphasizing the word friends and looked directly at Jasmine when he said it. Hopefully that would make her feel comfortable again.

An unrecognizable emotion shadowed her face. But like a quick cloud cover, it was there one second and gone the next. "Sounds great."

Jack picked up his coat and put it on, then unlocked the door. "Call me if you need me," he said, then turned toward Chloe. "Lock this door again. And keep it locked." Closing the door behind him, he shook his head, wishing he could shut the door to his heart as easily.

Chapter Eleven

Jasmine peered outside. The word deceptive came to mind as she stared at the clear blue sky, knowing the bright sun offered no warmth, and only a bitter freezing cold.

Her eyes followed Jack as he advanced toward his pickup. She forced down the longing to stop him from leaving, to call him back. If only Chloe hadn't interrupted them.

She couldn't believe Jack had almost kissed her. Even stranger yet, she had wanted him to, and that wasn't good. She should have never let down her protective wall and allowed her feelings to take over.

The empty bottle of pills next to Lori's limp form popped into Jasmine's mind.

Fear and confusion pinched her lungs. Jasmine moved away from the door and tried to get a handle on her emotions.

"Do you want to talk?" This time Chloe's question wasn't a demand—only a request.

"No." Jasmine shook her head. Her mind felt fuzzy. The emotional turmoil of the last few days had caught up with her, taking its toll on her body and mind. "All I wanna do is go upstairs and take a nap." She grabbed the gorgeous fire-and-ice roses Jack had given her and trekked her way up the steps.

Jasmine raised her hands in front of her, but she couldn't see them. A small, faraway patch of light beckoned her.

"Jasmine." She heard a ghost-like male voice coming from behind her. "I've come for you, my love."

"Wh—who are you? Wh—what do you want?" She turned, seeing no one, but felt his ghastly presence nearby. Frantically she gulped in huge quantities of air.

"You wound me deeply, Jasmine, that you have forgotten me so soon? But I haven't forgotten you. I've come for you just like I said I would." Was that a southern accent she detected?

Chills chased each other up and down her spine like icy footsteps. She glanced toward the light. Deep down inside, she somehow knew if she reached it, she'd be safe.

But no matter how hard she tried to move her legs, they wouldn't budge. They remained cemented to the floor.

Heavy breath brushed against her neck.

Her hair stood on end.

Her body felt like a million tarantulas were crawling on her.

Suddenly, someone grabbed her from behind and slapped a hand over her mouth. Terror, unlike anything she'd never known before, swept through her.

"I've got you now, my love." He kissed her cheek, leaving behind the scent of stale musk cologne and a sorely neglected mouth.

Her stomach lurched from his vile touch and odors. She jerked his hand off her mouth. "Jaacckk!" she howled.

No response came. Where was he? Why wasn't Jack answering her?

"Jack, where are you?" A heart-wrenching wail rose from the very essence of her soul.

"Don't waste your breath. Jack's gone," the man snarled.

"Leave me alone. I want Jack." She struggled to pull away from his strong grasp, but he held her tight.

"Too bad, Jazzy."

Jazzy? How did he know her nickname? A feeling of dread raced through her.

"You belong to me now." His evil laughter came from the very pits of hell itself. "You're mine. I can't wait until we become one." His terrifying words echoed throughout the black cave. "You're mine. I can't wait until we become one. You're mine. I can't wait until we become one."

Jasmine jerked from his grasp and whirled around.

"You're mine. I can't wait until we become one."

She spun forward.

"You're mine. I can't wait until we become one."

She whirled left.

"You're mine. And I can't wait until we become one."

She spun right.

Feeling his evil presence all around her and yet not seeing him made her head feel as though it would explode. Pressing her hands tight against her ears, she struggled to block out the tormenting words stabbing at her soul. No matter how hard she tried, the mocking words swirled around her until she thought she would go mad. The torture was more than she could bear.

"Stop it! Stop it!" she screamed at the unseen voice that wouldn't let her go. "No! No! You can't have me. I love Jack!"

Jasmine bolted upright, panting like an overheated mountain lion.

Her heart slammed against her ribs.

Her head throbbed with pain.

Chloe burst into her room.

Jasmine's hands flew to her mouth, and she muffled her scream.

Chloe rushed to her and wrapped her arms around Jasmine's trembling body. She held her just like their mother used to when she needed comforting. "You're okay, sweetie. It was just a bad dream." Chloe rocked her gently and whispered a prayer.

Jasmine pressed her head on Chloe's shoulder and held on tight. "It seemed so real."

It took several minutes for her body to stop quivering. Drawing in a shaky breath, she pulled away, and looked at Chloe. The concern on her sister's face crushed Jasmine's heart. She had to pull herself together and put on a brave front for Chloe's sake. She couldn't stand seeing her sister so worried and shaken up. And that she had caused it. Yanking courage to herself, courage she didn't feel, she forced herself to speak and to offer a reassuring smile. "Thank you. I'm fine now."

"Um huh. If you say so." Chloe stood. "Well, you know I'm always here for you."

Jasmine nodded. Love for her sister floated from her.

Chloe smiled, and Jasmine felt her love return to her in a comforting hug. "I know. Thank you. It was just a dumb dream. I'm fine now."

A moment passed and another. Finally Chloe nodded and walked to the door. "I'll be downstairs if you need me." She turned to leave but stopped. "Are you hungry? I made some soup earlier."

Jasmine glanced at the clock. "I can't believe it's a quarter after twelve already." She rubbed her eyes and face. "I'll be right down."

During a quiet meal of homemade vegetable beef soup in a bread bowl, Jasmine mulled over her dream and realized the ridiculousness of it. Of course she loved Jack. He was her best friend. It had to be all the stress, along with her head injury, playing tricks with her mind. She needed a reprieve for her maxed-out nerves. After thanking Chloe for lunch, she snatched up her laptop and headed upstairs. Simon was just the distraction she needed.

Jasmine shut the lid on her laptop and smiled. Simon was a fascinating person, and they had more in common than she'd ever imagined. She looked at the clock on the wall. 4:20. To remove the kinks, she rolled her head from side to side. A nice long bath sounded great. Once she had the claw-foot tub filled, she tossed in a bath oil bead and eased herself into the hot water.

Heat permeated her body and the steamy scent of Jasmine perfume penetrated her sinuses. She closed her eyes and allowed her mind to drift to her granddad's lake house.

Sweet magnolias and gardenias swirled around her senses as her skin soaked up the hot Louisiana sun. Sand squished between her toes as she strolled along the beach.

Jack stepped up alongside her.

They stopped.

His large hands cupped her face.

He lowered his head toward hers until his masculine lips took possession of her mouth— Jasmine's eyes sprang open.

Good grief.

That stupid nightmare had her mixed up something fierce. Kissing Jack was too bizarre for her to wrap her heart around. After all, they'd been best friends as long as she could remember. Then why didn't the kiss feel weird in her imagination?

She ducked her head under the water to rid herself of her wild imagination. There could never be anything between her and Jack. Never. Taking a friendship to the next level was too risky. No way could Jasmine handle the kind of pain Lori had endured. The similarities between their situations were too close for comfort. Lori and Steve's dreams and goals were polar opposite too.

Sure, Jasmine and Jack saw eye-to-eye on everything important in life, but sometimes he treated her more like a five-year-old niece than a grown woman. She wavered between liking the security of his protective stance and wishing he had more confidence in her. She figured his attitude would never change. They'd grown up together and formed opinions of each other long ago. There would be no changing of viewpoints now.

To protect her heart, she resurrected her reasons for not getting involved and for wanting to leave. Jack loved the mountains, the snow, and the bitter cold—and all the activities she loved but could no longer take part in, like cross-country skiing, snowmobiling, and ice skating on the river.

Revulsion for all of it twisted through her.

Nothing or no one would stop her from moving away from Steamboat Springs. A place she now loathed in the very depths of her soul. A place where she would always be known as one of the Moore triplets. A place where she was constantly smothered until the very life was being sucked out of her.

With her well-manufactured wall of protection back in place, she raised her head out of the water, filled her lungs with air, and resumed her restful position.

Jasmine wasn't sure how long she'd sat in the tub, but she realized the water had turned tepid. She stepped out onto the purple bath mat and slipped into her robe.

Dressing in heavy sweats, thick socks and a turtleneck with a sweater pulled over it, she dried her hair, brushed her teeth, and dabbed on a little makeup.

When she reached the bottom of the stairs, the doorbell rang.

Chloe slipped from the kitchen and opened the door.

"Hey, Chloe." Jack's tenor voice drifted through Jasmine's ears like a beautiful romantic melody.

The sight of Jack standing there sent her pulse racing faster than a professional Slednecks snowmobile racer. The words, I love Jack, rushed through her mind again.

Only this time she was 100 percent awake. *This is ridiculous, Jasmine. Stop it!*

"Get in here, and close the door. You're letting all the heat out," Chloe reprimanded him.

Jack threw up his hand in an okay-okay gesture, shut the door, and sat on the bench-seat.

Jasmine watched as he set a white square box on the floor to his left and the UNO card game on the opposite side.

"Where's dinner?" Chloe asked.

He glanced up. "It's being delivered around 6:30." He removed his boots and then stood. When he leaned over to pick up the UNO card game, the front door swung open, knocking him forward, off his feet, and headfirst onto her floor. His chin whacked against the hard wood. UNO cards flew out of the box and sprawled across the room.

Shanell stood inside the open door with wide eyes. "Oh, Jack. I'm so sorry!"

Jasmine rushed down the last two steps toward him as the three of them circled him like a flock of landing birds. "Are you okay?"

"I'm fine." He looked up at her sister, shaking his head. "Nice entrance."

Shanell held her palms up. "Hey, I'm sorry. I didn't see you." She leaned over him to assess the damage at the exact same moment Jack rose. The back of his head collided with her sister's chin.

"Ow." They both thundered in unison.

Jack plopped back down onto the floor, blinking, and shaking his head again.

Shanell rubbed her chin, frowning. "Jack!"

"Me? I didn't do anything."

Seeing the bewildered look on Jack's face, Jasmine struggled to suppress a rising giggle. "Are you two okay?"

When they both nodded, Chloe ordered, "Good. Now shut the door. It's fifteen below out there."

Shanell spun and shoved the door closed. She whirled back around. And when she did, she stepped on Jack's sock-clad foot.

Jack's eyes widened. "Shanell! Get off my foot."

"Oh, Jack. I'm so sorry." She took several steps backward. "Maybe you'd better move inside out of harm's way." Pressed against the door, Shanell gazed at them in apology. "Today's been one of those days. You know, the kind where you drop everything and spill everything."

Jasmine couldn't control herself any longer. She erupted into a spasm of laughter. When her guffaw ended, she noticed everyone staring at her. Judging by the looks on their faces, they thought she'd gone bonkers.

Her nose twitched.

She tittered.

Then laughter barreled out of her again. Before long, everyone had joined her. Her head throbbed from laughing so hard, but she didn't care. It felt great to laugh again. It felt like it had been forever since life didn't feel stacked on top of her.

After a couple of minutes, Shanell removed her winter outerwear, while the rest of them picked up the UNO cards.

Jasmine glanced over at Shanell, who stood statue-still, staring at the floor with a funny look on her face.

Jasmine followed her sister's line of vision and chuckled.

Shanell's foot lay smack dab in the middle of the pastry box. White and brown filling oozed out of the sides.

Jack and Chloe stopped also. One look and their mouths gaped open at Shanell.

"Oh, you've got to be kidding me." Jack rubbed the

back of his neck. "Man, I forgot about the dessert." He cocked a brow at Shanell. "I can't imagine how it slipped my mind."

Slipped? An understatement if Jasmine had ever heard one. Once again, she suppressed a giggle.

Shanell sighed and sent Jack a quirky grin. A playful smile spread across her mouth. "Like I said. 'It's been one of those days.'" She tossed her scarf over her arm and straightened her shoulders.

"Yes, well, I'd like to thank you all for coming tonight. My name is Miss Slippery, and I'll be your waitress for this evening." Shanell positioned one hand as if she were holding a pad in it and the other as if she had a pen in it. "Tonight's dessert special is: Squished Chocolate Delight." She tilted her head, as if listening. "Oh, yes. You heard me correctly. I didn't say Swiss, I said squished. Oh, but don't let that discourage you. I have it on the good authority of my foot that it's very smooth and creamy.

"Now, may I interest you in a slice?" Shanell glanced down. "Um." She quirked her lips sideways. "Make that a scoop."

They all burst out laughing.

Leave it to Shanell. Any time her zany triplet was around there was bound to be amusement. Shanell had a way of finding humor in any discomfited situation.

A cozy feeling wrapped around Jasmine.

Just like old times, the four of them were laughing and enjoying one another's company. She planned to keep it that way too. Never mind that stupid dream. Once again she reminded herself she and Jack were just friends, and that's the way it would forever be. Feelings of anything more be hanged.

Jack added logs to the fireplace, Chloe made hot chocolate, Shanell cleaned up the mess she had made of Jack's chocolate cream pie, and Jasmine set up the game of UNO.

Jasmine snuck over to the end table and grabbed a couple of acetaminophen. Her mind wandered to Simon and what he was doing now. With Chloe here, she didn't get to spend the time she wanted to with Simon. Her sister hovered around Jasmine like a predatory bird over its prey.

"Headache?" Jack's breath brushed her ear, sending goose bumps waddling across her skin.

She thumped her hand over her palpitating heart. "Jack! You just scared ten years off my life. Why do you sneak up on me like that?" *And why did shivers race down my spine when your breath whispered against my ear?*

"I don't. It's just that you're always so busy concentrating on what you're doing that you don't hear me coming." He shrugged matter-of-factly. "You looked a million miles away. Were you staring because your head's bothering you again?"

"Yeah, just a little." She downed the pills with a sip of water. "But don't you go tellin' Chloe, or she'll have me marching right up to bed. I am so ready for her to go home." Jasmine's eyes flew up to Jack's. She couldn't believe she'd just said that to him. She needed to be careful so they didn't discover all of her reasons for wanting to move. They would feel terrible if they knew how she felt. And so would she for saying anything. No, she'd bear that cross herself.

Jack settled his hand on her arm. "Look, Jazz, I know she can get a little bossy, but she's worried about you. We all are."

She knew that. And she hated that they worried about her. But would she ever be free from the guilt of making them worry so much? "You're right, Jack. I don't mean to sound ungrateful. It's just that I can't wait to—" She stopped suddenly and hiked a shoulder. She couldn't believe she'd almost blown it by telling Jack she couldn't wait to spend more time with Simon.

"Wait to what?"

She looked everywhere but at him. "Listen, just forget I said anything." She about-faced, but Jack stopped her by tugging on her arm. He turned her around, facing him.

"You didn't answer my question." His face was so close, she could smell his mountain-fresh aftershave and his cinnamon breath. "You can't wait to what?"

Uncomfortable with his nearness, she stepped back a bit and studied the button on his shirt. Knowing Jack wouldn't give up until she answered him, she reproached herself for not being more guarded with her words.

"You're staring again. Maybe we shouldn't play a game tonight so you can get some rest."

Not again! She couldn't even think without them panicking about whether she was alright or not. And yet she knew if she didn't do something quick, Jack would say something and then they would go home and another evening would be ruined.

In the time it took to draw in half a breath, she closed the distance between them and lowered her voice so Chloe couldn't hear. "Please, Jack. I need this." What she really wanted to do was yell at him to quit babying her and to stop trying to figure out what was best for her. That she was a big girl who could take care of herself if the three of them would ever let her. But that would cause a bigger scene than she wanted to deal with, so once again she caved in and kept her mouth shut.

"It's been a long time since the four of us have gotten together, and I don't want the evening to end because of me. The meds will kick in pretty quick, and I'll be fine. Please, I want to play and spend some time with all of you."

Frustration set in. Here she was a grown woman

begging them to let her play. It was maddening.

Jack glanced toward Chloe and then fixed his eyes on her, "C'mon, Jazz. It's only been a couple of days. A head injury isn't something to mess around with." He drove his fingers through his hair. "Don't you know you can have repercussions from this for several weeks? You've got to take it easy and start taking care of yourself. I don't want anything to happen to you." The soft, worried look in his eyes made her insides squirm.

She gave herself a mental slap. She'd heard that same tone and seen those pleading eyes millions of times, and she always fell for it, letting them make her decisions for her because of it.

In defiance she crossed her arms. This time it had no chance of getting past the protective wall she had erected.

"Jazz? I don't ever want to feel like I did the other day when I found you lying outside. I didn't know if you were—" He turned his head sideways.

She watched his chest rise and fall as he took in a deep breath. When he looked back at her, a shiny gleam filled his eyes. As much as she didn't want it to affect her, there really wasn't any other option. She opened her arms and stepped toward him.

Without question he pulled her into his embrace. She pressed her head against his chest and wrapped her arms around him. He pulled her tight against him and rested his head on top of hers. His accelerated heartbeat matched her own. The urge to kiss him again yanked at her until the rational side of her kicked in, screeching her to a halt and ordering her to push him away. But as much as she hated to admit it, wrapped like a cocoon in Jack's arms felt like home.

Home?

Jolted by the implication that single word implied, her mind screamed its objection. *No! You will not affect me this way. I won't allow it. I will not take the risk of*

losing your friendship or ending up like Lori and Steve.
Frightened by her building emotions and her apparent
lack of control over them, she cleared her throat, gathered
her wits, and stepped out of his arms. "Time to play
UNO." Knowing one look at him would melt her like hot
butter, she whirled and strode toward the table. She would
not give him a chance to weave his trance over her again.

Jack stared after her. What had just happened? One
minute she'd wrapped her arms around him, and the next
she fled like he had leprosy or something. Shutting his
eyes, he thought about how great she'd felt in his arms
and how her body molded into his as if God fashioned her
just for him. If only he could convince Jasmine they
belonged together.

"Jack! Hello!" Chloe chided.

"Yeah?" He blinked once, then glanced in Chloe's
direction. From her frustrated stance he realized he'd
missed something. "What?"

"Twice now, I've said we're ready, and you haven't
moved. Are you going to join us, or you just going to
stand there staring into space?" She smirked. "If I didn't
know any better, I'd think you were the one who hit your
head on the ice."

Inwardly he groaned. Chloe knew what was on his
mind. Over the past several years, the two of them had
spent hours talking about Jasmine. During those talks,
sometimes he'd caught Chloe staring at him like a
lovesick schoolgirl. But the only thing he ever offered her
was friendship. Like Jasmine offered him. Why did love
have to be so unbearably complicated? His heart
constricted with fresh pain. *Help me, Lord, to be strong
and patient.*

He plowed his fingers through his hair and ruffled the
back of his head. Too bad drug companies didn't
manufacture pain medication for aching hearts.

He went over, pulled out a chair, and sat across the table from Jasmine. When he looked at her, she quickly turned away. Baffled, Jack pressed his hands over his face. Tonight he had been sure he'd seen something akin to love in Jasmine's eyes. But judging by her actions now, it was only wishful thinking on his part.

"Jaaack. Pay attention. It's your turn." Chloe's no-nonsense tone broke through his musings.

Needing to lighten his mood, he playfully raised his hand to his forehead and saluted her. "Yes, sir. I mean. Yes ma'am." He jerked his hand away and picked up his cards.

Jasmine shot him a now-you-know-why-I-want-her-to-go-home look.

He understood Jasmine's need. But the very thought of her being here all alone sent a sinking feeling deep into his stomach, knowing that nutcase who had called her was still out there somewhere.

Chapter Twelve

Even after her doctor's medical release, it took several days for Jasmine to finally convince her reluctant sister she'd be okay by herself. Because there hadn't been any more strange phone calls and only a dull headache remained, Chloe left with Jasmine's promise to call her if she needed anything.

Jasmine traced the moose picture etching in her sparkling clean glass cupboard door. Chloe had shined all of the different animal-etched cupboards until they sparkled like glitter. It really was sweet of her sister to clean her house before leaving. Guilt nibbled at her conscience. "Lord, help me to change my negative attitude."

She reached inside and pulled out a purple mug. After fixing a cup of Irish crème coffee, Jasmine walked over to her breadbox, and opened the bobcat-carved lid. A white bakery box with a note attached to the top lay inside. She set her coffee down and lifted the box out. She removed the note and instantly recognized Jack's impeccable handwriting.

Jazzy, I gave this to Chloe when you were napping. I didn't want you to get up and have to think about breakfast. So, I bought you several of your favorite pumpkin chocolate chip muffins. Lunch and dinner will be delivered to your home today as well. Please take it easy, and let your body heal properly. If you need anything at all, don't hesitate to call me. I'm here for you... always.

Love, Jack

Her mind drifted back to the other night when she thought Jack was going to kiss her, and how she had closed her eyes and raised her chin toward him and— "Oh no!" Jasmine slammed her hand over her mouth. It was *she,* who had wanted the kiss, not Jack.

No wonder he'd left in such a hurry and had stressed the word 'friends' to her. Shame and uncertainty crashed into her thoughts.

She leaned against the counter and re-read his note. He signed this one, Love, Jack. Not, All my love, Jack. Did that mean something? Did it mean he really wasn't in love with her or that he was? And how would she ever know?

She pulled out a kitchen chair and plopped down.

How could she have let herself fall in love with Jack? She snorted. She knew how. Love had snuck in while she was sleeping. And now that it had, what was she going to do about it?

Oh, if only she could fall into his arms, confess her love to him, and live happily ever after, like storybook fairy-tales. But, this wasn't a fairy-tale. This was reality, and in reality things don't always work out the way we want them to.

Besides, even if Jack returned her love, love wouldn't prevent her misery if they stayed here, and she couldn't ask him to leave either. They would both end up resenting each other. It was a no-win situation all the way around. She would have to learn to survive without Jack, even though that thought felt as horrible as staying did.

"Oh, Jack. How could I ever forget you? What a mess this is. This is one time I wish you could fix it for me. But, I know it's impossible. Now that I've fallen in love with you, how will I bear leaving you behind? And yet I can't stay. I just can't." Heartbreak attacked her soul with the force of an F-5 tornado. Deep sobs tore from her. The throbbing pain pounding her eyes couldn't even begin to compare with the agonizing pain gripping her heart.

Rivers of tears wound their way down her cheeks. "God, please make this hurt go away. Please help me."

She drew in a deep breath, trying to calm herself.

A hiccup erupted.

She reached for her coffee and took a long gulp of the sweet brew.

First she would wash her face, and then she would go online.

Even though it broke her heart, the time had come for her to go ahead and make plans to move and never look back.

Starting today, she would work on emotionally separating herself from Jack.

She had to, for both of their sakes.

The phone rang.

Jasmine slowly padded across the room, wiping her damp eyes and blowing her runny nose.

"Hello?"

"Jasmine."

So, much for separating herself from Jack. She raised her hand and eyes heavenward, wondering why God had allowed this to happen. Didn't He care?

"Jazz, you there?"

"Yeah. I'm here." Her voice sounded nasally.

"Are you okay?"

"I'm fine," she lied. She'd never be fine again. Her world had just crashed in around her, and there wasn't a thing she could do about it.

Yes you can. Follow your heart and trust Me.

The heart is a wicked thing, Lord. You said so yourself in your Word.

"You don't sound fine. I'll be right over." He hung up before she had a chance to let him know he didn't need to come.

She rushed the stairs two at a time, grabbed some clothes from her dresser, and after a quick shower, she stared at her reflection in the mirror. Red puffy eyes stared back at her. She didn't want Jack seeing her in this wretched state.

She couldn't lie to him and say everything was all right. He'd see right through her the second he got here. She had to think of a believable reason for being so upset.

"I know. I'll just say his muffin gesture made me cry. That isn't a lie, and nothing says I have to reveal all the rest."

Tell him the truth.

"I can't do that, Lord. I can't jeopardize my friendship with Jack and end up hurting as horrific as Lori did."

Aren't you endangering your friendship by moving?

"It's not the same, Lord. Just because I'll be moving to another state doesn't mean Jack and I will stop talking and spending time together. It just won't be as often is all." That thought broke her heart, but it would destroy her completely if she and Jack never talked or saw each other again.

Besides, she had seen what happened once a person crossed over the line of friendship in to love. Chunks of fear bit into her soul just thinking about the consequences of what could happen if she did allow anything more than friendship to develop between them, and she shuddered. "I'm sorry, Lord, I can't do it. I can't tell him why I'm upset. Forgive me, Father. Forgive me."

After her conversation with the Lord, she needed to give herself a good talking to before Jack arrived. She planted her palms on her sink and leaned toward the mirror. "Listen here, girl. You can do this. Just go back to looking at seeing Jack as your best friend. It shouldn't be that hard."

Yeah right. Ack!

The doorbell chimed, and her heart flipped. She flew downstairs and after turning all the front door locks and removing the heavy-duty chain, she swung the door open. Bitter cold rushed in, chilling her instantly. And a new resolve funneled over her. She detested the cold, loathed being smothered, and craved her independence. Nothing would stop her from leaving. Not even Jack.

One look at Jasmine's blotchy face and Jack knew she'd been crying. He shoved the door closed and pulled her into his arms. "You okay? Did you get another strange phone call?" He tilted her chin to see her reaction.

Jasmine stiffened, then slipped out of his embrace.

Not the reaction he expected, worry pounced on him. "Jasmine, tell me. Did you?"

"No." She plastered a smile on her face and wrapped her arms around her stomach.

He knew that stance well. It said, let's pretend everything is all right.

Well, Jack didn't believe in pretending. Communication was a major part of any relationship. They may not have a relationship the way he wanted one, but she was still his dearest friend. And friends shared. Friends helped one another. When one was down, the other picked them up. That's what he and Jasmine had always done. Until lately, when Jasmine had started pulling back. He wished he knew why. But all he could do now was hope and pray that in time she would tell him. "You've been crying. What's the matter?"

She chewed on her thumbnail and turned her back toward him. That meant she wasn't going to tell him everything. It was her way of protecting herself and the ones she loved. Who was she protecting this time? Him? Or her? He shrugged out of his coat and hung it up.

"I was so touched by your thoughtfulness this morning," she said, facing him. Again she draped her arms around her stomach, then looked down. "I don't really know what to say. That was so sweet of you."

Keeping her head down, she lifted her eyes toward him. "And your note was so perfect. Except I wished you would have signed it—" Her head jerked up, but she quickly glanced away, her body turned with it.

Jack caught her arm. He cupped her chin and forced her to look at him. "You only wished I'd signed it like what, Jasmine?"

When she looked at him, sorrow filled her eyes, and if he wasn't mistaken, longing.

"Just forget it, okay?" She shrugged off his arm and walked into the kitchen.

No way would he forget something so important. With determined steps, he trailed her into the kitchen. Everything inside him wanted to pursue what she had almost said, but knowing Jasmine, asking her would get him nowhere. Her protective façade was in place. Yet somehow, he had to figure out a way to break through her barrier and get her to open up to him. If she had been about to say what he had hoped to hear, well—

She stopped and spun around.

Jack clutched her elbow. Lightning bolts charged up his arm, piercing straight into his heart with a longing so deep he thought he would short circuit under its power.

Did she feel the same strong current he had? By the stunned expression on her face, he was almost certain she had. Almost.

Jasmine pulled her arm from his grasp and moved away. With her back to him, she plucked off a chunk of muffin and shoved it into her mouth. "I was just going to nuke my coffee and eat a muffin. These are delicious by the way." She tried acting normal, but Jack knew she was as nervous as he was. "Can I get you some?"

He wanted to touch her again and watch her reaction, but his stomach chose that moment to rumble loud enough it echoed in the room.

Jasmine turned around with a wry smile painting her

beautiful face. "Hungry are we? Sit down." She pulled out a chair for him. "I'll get you some coffee."

Jack watched her scurry toward the storeroom. No way would he be able to sit. He had unfinished business to tend to. She wasn't getting out of it that easily. After all, he knew Jasmine well enough to know she had felt something too. Or maybe it was just wishful thinking on his part. Either way, he had to find out. In four long strides, he stood behind her.

"Is decaffeinated Orange Mocha okay?" she asked from inside the pantry.

"Sounds good."

With a jerk, Jasmine twisted around. In the confines of the pantry, only a hand's length separated her face from his. Her wide eyes stared up at him, blinking. Her eyes slid from his to his mouth. His did the same. Nothing had ever felt so right or so natural. Without really thinking it through, Jack leaned toward her, and his lips parted.

As if caught in a trance, Jasmine tilted her chin upward, inviting him to kiss her. Jack thought for sure his heart had stopped beating as his dream was about to come true. Careful to not give in to the strong urge to kiss her with all the pent up passion he had bridled inside of him, he gently lowered his mouth on hers. Their sweet contact caused his insides to tremble and his heart to soar to the heavens. Jack drew her closer and deepened the kiss. As his lips played over hers in a loving caress, a massive firework display exploded throughout his body.

Jasmine matched his every caress, and he battled to tamp down the deep groan of contentment aching for release as his mouth continued to taste of her sweetness. Jasmine slipped her fingers through his hair and captured his lips in hers, sending his insides into fits of shuddering spasms, and this time he could do nothing to stop the moan from escaping.

Jack crushed her into his arms.

A loud crash echoed through the tiny space.

Jasmine jerked back with a yelp.

"I'm sorry. Did I hurt you?" he asked through ragged breaths.

"No." She sounded as breathless as he did. "The can of coffee fell on my toe." They both looked down at the brown powdery substance sprawled around her feet.

"You okay?" Jack took a couple of steps backward.

"I'm fine," she answered, not looking at him. Jasmine grabbed the broom and dustpan from the hook on the door and started sweeping up the mess.

Jack took the broom from her, grasped her hand, and helped her step over the coffee. "Here. Let me."

Neither spoke while he cleaned the mess. From the corner of his eyes, he watched her, trying to gauge her reaction.

Jasmine gnawed on her thumbnail at record-breaking speed.

A sinking feeling pressed in on him. Although she'd responded to his kiss, he could tell by her present actions, she was extremely uncomfortable.

Did she regret kissing him?

That thought ripped and stabbed its way through his soul. He had finally gotten to feel her soft lips under his. Her kiss was everything he had imagined, and much, much more, but now she looked ready to bolt. *Dear God, is there anything I can say or do to put her at ease?*

Jasmine's insides quivered and her knees wobbled as if they were a piece of soft rubber. She leaned against the counter, stunned and dazed. The moment Jack's lips had touched hers a tingling sensation had spread throughout her body. Never had she experienced anything so wonderful. Or so passionate. His lips were silky soft and very kissable. She sighed, dreamily. And what a kiss.

Jasmine touched her fingertips to her lips. Her mouth still tingled.

Now she was more confused and torn than ever before. Without a doubt, she was irreversibly in love with Jackson Neil Warren. And judging by that kiss, he felt something for her too. Which made things even more complicated.

Jack's finger touched her chin. He raised her head up. "Look at me, Jazz."

What was she going to do? If she looked at him, he would know the depth of her feelings for him. For both of their sakes, she forced a shield of nonchalance into her eyes, then she looked at him.

"I'm sorry. I shouldn't have kissed you. I—"

The words of apology slashed through her, but she jerked those emotions up short. "Don't worry about it." She cut him off with a wave of her hand. "I don't know what came over me either." She wanted to run and hide. "It was an impetuous mistake. That's all." Instead of allowing commonsense to dominate her emotions, like a dummy, she had let her heart rule and had returned Jack's kiss. Well, her heart would not get the best of her senses.

A flashback of Lori's limp body lying on the floor flickered through her mind, giving Jasmine the courage she needed to force the words she didn't want to say past her lips. "Trust me, Jack, it will *never* happen again." *Except in my dreams.*

Stung to his core, Jack dropped his finger from her chin and stepped back. Before she had cut him off, he was about to explain why he shouldn't have kissed her. But her words, 'It was an impetuous mistake. That's all.', and 'it will never happen again', had felt like a machete hacking away at his heart, wounding him deeply.

Judging by the forced smile on her face, she had slipped into her let's-pretend-every-thing-is-fine mode again, but again pretending just wasn't his style. He liked things out in the open. But right now, he felt in his spirit he needed to let the subject drop, or he would risk pushing her away from him forever.

Jack forked his hands through his hair as silence stretched between them. "I guess I'd better go. Enjoy your breakfast. If you need anything, holler. I'll be at my drawing table until three this afternoon. Then I'll be out of the office for about two hours. But you can reach me on my cell phone."

"Meeting with Monroe again?" Jasmine asked.

Jack hated seeing her uncomfortable, which seemed to happen a lot lately. He had to figure out a way to make things right between them again even if it meant not kissing her anymore. From now on, he would rein in his emotions and force himself to see her as a friend only. That thought hurt worse than an ulcer attack, but he would rather have her friendship than lose her completely. "No. My meeting is with Miss Collinsworth."

"Oh." Jasmine's eyes widened for a second, and he noticed the tightness of that word. "Listen, I— What I'm trying to say is. I don't want you to go."

Seeing her discomfort twisted the blade further into his already bruised heart. He should have never given into his urges and kissed her. Didn't matter that she welcomed it, he should have controlled himself knowing her vulnerability because of all she'd been through lately.

"I could make a pot of decaf." Her throat muscle twitched. "Besides, you really shouldn't leave without trying one of those muffins." Biting her lip, she looked away.

Jack rubbed the back of his neck. The last few days had been rough. Even though she chose not to talk about what was happening between them, he still had time before his meeting, and he really did want to stay in hopes of easing the tension between them. So stay he would.

"I saw some Irish Crème on the shelf. How about a cup of that instead?" He sent her an I'll-drop-it-for-now smile. "I'll get it. You're supposed to be taking it easy, remember? You need to relax. Now sit, or I'll call Chloe."

She turned her head toward him with wide playful eyes. "You wouldn't dare do that to me. Would you?"

He waggled his eyebrows. "Do you want to find out?" He chuckled, then gave her a mock serious look. "I will if you don't park yourself right here." He motioned toward the chair already pulled out, his eyes twinkling.

She held her hands up and shook them. "Okay, okay. I give." She plunked herself down on the chair. "Boy, bossy. I can see you've been taking lessons from Chloe."

They both sniggered. Jack fixed himself a cup of coffee and nuked hers before handing it to her.

"Thank you, Jack. You always think of everything." She gave him a grateful smile.

He grabbed a couple of napkins. Making sure Jasmine had her muffin, he snatched one for himself and sat down next to her.

As was their habit, they bowed their heads.

"Father, thank You for this food. Restore Jasmine to total health, and keep her safe. In Jesus' name amen." Under his breath he mumbled, "And let her know I love her."

"I'm sorry but I didn't hear the last part? What did you say?"

"Nothing for your ears." He peeled back the paper, tore off a big piece of muffin, and tossed it into his mouth. "It's between me and God."

CHAPTER THIRTEEN

Jasmine stepped down into her favorite room. She parked herself Indian style on a beige, high-back wicker chair and raised her face toward the skylights. The afternoon sun penetrated the thick glass, filling the room with penetrating warmth. The bright red rhododendrons, pink azaleas, purple orchids, bird of paradise, bromeliads and other blooming plants transported Jasmine to somewhere in the sun-kissed tropics.

Three years ago Jack had built this room for her. She remembered the day he finished it as if it were yesterday.

That day, Jack had arranged for Shanell to take Jasmine shopping. When she walked in the door and sniffed the air, it was as if she had walked into a flower shop.

Jack stood with a silly grin on his face, holding a batch of cut flowers in his hands, and looking rather pleased.

"What are you doing here?" Jasmine asked.

"Well, if you'd just go on in you'd find out." Shanell pushed her inside the door.

Jasmine looked sideways at her sister, squinting. The two of them were up to something.

"Hi, Jack." Shanell peeked around her, giving a quick wave. "Well, gotta run." Shanell winked at Jack and then rushed out the door without even saying goodbye or looking back.

Jasmine stared after her, brows raised. She faced Jack. Landing her hands on her hips, she tilted her head, and opened her mouth to speak.

"I know." Jack ventured. "You're wondering what

I'm up to, right?"

She quirked her mouth and shook her head in disbelief. He'd done it again. He knew her thoughts before she even had a chance to voice them.

"Well, I'll tell you. But first I want you to close your eyes, okay? And just to make sure you don't open them until I tell you to…" He set the flowers on the wooden bench in her entryway and set aside her packages. He reached behind his back, pulled a flannel scarf from his back pocket and turned her around. Making sure her eyes were completely covered, he secured it by tying a square knot. "Is that too tight?"

"A little, but it'll be okay." Jasmine felt like she was getting ready to play pin-the-tail-on-the-donkey. "Do I get a prize if I get the tail on right?" She giggled.

"What?"

"Never mind," she said through a titter.

"Can you see anything?"

"Nope."

"Good. Okay, I'm going to spin you around so you won't know where I'm taking you."

Jasmine felt like a spinning top. "Okay, okay. You're making me dizzy. If you don't quit, my lunch is gonna come back up."

"That's a disgusting thought. You win. I'll stop." He chuckled.

Jack clasped her hands with his clammy ones. That meant he was either excited or nervous or both. Taking choppy steps, she tried to figure out where Jack was leading her. When they stepped down two stairs, she knew exactly what part of her house they were in. Jack had added the final carpentry touches to the empty room two days before. But something was different about the sunroom today.

Humidity filled the air. Fresh potting soil and a sweet flowery fragrance teased her nostrils, reminding her of an exotic plant nursery. She titled her head, listening. The sound of running water drifted through her ears like harmonious music. A strong urge to rip off the scarf tugged at her.

Jack urged her forward a couple of steps and then stopped. He released one of her hands and shifted around her until his chest touched her back.

"Don't move." He released her other hand. "And don't open your eyes until I say to, okay?"

"I won't." Her heart pounded with anticipation.

Jack wrestled with the knot.

"Here let me do it." She reached behind her head and worked on getting it loose. "Boy, Jack. When you tie a knot, you tie it good."

"Well, I didn't want you to see."

"I can tell." Jasmine giggled as she pulled on the knot until it relaxed.

Jack grabbed her hand, stopping her from removing it completely.

"It sure smells good in here," Jasmine said, sniffing the air.

Jack slipped off the scarf. "Okay. You can look now."

She opened her eyes. Her mouth fell open, and her eyes widened at the sight. "Oh, Jack." Tenderness and awe wisped through her voice.

In the center of the room sat four, beige, high-back wicker chairs surrounding a round table with a square, white lacey tablecloth draped over it. A decorative heat lamp hung several feet above the table. In the center rested a purple vase filled with fresh-cut spring flowers. Jasmine picked up the vase and sniffed several of the posies, enjoying each delightful fragrance before perusing the room again.

Filling the corner to her left stood a large marble fountain that looked like a Hawaiian waterfall surrounded by exotic plants, trees, toucan birds, parrots, and butterflies. She swiped at the tears of joy trickling down her cheeks. She had stepped into her own tropical paradise.

Various plants lined the windowed walls. Jasmine made her way along them, feeling the leaves, smelling the blooms, and admiring the different shades of pink, purple, yellow, orange and red blossoms that cheerfully greeted her.

When she reached the fountain she stopped and ran her hand over the smooth, wet marble.

Jack came up behind her and positioned his hand on her shoulder.

Jasmine quickly placed her hand on top of his and gave it a squeeze. Deeply touched, she wanted to say something, but the words wouldn't come.

"I know how much you hate the cold," he spoke softly. "So, I thought during the winter you could come in here and sit. You could close your eyes and imagine you're on a beach somewhere in Hawaii or the Bahamas. Maybe it'll help you through the long winter months." His voice exuded tenderness.

Never had Jasmine been so touched in her life. She spun and threw her arms around his neck. "Oh, Jack. Thank you. Thank you so much."

"You like it?"

She pulled back and looked into his face. "Like it? I love it!" She gave him a quick hug, stepped out of his arms, and glanced around. "It's the most beautiful room I've ever seen."

Jack leaned over and grabbed a beige wicker basket from behind a tall rubber tree plant next to the fountain. He clasped her hand and led her to the table.

"How about a picnic?" he asked, flashing her a teasing smile. He set the picnic basket on the table, reached inside and pulled out three sealed, see-through containers with fried chicken, Greek salad, two slices of Cherry Chocolate Cheesecake, plates, silverware, napkins, and iced tea.

As they sat eating their meal, Jack pointed to a long box on the floor between two Areca Palm trees, filled with white sand and seashells. "That's your own private little beach. You may even find some sharks teeth in the sand. I had the sand and seashells shipped in from Florida."

All she could do was stare, as she was utterly speechless at the lengths Jack had gone through just to make the room special.

It took several minutes for Jasmine to compose herself before she could thank him again. That was one of the most thoughtful, sweetest things anyone had ever done for her.

Jasmine had long since tucked that special day in her treasure-chest of memories. Every time she stepped into the room, she thanked God for her precious friend.

Pulling her mind back to the present and onto Jack's kindheartedness, she wondered what to do about him. He always did things to make her world better. She tried to do special things for him too, but all her efforts paled in comparison.

Sure he appreciated it when she baked his favorite goodies and foods for him, bought him season tickets to the Avalanche and Bronco games, designed special images on his snowmobile and helmet, and dealt with all the arrangements for his company's parties. And when sickness overtook his body, she made sure he had medicine and nutritious food, like homemade chicken noodle soup. But still, it came nowhere close to what he did for her.

Too bad he loved Steamboat Springs like he did. If he didn't, she'd ask *him* to marry her and move away. She laughed at that thought. But the truth was, he did love

Steamboat Springs. Not only that, she got so many mixed signals concerning his feelings toward her, discerning what he felt about anything was a challenge. Like their shared kiss earlier. By the passionate way he had kissed her, she thought he felt something for her too. That is, until he apologized for his actions.

Jasmine pressed her fingertips on her lips as she relived that reach-for-the-stars kiss. Regret for ever experiencing Jack's amazing kisses streamed over her like the water flowing down her marble fountain because now she knew the satisfying depth of being held and kissed by the man who now forever imprisoned her heart. The saddest part of all, he didn't even know it—and never would. Her heart couldn't risk it. She had to let him believe their kiss had been a mindless gesture. A mistake.

Not wanting to dampen her spirits any further by meditating on what could never be, she picked up her laptop. Windows seemed slow booting up. She chalked it up to her desperation in trying to get her mind off of Jack.

She checked the time on her computer. 3:10. That time meant something. But what? She rummaged through her memory banks trying to remember. Jasmine closed her eyes and groaned. Jack had an appointment with a Miss Collinsworth at three o'clock today.

Jasmine remembered meeting Miss Collinsworth at Jack's office. The could-be model with her waist-length black hair, violet eyes, and long shapely legs, caused a slithering snake of jealousy to wind its way around Jasmine's mind. Jack sure had a lot of appointments with that woman—more so than any of his other clients. Maybe he was interested in Miss Collinsworth. Why hadn't Jasmine thought of that before? Could that perhaps be the reason why he was sorry he had kissed her?

A feeling of insecurity wrapped around her like a mummified body wrap. Never before had she experienced this kind of emotion where Jack was concerned. And she didn't like how it felt. Not one little bit.

"What he does is none of your business, Jazz. So, just get over it." She marveled at how much she seemed to be talking out loud to herself lately.

Bougé jumped on the table and laid down in front of her, wanting a rub down. After Jasmine finished petting her cat, she brought up her instant chat messenger.

"Great. He's online," she told Bougé.

Good afternoon, Simon. How are you today?

Jasmine clicked, Send.

She took a drink of water and flicked her thumbnail with her teeth, waiting to see if he'd answer.

Hello, Jasmine. As always, it's a pleasure to hear from you. How are you feeling? Are you doing any better?

She closed her eyes, smiling. How sweet of him to ask.

Jasmine placed her fingers on the keyboard and typed.

I'm feeling much better. It's nice to have my house back to myself again. How about you? What have you been up to?"

Send

Jasmine tipped her glass to take a long gulp of water. It spilled out the sides and ran over her chin, dripping onto her sweatshirt. She patted it off with a napkin and glanced at the screen.

I'm so glad you're feeling better. I was worried about you. As for me, other than working, I haven't done much else. I did get an opportunity to go to a local dinner theater last night and watch the play: Seven Brides for Seven Brothers. How about you? What have you been doing?

Jasmine wondered who he'd gone with. Did he have a girlfriend?

I'm jealous. That's one of my favorite shows. I've

about worn out my DVD copy. I love going to dinner theaters. Did you go with some friends?

Send.

Jasmine sucked in one side of her lip and gnawed at it until it ached. Her eyes never left the screen.

A client gave me a couple of tickets, so I took my friend with me. Last time when my friend had free tickets, I was invited. It was only fair to return the kind gesture.

He didn't say if the friend was a she or he. Her curiosity got the best of her.

How thoughtful of you. A dear friend of mine takes me down the mountain a few times a year to plays and ballets. He doesn't care for ballets, but he knows I like them so he tolerates them just for me. Sometimes we go to the Country Dinner Playhouse or the Heritage Square Music Hall. You asked what I'd been doing. Not much, except for last night. It was the first time in several days that I found myself laughing and having a good time.

Send.

What friend is that? Have you ever mentioned him before?

Her plan worked. If he could ask, well, so could she.

My friend Jack came over. My sisters were here too. We played UNO for two hours. Did your friend enjoy the play? Was the food to her liking?

Send.

Hehe. You are a sneaky one, Jazzy. My friend's name is Kailee. We've been friends since junior high. She'd like more, but she's like a sister to me. We hang out together a lot, but we're strictly friends. How about you? Is Jack your boyfriend?

Jack? Her boyfriend? Only in her dreams. And her nightmares.

She turned her mind to Simon's message. It tickled her that he caught her real motive. What a great friend Simon was turning out to be.

No, we're just super close friends. We've known each other since elementary school. He rescued me from a bully that knocked me down and ran off with my Valentine's candy. Jack chased him down and forced him to give it back to me and then made him apologize.

Send.

A message screen popped up from RodeoCowboy. Shivers crawled through her spine and a pit filled her stomach. She remembered that dreadful phone call and the slight southern accent flowing through the man's creepy seductive words. Time and time again she wondered if RodeoCowboy was the one behind those calls.

This wasn't the first time RodeoCowboy had sent her messages while she was talking to Simon. Out of curiosity, she had read the first couple, but after that, she'd stopped reading them. His messages about knowing where she lived gave her the creeps.

She clicked on the X to disengage RodeoCowboy's screen.

Is there a way to block someone from contacting you?

Yes. Why do you ask? Are you planning on blocking me? hehe

No, no. There's a person who keeps messaging me, and I want nothing to do with him. He scares me.

Whew. I'm glad it's not me. <grin> I'm sorry that someone is harassing you. You can add him to your ignore list, and that will prevent any more messages from coming your way.

Simon walked her through the process. What a relief.

Thank you so much for helping me. I feel so much better.

The phone rang. "No. Not now," she groaned, not wanting to be interrupted. Lickety-split she typed: *Hang on please. Don't go away, Simon. I have to answer the phone. brb (be right back).*

She snatched up the portable phone and clicked TALK. "Hello?" Nothing. "Hello," she repeated. "Is anyone there?"

Heavy breathing filtered through the earpiece. A knot formed in her throat. "W—what do you want?"

"You." The voice on the other end said.

Instead of allowing fear to take charge this time, she got angry. Who did this person think she was? Some toy he could play with? Well, he had another think coming. "Who are you?" she demanded.

"It doesn't matter who I am. What's important is… I know who you are. By the way, you looked cute sitting Indian style in that beige wicker chair."

Jasmine mashed the OFF button. As if the phone were as deadly as a brown recluse spider, she flicked it far away from her. Her eyes darted around the room, looking out the windows for someone watching her. Jasmine raced through the house, bolting all the locks on her doors, checking all the window latches to make sure they were locked, and closing all the blinds and curtains.

Who was this, and how did he know about her wicker chair?

Her breathing became shallow.

She gasped, struggling to draw air past the lump of fear lodged in her wind pipe.

What should she do?

Should she call the police?

And just what would she tell them? That someone was playing a sick joke on her?

Jack. She needed to call Jack. He would know what to do.

In hopes he would be finished with his meeting, Jasmine scrambled up the stairs and into the kitchen. She snatched up the wall phone and quickly punched in Jack's office number.

While waiting for him to answer, she drew in slow steadying breaths to try and calm herself.

His secretary answered the phone on the third ring. "Mary, this is Jasmine. May I please speak with Jack?"

"He's not here. He took a client out for an early dinner."

Oh no. He was still with that woman. Jasmine's heart plummeted.

"Are you okay, Jasmine? You don't sound so good."

She pressed her fist against her lips, wondering what she would do now? "I—I'm fine. Tha—thanks, Mary. I'll try—try him later." She put the phone back in its cradle.

Afraid to go back into her sunroom, she debated what she should do now.

Call her dad? No. She refused to bother him because he hadn't been feeling too well lately.

Chloe. No. She didn't want to impose on her sister again. Besides, who knew how long this thing could go on?

She had to figure something else out.

And quick.

"Oh, Jack. Where are you?" she whispered into the empty room. If only she could call his cell phone. But, she promised herself a long time ago she would never bother him when he was out with a client.

Usually he had an uncanny knack of knowing when she was in trouble or when she needed him. But not today. He was probably enjoying his time with the gorgeous Miss Collinsworth. Against her will, bitter envy jabbed her in the chest. *Stop it!* She beckoned her mind back to what she needed to do about the phone call.

In the dimly-lit living room, she curled up in her over-stuffed chair, and pulled a blanket over her lap. What she really wanted to do was pull it over her head. She couldn't believe she'd lived alone in this place for eight years and had never been afraid. Until now.

Who was this man?

And why her?

Messages from RodeoCowboy played through her mind. He said he knew where she lived and she'd be sorry she had scorned him. Was it him?

The local newspaper article flashed through her mind. Could it be the Steamboat Springs Peeping Tom? Did he call his victims?

She gulped down the fear closing in on her at a high rate of speed.

A knock sounded at her door.

She jerked the blanket to her mouth, pressed it tightly against her lips, and stifled a scream as she stared at her front door. *Lord! Help me!*

CHAPTER FOURTEEN

Something wasn't right. Jasmine never closed her drapes during the day. Jack's pulse pounded hard against his throat. "Jasmine!" he hollered, pounding on the door. "It's me, Jack. Open up."

Within seconds he heard the swift turning of locks.

The door flew open.

Jasmine dashed into his chest, throwing her arms around him, nearly sending them both crashing to the ground.

He stumbled to catch his balance.

Her wild eyes darted toward the stately pines as if they were evil.

She yanked him inside, slammed the door shut, locked the locks, and secured the chain. She whirled, and in the time it took to draw a breath, she had her arms around his waist, pressing her body against his, and hugging him so tight he could barely breathe. "Hey. Hey." He wrapped his arms around her trembling body and rubbed her back in soothing circles, his face rested near her ear.

"Oh, Jack," she sobbed. "I'm so glad to see you. How did you know to stop by?"

"Mary called me on my cell phone. She said you sounded upset and that I'd better check on you."

"Wait." She looked up at him with a tear stained face and terror-filled eyes that brought out his protective instincts again.

He wanted to shield her from whatever had caused her such torment.

"I thought you had a dinner date."

"I did. After Mary called, I cancelled my appointment."

"I'm so glad you're here, Jack. I've never been so scared in my life." She buried her head against his parka.

"What's going on?" Careful to keep one arm securely around her, he shrugged out of his coat, and then tucked her tightly under his arm as he led her into the living room. "Why is it so dark in here?"

"I'll tell you everything in a minute. But first I have to use the bathroom. Don't leave. Please!" Her terror stricken face gawked up at him.

"I won't." Reluctantly he let her go. Jack paced a moment and then decided to check things out. When he stepped down into the sunroom, he paused, looking around. All the blinds were drawn there too. And Jasmine had never shut the blinds in this room before.

His focus dropped to her laptop. He looked toward the bathroom door then stepped up to the table. The instant chat messenger with Simonrapport's nickname filled most of the screen. Not wanting to snoop but wondering if there might be a clue as to why she was so frightened, he glanced over his shoulder before turning back to read her messages.

Frustration swelled inside of him when he noticed how chummy they were getting.

He continued alternating between looking at the bathroom door and reading her message.

You've got to be kidding me. He couldn't believe she'd told Simonrapport he had taken her down to the mountain to Heritage Square Music Hall and the Country Dinner Playhouse.

What had she been thinking by telling him that?

How could she act so irresponsibly? Something so out of character for her. She was one of the most responsible people he knew. That was one of the things he loved about her.

He read more.

Her last message said she had to answer the phone. Then Simonrapport replied he needed to go, and that he'd talk to her later.

Jack's awareness snagged onto her ICM contact list. Curious about RodeoCowboy, he glanced at the bathroom door again and clicked on the nickname.

As he flew through the messages there, he clamped down so hard on his teeth they started to ache. How dare that man threaten Jasmine.

The toilet flushed.

Not wanting Jasmine to know where he'd been, Jack took both steps in one sweep and waited near the bathroom for her. He hated his sneakiness, but right now he was more concerned about Jasmine's welfare than invading her private life.

Jasmine stepped out of the bathroom and turned toward him. She looked more ragged than he'd ever seen her before.

He closed the gap between them and pulled her into his arms. The smell of sweet strawberries drifted up his nose.

Seconds later, he settled the two of them on the loveseat and fixed his eyes on hers. "Tell me what happened."

"I had another phone call."

"The same as before?"

"Yes."

Every nerve in his body stood on end. "What'd he say?"

Tears pooled her eyes.

A feeling of helplessness swooped down on him.

"He said he knew who I was and that—" Jack struggled to hear her broken whisper. "He—he liked the beige, wicker chair I was sitting Indian style in." She burst out crying.

Jack wrapped his arms securely around her.

How did the man know about her sitting Indian style in her wicker chair?

And who was this person?

Was it the psycho Peeping-Tom he'd read about in the local paper? Everything fit that guy's M.O., his profile.

Or was it that dirt-bag RodeoCowboy from online, who said he knew where she lived and he'd get even with her?

Realization belted him upside the head. Nothing like this had ever happened to Jasmine before she'd met Simonrapport.

Could Simonrapport be here in Steamboat?

Dread plopped into his burning gut. With all the stress he'd been under lately, the prescription medication hadn't had a chance to heal his ulcer.

Jasmine shifted back in his arms and gazed up at him. "Jack. What am I going to do? How did that man know how and where I was sitting?" With a panicked look, she glanced around the room.

He struggled to not show his fear for Jasmine's safety. He had to be strong for her. Tomorrow he would talk to Stan and ask him to step up his investigation to find this man. And to check on some jerk named RodeoCowboy. "Don't worry, Jazz. He can't see in here now. Besides that, if I ever catch him I'll—" His jaw tensed as he crammed down his rising anger. "Think, Jasmine. Have you mentioned your wicker chair to anyone? Maybe this guy hasn't really seen it but is using information you've given him. Or have you had any service men in the house lately?"

"I called a plumber last week, and he came here a couple days ago."

"Why didn't you call me?"

"You do too much for me already."

Jack pressed his hand down over his face. "Next time call me. You know I love to help."

"I know, and I appreciate all you do for me, Jack."

"So, who did you call?"

She named a plumbing business he didn't recognize.

"What was the name of the guy who came?"

"I don't know. I've never seen him before."

"Well, I'll check them out. Chloe was still here, so I'll talk to her, too." *And while I'm at it, I'm going to talk to Stan and see if he can tap your phone. At least we might be able to track where the phone calls are coming from.*

"I don't think that'll help. The guy said that was his last day. He was moving that weekend to Florida." A wistful look came over her face. Knowing how badly she wanted to move, would these phone calls push her in to moving sooner? He couldn't think about that now. He needed to keep his mind clear so he could get to the bottom of things. "Well, I'm still calling them. Anyone else?"

"No, not anyone I can think of off hand." Jasmine stood and paced the floor. "Wait. I did mention to—" She stopped and glanced at him. "Now, don't get mad at me, okay?" She put both hands up in a defensive gesture.

Jack's patience was wearing thin. He rose and stepped in front of her. "Tell me."

"I didn't think it would hurt to tell..." She looked down and scraped her thumbnail against her teeth. "To tell Simon." She shot Jack another quick glance and looked away.

"Simon? Who's Simon?"

"My new Internet friend."

"What?! Have you lost your mind? Whatever possessed you to do such a thing?" Shaking his head, he pressed his lips together. "What else did you tell him?" Jack's blood boiled like a whistling teapot. He just knew she would get sucked in. As responsible as she was, she was pretty naïve when it came to things like this. Jasmine believed the best of every one, which wasn't a bad thing, but in this instance it definitely could be.

"I didn't give him any private information, Jack." She jumped to her feet, slammed her hands on her hips, and glared at him. "I'm not stupid," she huffed. "Besides, there's no way he could find my phone number. He doesn't know my name, where I live or anything."

Oh yeah, what about the messages I read? "We need to talk." He pulled her to the sofa, motioned for her to sit down, and then joined her.

Her blue-green eyes settled on him.

"I saw the message screen on your laptop." He held his hand up. "Before you blow your top, hear me out. First, your nickname is Jazzy."

"So." She stared at him with a baffled look on her face.

"Did you ever tell him what you do for a living?"

The blood siphoned from her face.

He had his answer. "I thought so. Listen, if the guy is computer savvy, then he might think to run a check on any greeting card or artists with the name 'Jazzy' in it." He let that sink in. "Now, did you tell him anything that would indicate where you live?"

Jasmine thought about his question.

"I told him I hated living where it's cold and—" She stopped, and stared up at him with guilt written all over face. "I said my friend takes me down the mountain to see plays and stuff. But I didn't mention a city. Besides, I'd just told him that today. There's no way he would have had time to track me down."

No, but you gave him names of the places I took you, he thought but didn't say anything. He wanted her to trust him enough to tell him herself. It disappointed him that she didn't. "Did you mention anything about your family at all?"

"Like what?" She looked perplexed.

"Well, that you're an identical triplet. Or that your sister owns a gift shop or a restaurant at the ski resort. Anything like that?"

Her gaze dropped to her lap, and she sucked in her lower lip.

"You did, didn't you?" Jack stated, more than questioned, but in a non-condemning tone.

"I told him I was an identical triplet and that I felt like a freak because my sisters loved living in this frigid ski-resort town, and I didn't." She queried him with her eyes. "But surely that wasn't enough information for him to find me. There are scads of mountain ski resorts. Besides, Jack, he seems like a really nice guy." She raised her thumb to her mouth but scratched her chin instead.

"That's exactly what men on the Internet want single ladies to believe. And that's why the Internet is so dangerous. There's no way of knowing for sure if the person you're talking to is indeed who they say they are. Don't get me wrong, I'm not saying that all people on the Internet are bad. There are many good and wonderful people who use the Internet. I'm just saying that you just can't trust everyone on there, Jazz."

Her lids lowered. "Chloe said the same thing."

Jack lifted her chin up with his finger, coaxing her to look at him, but her eyes remained downcast. "I need to ask you one more thing."

She raised her eyes to him and nodded.

"Did he tell you what he does for a living?" Jack knew the answer, and Jasmine did too, but he wanted her to think twice before she talked to that man again. He watched her process the information.

A sinking feeling shadowed her face. She nodded and drew in a shaky breath. "Yes, he told me. But I already knew from reading his personal information that he's a computer analyst. But surely Simon wouldn't—" A glazed look of despair spread over her face. She pressed her lids tight before looking at him.

"I've only known him a few days, but we've talked for hours. He wouldn't scare me like this. It can't be him." Her eyes pleaded with Jack to reassure her, but he couldn't.

"Listen, Jazz." He purposely kept his voice gentle. "I know you want to—"

The ringing telephone caused Jasmine to screech. She stared at it as if it were a boa constrictor ready to swallow her up.

Jack shot up. "Stay put. I'll get it." He stormed over and snatched up the receiver.

Chapter Fifteen

"Hello," Jack ground out.

Jasmine held her breath, wondering if it was 'him' again.

When Jack relaxed his stance and said, "Oh. Hi, Mrs. Moore." She closed her eyes and breathed.

He covered the mouthpiece with his hand and mouthed, *You want to talk to her?*

Jasmine nodded and headed toward him.

"She's standing right here. Just a minute." He handed Jasmine the phone.

"Hi, Mom."

"Hello, sweetheart. Boy, Jack sure sounded grouchy. Is he okay?"

"Yeah. He's fine." She refused to explain why he sounded so testy. Her mother had enough on her plate with her dad's health issues. She didn't need to be worrying about Jasmine too.

"Oh good. I'm glad to hear it. Listen, I just called to see how you were doing and if you needed anything." Her mother's kindness wrapped around her like a security blanket.

"I'm doing fine." She glanced up at Jack.

He raised a brow and crossed his arms over his chest.

Jasmine gave him a quick shrug and looked away. "Right now I don't need a thing. But thanks for asking, Mom. How's Dad feeling?"

"He's doing pretty good. The new blood pressure medicine seems to be working."

"I'm so glad. I've been so worried about him."

"Me, too. But he seems to be feeling much better

now. Well, listen, sweetheart. I won't keep you. I know Jack's there. If you need anything, give me a holler."

"Thanks, Mom. I will. Tell Dad hi for me. I'll call you later. I love you."

"Love you, too."

Jasmine hung up the phone and spotted Jack in her kitchen. A few minutes ago, when he'd questioned her, she'd wanted to tell him about RodeoCowboy, but with his ulcer acting up from worrying about her, she didn't want to stress him out further. Plus, he would just tell her how he had warned her stuff like that would happen. Well, she refused to believe everyone from the Internet had evil intentions. Okay, in all fairness, Jack did say that not all people online were bad and that there were many good people out there, and that he just wanted her to use caution. Surely Simon wasn't in the bad category. Was he? She blotted that thought out.

She walked up next to him. "What are you doing?"

"Just checking the locks on the door."

She smiled. "Like I told you earlier, you think of everything. Thank you."

"No problem."

She watched him twist the locks, making sure they went into the doorjamb.

"I got to thinking about something." She tilted her head and sent him a slight smile. "When I got that call today, I was talking to Simon online, so it couldn't have been him." She was grappling with hope, but she couldn't bear the idea Simon might possibly be the one harassing her.

Jack stood up straight. "Look, Jasmine." He led her to the kitchen table and pulled out two chairs.

They sat facing each other.

He clasped her hands between his and looked her square in the eye. "I know you want to believe it's not him, but your message back to him said—" He stopped, guilt written all over his face.

"How dare you read my messages!" She jerked her hands free.

"When I glanced at your screen and saw that you were talking to him. I got nosy. So, shoot me. I care." His voice held no apology.

How could she be mad at him when he really did care? He showed it every day in the things he did for her and the way he treated her. But still, it annoyed her that he thought she couldn't handle herself. And she was beginning to wonder if she ever would.

No! I will. I know I can. Sure I'm struggling with some psycho right now, but this isn't your typical everyday problem. This too shall come to pass.

"Just go with me on this," he continued. "Your note to him said you had to answer the phone. Knowing he was talking to you online, what if he dialed your number to see if you would say anything about the phone ringing, then he'd know for sure it was your number."

"That's ridiculous!" She jumped up, sending her chair whacking against the hardwood floor.

"Is it, Jasmine? Think about it." He stood and righted her chair. "Is it so out of the realm of possibility?"

She would think about it all right. And then she'd figure out a way to prove Jack wrong. "Can we just drop this for now?" She walked away and then faced him. "Look, I'm hungry. Why don't we order takeout?"

"It's almost six o'clock. The pizza should arrive any minute now."

The pizza. One more thing Jack had taken care of. Times like these she wasn't sure if she should be mad about his interference or grateful for his thoughtfulness. "I forgot you arranged for food to be delivered. That was really sweet of you, Jack, to order lunch and dinner for me today. Thank you. And thanks for always being here when I need you and for caring about me." She closed the distance between them and hugged him. "You're the best friend a girl could ever have." Jasmine dropped her arms from around him. "I don't deserve you."

Jack stopped her and pulled her closer.

Puzzled, with a tilt of her head, she leaned back and looked up in to his face. "What are you doing?"

"Just returning your hug."

"Oh." Jasmine hoped her disappointment didn't show. She thought maybe he wanted to hold her, and it would lead to another lip-tingling, toe-curling kiss. It was impossible to think rationally with him so close and with his rock solid arms around her.

He gently pressed her head against his broad chest. His heart pounded a soothing rhythm, and his flannel shirt felt warm against her ear. A lingering pine-like scent intoxicated her senses, and a sigh of contentment slipped from her.

Against her will, and her better judgment, she found herself longing for him to kiss her again. Just one more time, then she would let him go on with his life, and she would go on with hers.

After all, if her plans worked out, when summer rolled around, she would be gone. Jasmine pulled back a couple of inches and glanced into Jack's hazel eyes. What she saw there stopped her. The intenseness of his gaze pierced into her soul like Cupid's arrow. She should look away but felt powerless to do so.

His eyes willed her closer, drawing her into their depths. Spellbound, she leaned into him.

He lowered his head, never breaking eye contact.

In anticipation of what was coming, bubbles of excitement exploded inside her one right after another.

Jack's lips parted before his mouth staked his claim on her. His lips slowly glided over hers in a gentle massage. Her insides melted like snow on a warm spring day. She slid her arms around his neck and her fingers brushed through his soft hair.

Her insides trembled, and her knees liquefied. His powerful arms pulled her closer until their heartbeats had become one.

Nothing had ever felt so right or so good.

Their kiss deepened, and bells rang in her head.

Her heart strummed to the tune of a love song. The only other time she'd experienced something this wonderful was the last time Jack had kissed her.

Her breathing increased, and the bells sounded again.

Oh no, she inwardly groaned. Someone was at her door.

It took every ounce of restraint she possessed to break the kiss, but her mouth still felt the pressure of his lips on hers.

"Jasmine." Jack sounded husky. "I—"

She pushed away from him for she couldn't bear the thought of Jack telling her he was sorry for the kiss they had just shared. "I need to answer the door."

Each step she took, her knees wobbled like wet noodles. When she reached the door, the second she swung it open, cold air smacked her, making her shiver. After grabbing the pizza box from the teenage boy, she turned and set it down on the bench and grabbed her wallet off the dumbwaiter. "No ma'am. It's already taken care of."

"Well, just let me give you a tip."

He waved his hand and shook his head. "No can do. Mr. Warren took care of it and left strict orders you were to do nothing." He flashed a toothy grin, spun around, and trotted off.

Jasmine rubbed her hands up and down her arms, trying to circulate her blood. All the warmth that had radiated throughout her body before she'd opened the door had fled. How she despised the cold. Somehow it had a way of bringing reality back with a slap.

Snatching up the large box, she decided tonight she had to put an end to whatever was happening between her and Jack. She refused to live the rest of her life freezing to death in a place she despised more and more with each passing day. But doing that would be the hardest thing she ever had to do in her life.

On the way into the kitchen, sadness gushed over her like a broken dam, crushing her spirit under its weight. *God, give me strength. I can't let this thing with Jack go any further.*

~⁀ᴄᴏ ᴏᴄ⁀~

Jack collapsed onto the chair. Placing his elbows on his knees, he clasped his hands, and stared at the floor. He'd never had a kiss affect him like that before. Now what was he supposed to do? He wanted to slap himself upside his head for yet again taking advantage of her at a vulnerable time. No wonder she scrambled to the door like a frightened kitten.

He looked up when he heard her enter the kitchen. He wanted to stand and take the pizza from her, but his knees had no strength in them.

She set the box on the table and glanced at him.

This time she was unreadable. Even for him.

"Jack."

Still dazed, he forced himself to look at her even though he knew his heart would expose his true feelings for her.

She turned away from him and wrapped her arms around her stomach. *That wasn't good.* "I think you should know. I'm moving away from here this summer."

That was the last thing he expected to hear. His brief encounter with hope vanished.

"I can't bear this cold any longer," she ground out while rubbing her wrist and fingers. "I'm going to try and buy Granddad's lake house. But even if that doesn't work, I'm still moving someplace warm. And I've already got a buyer for this house when I'm ready to sell."

As if someone had set off a bomb under his backside, Jack shot to his feet and grasped her shoulders. "That's it? Just like that. What about me, Jasmine? What about us?" Heat blazed from his eyes. "We've been friends a long time. Are you leaving me behind too?" Anger slithered through his voice, but he didn't care. How could she just blurt it out to him like that and act as if all the years they'd shared together were nothing? As if that kiss they'd just shared meant nothing to her?

She looked up at him with sad eyes. "It's not that easy for me to leave. But it's harder for me to stay. I don't want what happened to—" Pain replaced the sadness in her eyes. "Can't you see how miserable I am? I've made my decision. I don't want to be here anymore. And nothing's going to stop me this time." The look she passed him said not-even-you.

Right before she'd spoken her last words, Jack had been about to tell her if she loved him, they could marry and move away together. But her brook-no-argument words and look shot that idea down. It crushed him how she could just walk away and forget him so easily. That moving was more important to her than he was, and that she didn't even give him a chance to see if they could work something out.

Jack's heart couldn't handle much more of this up and down emotional roller-coaster ride. "Okay, Jasmine. If that's how you want it, that's how it'll be." He turned and stalked out of the room, jerked on his coat, and slammed the door behind him. The cold outside smacked him, but he barely felt it as he stormed to his truck and spun out of her driveway.

On the way home, anger and heartbreak wreaked havoc with his mind and heart. He didn't understand how Jasmine could return his kisses with such passion one minute, and then act like they meant absolutely nothing to her the next. Was he missing something here?

And what had she been about to say when she blurted, 'she didn't want what happened to'? He wanted to ask, but her words about nothing stopping her from leaving had crushed him too much to think straight.

He slammed his hands on the steering wheel.

Couldn't the woman tell how much he loved her?

He had put every ounce of love for her in to his kisses. Was she aware, or did she even care what she did to him? Did she really only kiss him because he offered her comfort? Her desperation to move from here sometimes drove her to act irrationally. Was this just another one of those times?

Jack pulled into his driveway and shut off his truck. He leaned his head back against the headrest. "Oh God, You know I love Jasmine more than my own life." With an angry swipe, he brushed away his tears. Tears he was tired of shedding. "There isn't anything I wouldn't do for her, Lord. But I can't make her love me, so what am I going to do?"

While he pondered what to do next, he grabbed the roll of antacids out of his front shirt pocket and tossed three into his mouth. The powdery substance felt like gravel.

Perhaps if he gave her some space and stayed away, then maybe, just maybe, she might miss him enough to call. If not, she would at least see what life would be like without him. He rubbed his fingers over his eyes. Unfortunately, that also meant he'd find out what life would be like without her too. That idea ripped his being into shreds. But he had to face the truth.

"God, give me the grace to stay away." The unknown of what would happen to their relationship settled inside him like an unwanted virus. Ever since they were little, they had talked or had seen each other almost every day. They'd even gone to the same college together. But now, she was moving hundreds of miles away.

At that moment, Jack wondered how she was going to feel when she found out her granddad's lake house was already sold. To him.

...she was actually frantic that morning. But at that point... it was clear... how this way got to feel when she knew... persuaded Tate.

CHAPTER SIXTEEN

Three weeks later, Jasmine sat in her sunroom. With complete confidence in her God-given talents, she added the finishing touches to the life-sized celebrity portrait. Today was one of the rare days when her fingers didn't hurt and she didn't destroy another piece of artwork.

She stared at the portrait and marveled how exquisite the ebony-haired actress looked and how her emerald-green gown brought out the sea-green in her full, bright eyes.

The actress's screenwriter husband had called her after he'd seen her artwork in Chloe's Gift Shop. He had ordered and paid for an original greeting card and the life-sized portrait of his wife.

This had definitely been one of her biggest challenges and biggest commissions, but with the Lord's help, she had succeeded.

She glanced at her calendar. Today was the fifth of February. Sometime before February 14th he would be picking up his order to give to his wife for Valentine's Day. The twenty-thousand dollars he'd paid was stashed away to help pay for her granddad's lake house. At least the amount he'd said he would ask if he ever did sell the place.

Excitement surged through her. She was one step closer to making her dream a reality. Now if she could just convince Granddad to sell to her.

The mid-morning sun beamed through the skylights, warming the room to a toasty ninety degrees. A smile spread across her face, knowing the bitter cold weather would soon be over and spring was just around the corner.

The telephone rang.

Jasmine snatched up the hand-held receiver. "Hello," she answered cheerfully, hoping it was Jack. She hadn't heard from him or talked to him since he walked out her door three weeks before, and she couldn't decide if that was a good thing or a bad thing.

"I've missed hearing your voice. But it won't be long now before we'll be together, and I can have you all to myself. I can hardly wait." The twisted man's voice sounded slippery and husky.

Jasmine shuddered with repulsion. But having had enough of the man's obscenities, anger replaced her repulsion. "Get a life." She mashed the OFF button and checked the caller ID. It showed, private. She should have checked the number before answering. Ever since she had caller ID installed two and half weeks ago, anytime it showed unavailable, private, or some number she wasn't familiar with, she let it go to her answering machine.

The infuriating man had left several disturbing messages on her answering machine. At first she'd been terrified, but then she decided if the guy had planned on hurting her, he would've done so by now, so the calls no longer frightened her. Instead, they made her angry. Plus she refused to let fear rule her life any longer.

At least she'd finally ruled out it wasn't Simon calling her. They'd shared many long chats over the last several weeks, and Simon showed nothing but kindness and consideration, and her fondness for him deepened. Before Jack stormed out of her life, she wondered if Simon might be an answer to her prayers. But as much as she enjoyed Simon, he didn't fill the void left by Jack's absence.

Jasmine absently rubbed a coleus leaf between her fingers. The coleus Jack had given her. Each birthday and each special occasion, Jack added a new and different kind of plant to her sunroom. But somehow these plants didn't seem as bright as they once had. In fact, without Jack, everything in her life had dulled. "Oh, Jack. I miss you," she whispered. Sadness drizzled over her like the fine mist at Niagara Falls.

She shifted in her seat and stared at the number touchpad on the phone. Over the last few weeks, many times she'd picked it up to call Jack but then couldn't go through with it because he obviously no longer wanted anything to do with her.

How ironic. The one thing she had feared and wanted to avoid had happened. She'd lost his friendship. Her heart felt as if someone had cut it open without the aid of any anesthetic and slowly, torturously, sliced it into a million tiny pieces.

Bougé rubbed up against Jasmine's leg. She leaned over and picked up her long-haired cat. "You always seem to know when I need comforting." She hugged Bougé close and gave her an Eskimo kiss. Bougé's purring had a comforting effect.

Minutes later, she gave her pet a gentle squeeze and placed her on the floor. "I've been cooped up in this house too long. I'm going for a walk."

Jasmine checked the temperature: thirty-five degrees—a whole lot warmer than twenty below. She hustled upstairs, dressed, then flew downstairs where she slid into her outdoor winter garb.

Making sure she had her house keys and binoculars, she grabbed her gloves and opened the door.

For once, it wasn't horribly glacial outside. She smiled, pulled the door closed and locked it. At the bottom of the steps, she turned her face toward the mid-morning sky and closed her eyes, soaking up the sunshine. The warmth felt so good on her face that the yearning to relocate grew even stronger inside her.

She couldn't understand her granddad's hesitancy in making his decision. "Lord, would you please talk to

Granddad about selling the cabin to me, or don't You care how miserable I am here?"

I care about every aspect of your life, God whispered to her heart.

"There was a time when I believed You cared. But now I'm not so sure. Every time I pray, my prayers seem to hit an invisible steel wall." She turned her face upward again and stared at the endless, clear blue sky. "And yet I know You're out there somewhere."

I'm only a whisper away. My Spirit lives inside you. I will never leave you nor forsake you. Even though God's words wrapped around her, she felt no security in them.

"Then why, Lord? Why aren't you answering my prayers? You know all the reasons why I want to move, and yet You choose to leave me here. I don't understand," she whispered. "And now with the situation with Jack, living here has become even more unbearable."

Jack. He was never far from her thoughts. How she missed him. She still couldn't believe he hadn't called.

Jasmine shook her head to clear away the unpleasant memories. Today was a beautiful day and she intended to enjoy it.

The hard crusted snow crunched under her feet as she headed north. Pine mingled with crisp mountain air brought a lilt to her steps as she followed the narrow path the cross-country skiers and snowmobiles had made through the aspen and pine trees.

Hiking through woods, communing with nature, always gave Jasmine a sense of freedom and a reprieve from her winter confinement. She smiled when a jackrabbit scampered through the trees.

As she continued her hike, she thought about Jack and how the two of them had climbed this mountain together every year. But not this year. This year she would be gone.

The idea of never seeing Jack again caused a heavy

shadow of sadness to loom over her like the tall awning of trees above her. How she wished she could tell him the real depth of her despair. But knowing Jack's unselfish nature, he would offer to leave the place he loved, just for her. Often she had longed for that very same thing, but she loved Jack too much to allow that to happen.

And if she explained her fear of ending up like Lori and Steve, Jack would deny something like that would ever happen to them.

She snorted. "I've lost him already, and our goals and dreams haven't even entered into the equation yet."

Only one other choice remained. Move on with her life and forget him.

All of a sudden, the fine hair on the back of Jasmine's neck and arms rose.

She froze.

An ethereal feeling of being watched settled over her.

Unzipping the inside pocket of her parka, she pulled out her pocketsize binoculars and scanned the small clearing ahead. Her eyes trailed up the tree line to a set of protruding rock formations.

Jasmine gasped.

Lying on one of the escarpments was a mountain lion, devouring something. Adrenaline rushed through her body. *Don't panic. Calm down so you can think clearly.*

She knew she didn't dare turn and run or the lion would chase after her. She needed to back down through the trees. That's what the game wardens said to do.

With each step, she fought the urge not to spin around and run for dear life.

Why hadn't she listened to Jack? The day before their disagreement, he told her about the fresh mountain lion tracks around her place, and warned her not to go near the woods until the Division of Wildlife captured it. She scolded herself for being so stupid and forgoing his warning.

The thin air made it difficult for her to breathe. Hot from the fear and physical energy, she unzipped her coat and tied it around her waist.

When she spun to see how much further she had to go, a sharp stabbing pain rammed into her neck.

She touched the spot with her glove and felt something sticking out.

Crimson stained her glove.

Her pulse fired like a machine gun, knowing if the mountain lion got a whiff of fresh blood, she'd be a goner for sure.

She whirled around and fled the rest of the way down the mountain, praying the large cat wouldn't catch up to her and attack her.

Her lungs burned from the exertion.

Several times she stumbled until she finally made it out of the woods.

From the corner of her eye she noticed a flash of something moving. She darted a quick glance in that direction, but she didn't see anything.

Onto the porch she dashed.

Her eyes darted about the area.

While fumbling to get the key into the lock, she pulled air into her deprived lungs.

Finally, the lock turned. She finished unlocking the others and jerked the door open. She leapt inside, slammed the door shut, and secured all the locks. Jasmine braced her hands on her knees and closed her eyes, panting.

Bougé growled and hissed.

Jasmine's eyes flew open. She spotted her cat under the end table. Her glassy eyes were red and blazing, the hair on her back stood straight up, and her ears were pinned against her head.

Jasmine followed Bougé's line of vision.

A figure ducked behind the large blue spruce in her

yard.

Not a mountain lion, but a man.

Jasmine slunk to the floor and crawled to the kitchen doorway. The sunlight streaming through the windows made it difficult for anyone to see her.

Bougé continued growling low and deep.

Jasmine stood, drew in a deep breath, and scoped the area. When she didn't see anyone or anything, she convinced herself her imagination was working overtime and that Bougé was growling because she sensed the feline predator.

But wait. That didn't make sense. Bougé didn't growl the day Jack noticed fresh mountain lion tracks in her yard. And the figure she saw was too tall to be a mountain lion.

Memories of the past week played through her mind. Every time she had gone out, she noticed a black car with dark windows had left when she did. At the time she'd blown it off as coincidence, but now she wasn't so sure.

She gnawed at her thumb in the same manner the hungry mountain lion had chomped on its prey. The movement caused a sharp pain in her neck. Rather than take care of it right now, she wanted to check something out first.

Jasmine stealthily made her way to the sunroom. Hiding behind a large plant, she peered out the window and gasped. Up the block and across the street sat that same black car.

Not caring if anyone saw her, she darted through the house drawing shades and making sure all the windows were locked.

After she had finished, the urge to call Jack burned inside her, but she didn't because he wasn't speaking to her.

Her chest rose and fell with a heavy sigh. Once again she found herself in another situation where she needed help. No wonder her sisters and Jack treated her like they did.

Constant ticking of the battery-operated clock pecked away at her fraught nerves, and waves of pain in her neck throbbed in tune to the clock's rhythm. Throb—throb, throb—throb, throb-throb.

A cracking noise outside snatched her attention.

She peered out her living room window.

Bougé growled and hissed.

Paranoia wound its way around Jasmine's spine like a slithering snake winding its way around its victim. "Jesus, help me. I'm so scared. Show me what to do."

She crawled to the phone and grabbed it before she huddled in the corner behind the end table, wondering who she should call.

If she called the police, what would she say? That she *thought* she saw a man outside her window. After the Peeping-Tom article, Jasmine bet the police station had been over-run with phone calls from single women who noticed any male stranger even remotely near their places.

But what if she called them about the mountain lion? If she did, then she wouldn't look like some jumpy psycho woman. And when they came, they would see the same tracks Jack had. Her mind made up, she punched 911.

❦

Jack settled in his black, down-filled office chair and thought about Jasmine. Something he'd done more than ever before. The last three weeks without her had been the longest and darkest time of his life. Everywhere he looked reminded him of her. From the bald eagle picture soaring above a snowy field that Jasmine had purchased because she knew he loved eagles, to the down-filled red suede couch with the high back and arms she had talked him into because he loved red.

His intercom buzzed.

He pressed the button. "Yes."

"Jack, Stan's on line two," his secretary said.

"Thanks, Mary." He pressed line two and jerked the phone to his ear. "Hey, Stan, did you find out anything?"

"Not about Simon, RodeoCowboy, or the plumber yet, but I thought you might like to know I just heard over the police scanner a woman reported seeing a mountain lion. The address was Jasmine's."

Jack yanked up straight in the chair. "Thanks for letting me know, Stan."

"You're welcome. Look, I gotta run. I have another phone call. I'll let you know as soon as I find out anything about those three."

"Okay, thanks, buddy." Jack hung up the phone and sat back in his chair.

Had Jasmine seen the mountain lion in her yard? Or had she gone hiking when he'd warned her not to? He fought the urge to dash over to her house. She may not want him around, but he had to know if she was okay, so he picked up the phone and punched in a number.

"Chloe's Gift Shop, how may I help you?"

"Chloe, this is Jack."

"Hi, Jack. What can I do for you?"

"I called to ask a favor."

"Sure, just name it."

"Stan just called and said he heard over the scanner that Jasmine had spotted a mountain lion. Would you call and make sure she's all right?"

Chloe exhaled sharply. "I wish you two would put your pride aside and talk to each other."

"Chloe, can we not get into that now? I want to know if she's okay." He doodled on a yellow legal pad.

"Okay, okay. I'll run over there and see and get back to you." He heard her sigh again.

"Thanks, Chloe. I owe you one."

"Jack. I don't know what's happened between you

two, but don't give up on my sister. She's just confused now, but I know she loves you."

"Maybe. But not enough, Chlo. Not enough." He tossed the pen down and ran his hand through his hair. "Look, please call me as soon as you can. And please don't tell Jasmine I called."

"Okay. I'll figure out something so I don't have to lie."

Jack hung up the phone and swiveled his chair around. Had it not been for Chloe updating him these last three weeks, he wouldn't have been able to handle staying away from Jasmine. But Chloe had assured him Jasmine seemed fine, and as far as she knew, Jasmine hadn't received any more threatening phone calls.

He stood and paced the floor.

It took every ounce of willpower he possessed not to call Jasmine. He had always been there for her, and she had always been there for him. When he got the flu, she nursed him back to health and never once complained when she ended up getting it herself. She made him special gift cards. Brought him homemade baked goodies. On stressful days, she massaged his neck and shoulder muscles. So many times she surprised him by bringing dinner to his office when he had to work late. All these things said she cared, but unfortunately, not enough.

Stopping in front of the window, he stared blankly outside. Could he bear it if he never saw Jasmine again? Never heard her voice or heard her soft laughter again?

Needing some kind of connection to her, he envisioned the soft tendrils of wispy hair down her graceful neck. Her blue-green eyes that sometimes appeared translucent. Her perfectly shaped lips that had proved as kissable as they looked. He forced his mind not to stray that direction. Instead, he thought about the way she chewed her thumbnail when she was nervous or uncomfortable. He grinned. That always tickled him.

And how it upset her when he seemed to read her thoughts. Of course he couldn't read her mind. He just knew her. And loved her. *Oh, Jasmine. My sweet, Jazzy. I miss you so much.*

His back burned from his ulcer, but not as bad as it used to because it had finally started to heal. He reached for his antacids and tossed a couple into his mouth.

Jack needed to get his mind off of her so he wouldn't fan the flames of his ulcer any further. He sat at his drawing table and picked up a lead holder. He set to work on the Manson's design, but no matter how hard he tried, he couldn't concentrate. He got up and went back to the window, staring in the direction of Jasmine's house.

If only she'd call him. To let him know she still cared about him. Still wanted him around. Her silence proved to him she didn't. And he wasn't the kind of man who went where he wasn't wanted.

Grief barreled over him. He collapsed into his chair. Leaning on his elbows, he placed his head in his hands.

"Lord, what am I going to do? You said to be patient, but she doesn't want me. This whole thing is so tormenting. I've never felt so alone in my whole life. Show me what to do, Jesus."

His eyes stung, but he refused to cry. Instead, he reached for his Bible and let it fall open. The words, "Delight yourself in the Lord and He'll give you the desires of your heart" leapt off the pages. He muttered those words until God's peace filled the emptiness inside him. "Thank You, Lord. I won't give up. She's worth waiting for."

Jack returned to his drawing table, straddled his bar stool, and had started working when his phone rang.

He jumped up and sent the stool crashing to the floor. "Hello."

"Jack, this is Chloe."

"What'd you find out? Is Jasmine okay? Are you

there now? What happened?"

"Jack! I can't talk if you don't shut up."

"Sorry. How is she?"

"I'm at the hospital with her now."

"Hospital!" Panic smacked him upside the head. "What's she doing there? Did the mountain lion attack her?" His stomach felt woozy. "Is—is she okay?" He held his breath with trepidation as he waited for Chloe's answer.

CHAPTER SEVENTEEN

Jack stared at the wildlife photo of a mountain lion hanging on his wall. Seeing its menacing scowl and sharp fangs, the phone he held next to his ear felt like a hundred-pound dumbbell as he waited for Chloe's answer.

"She'll be fine," Chloe said.

Jack closed his eyes and started breathing again.

"She's in getting checked now. A small branch is lodged in a muscle in her neck."

"Jasmine has a branch in her neck?" That image made him cringe. "What happened?"

Chloe briefly filled him in about Jasmine's walk, and the mountain lion, and how she got the twig in her neck.

"Why didn't the officer call an ambulance?"

"Jasmine told them I would take care of her. It was hard seeing it, but she's here now, and they're taking care of her."

Jack pressed his hand over his chin. If only he would have controlled his emotions and been patient like God had told him to, then he would have never kissed Jasmine, and she would have called him instead of the police. And Chloe would have never had to go through this either. The woman couldn't stand the sight of blood. He could kick himself for being so pigheaded.

"Jack? Are you listening?"

"Sorry."

"I don't care what happened between you two, you need to get your behind down here right now. Jasmine needs you."

"I don't know." As much as he wanted to be with her,

he wasn't sure that's what Jasmine wanted.

"Listen. You and Jasmine have been friends far too long to let whatever happened between the two of you keep you apart. Can't you two work it out?"

Jack didn't know how to answer her. *What should I do, Lord? Please, show me.*

Go to her.

"How long will you be at the hospital?"

"I don't know. I'm not sure if she'll need stitches or surgery. They don't know how deep the stick went in. I need to get back to her now, Jack. Won't you please come?" The tone she used let him know *she* needed him, too.

In one breath the decision was made. "I'll be there in ten minutes."

Once again, Jasmine found herself at the hospital. She stared at the drab tan, yellow, and sea-green privacy curtain, wondering when she could get some pain medication. The thought of a twig wedged under the skin of her neck made her stomach queasy. *Ewww.* She cringed. *Focus on something else, Jazz.*

Jasmine thought about Chloe's timing. Thank the Lord, she had shown up when she had. Like she had so many other times before, her sister had probably sensed something was wrong and rushed right over.

A middle-aged nurse pulled the hospital curtain back, stepped next to Jasmine's bed, and drew the curtain closed again. She had the same blond colored hair as Jack's.

"Hello, my name is Sandy. How are you doing?" Her genuine concern touched Jasmine.

"All right I guess. My neck's pretty sore." Jasmine reached up to touch it, but the nurse tugged her hand away, and placed it beside Jasmine's leg.

"We'll get you something for pain. But I need to find

out if you've had a tetanus shot in the last ten years."

"I don't remember ever having one."

"Do you have any allergies?"

"No."

"What happened?"

Jasmine relayed the whole event. "This sort of freak accident is something that would happen to my sister, Shanell, not me." She chuckled, then stopped when an onslaught of fresh pain accosted her neck.

The nurse patted her hand. "The doctor should be in here any minute. We'll take good care of you." She pulled the curtain back and glanced at Jasmine and smiled. "Believe it or not this type of thing happens often with all the short, broken branches there are around here. I'll be right back." She slipped through the curtain and closed it.

Jasmine ran her fingers over the crisp white sheet, glanced at the monitors and machines, and perused the whole room until there was nothing else to see. The stinging pain in her neck grew. What was taking them so long?

She stared at the curtain and tried to create pictures out of the faded design while waiting for the nurse to return. Minute after minute ticked by and still no nurse. She scooted down to find a more comfortable position. Finally, the curtain moved. A doctor, who looked to be in his early sixties, walked up next to her bed and extended his hand. "Hello, Jasmine. I'm Doctor Mitchell."

She smiled, returning his handshake.

"I heard you spotted a mountain lion. You're one lucky lady. You know that, don't you?" His friendly smile and kind voice reminded her of her granddad.

A memory flashed through her mind. At the age of six, her older cousin Lex had accidentally hooked his fishing lure in the back of her head when he tried casting out his line. All the way to the lake house, she had remained calm. But one look at Granddad, and she broke down crying, knowing she no longer had to be brave because her granddad would take care of everything.

This doctor had the same effect on her. He would take care of her. She could stop being brave now. When she relaxed her tense body, it started quivering uncontrollably.

God, please don't let me hyperventilate.

"Are you cold?" the doctor asked.

"Yes." Embarrassed, she lowered her head, "Plus, I'm so scared." She couldn't keep the quiver from her voice.

He patted her shoulder. "We'll give you something to calm you down." He looked at the nurse. "Give her a shot of valium and Toradol, and grab a blanket out of the warmer."

Within seconds, Sandy draped the warm blanket over her. The heat penetrated Jasmine's skin, and within minutes it soothed away even her fear.

She winced when the nurse gave her the shots, but within seconds, the pain slipped from her body. Her arms, her whole body felt heavy and limp.

She strained to keep her eyelids from bobbing up and down as she watched the doctor and nurse put on rubber gloves.

The doctor pressed lightly around Jasmine's neck. She recoiled, not from the pain, but from the idea of what was happening. How she wished Jack was standing next to her, holding her hand, and talking to her in that unique way of his. The way that made her feel protected and that all was right with the world.

"You realize how lucky you are this branch lodged in your trapezius muscle, don't you? If it had hit your jugular vein, it would have been life threatening. God was sure watching over you, young lady."

"Thank you, Lord," Jasmine whispered.

The nurse injected something close to where the stick

had gone into her neck. Jasmine surprised herself at how calm she remained. Her eyelids drooped with heaviness.

On the table next to Jasmine's bed, Sandy placed a small basin of saline solution and a syringe.

"We're going to remove the twig now. You'll feel some pressure and a slight amount of discomfort," the kind doctor informed her.

Jasmine held her breath as he pulled the stick out. Just like he'd said, she experienced a slight amount of pressure and nominal pain.

"Now that wasn't too bad, was it?" He smiled at her.

She tried remembering his name but couldn't. She glanced at his name tag. "No, Doctor Mitchell. Not as bad as I thought it would be." In her medicine-induced, dream-like state she didn't think anything would hurt.

He filled the syringe with the clear liquid. "Okay, now we're going to irrigate your wound so we can get any remaining particles out. We don't want any infection setting in." He turned his kind eyes on her. "You doing okay?"

"Yeah," she drawled.

He smiled and then glanced at the green-eyed nurse. "I need more light please."

She left and came back a minute later, placing the bright light above Jasmine. After the doctor irrigated the spot in her neck several times, he picked up some instruments. She felt him exploring around in her wound. It didn't hurt, but the thought made her skin crawl and her stomach woozy, so she silently prayed she wouldn't throw up or pass out.

"It looks pretty clean, and the muscle isn't torn. I'm going to close the hole with a couple of sutures."

She watched him head toward her neck with a needle and thread. Her mind whirled as she thought about what he was about to do. She pressed her eyes shut and willed her stomach to not empty its contents. If only Jack were here. Right now she'd even settle for Chloe. But no one or anything would be able to persuade her sister to come into the room with her. Chloe might be a strong person, but Miss take-charge couldn't control her reaction to the sight of blood or stitches. Usually she slumped to the floor in a heap. Jasmine chuckled.

"What's so funny?" the nurse asked.

Her eyes opened. "Just thinking about my sister. If she were in here, she'd be on the floor right now, and you'd be tending to her instead of me." She snickered.

"Is she the one who brought you in?" Sandy asked.

"Yes."

"Are you identical twins?" she inquired while handing the doctor a piece of sterile bandage.

"No."

The nurse's eyebrows shot under her bangs.

Jasmine giggled. "We're identical triplets."

A smile of understanding lit across her face. "Ah. I see. I knew you had to be identical something." She laughed and handed the doctor a couple strips of tape.

"There, young lady. You're all set. We need to keep this wound clean so infection doesn't set in." He laid his hand on her arm. "You're going to experience some soreness for a few days." He patted her gently, his eyes exuding compassion.

Jasmine felt too good to care about how she'd feel later or about anything else right now.

"Now, if you have any trouble with a rise in temperature, drainage, redness, infection, or increased pain in the next twenty-four hours, I want you to go see your family doctor right away. If not, then do a follow up with your PCP in a week. Sandy will give you a tetanus shot and further instructions." He gave her a sly smile and playfully shook his finger at her. "Now, no more playing with them mountain lions, you hear me?" He winked, then chuckled. "I heard the Division of Wild Life has been trying to trap it for some time now because it's too close to the residential area." Squeezing her hand, he added, "You take care of yourself, and do what my nurse tells you to."

"I will. Thank you, Doctor."

"You're welcome," he tossed over his shoulder and left.

"He's really nice," Jasmine said to the nurse.

"None better, that's for sure." Sandy's smile showed her respect toward him. "Okay. Here's what you need to do." She handed her a small package with six prescription pain pills in it. "You probably won't need these. Advil should work just fine. But I'll give them to you just in case." She continued giving Jasmine instructions, telling her not to get the wound wet and what signs to look out for that would indicate an infection.

After receiving all the information and the tetanus shot, Jasmine was free to go. When she swung her legs around and stood, a touch of lightheadedness dizzied over her. She braced herself against the bed as the room continued to move.

Sandy held her arm. "Do you have someone to drive you home?"

"Yes." She nodded and gave the nurse a silly grin. "But the way I feel, I could just float home." Her giggle sounded goofy even to her own ears. But she couldn't help herself. That medicine was something else.

"Everyone's reaction to the pain medication is different. Enjoy, because the effects will wear off before long." She smiled and pulled back the curtain. Supporting Jasmine, she helped her safely out of the room.

In her dream-like state, wobbling her head like a newborn kitten trying to hold its head for the first time, Jasmine scanned the waiting room, searching for Chloe. Instead, her eyes landed on Jack. At least she hoped it was him and not a hallucination. Several blinks later, she rubbed her eyes. It took a few seconds for her to realize she wasn't seeing things. Her heart skipped and then sped up.

Jack had his head down, and he hadn't noticed her yet, so she drank in the sight of him. He looked so handsome in his gold flannel shirt. It brought out the yellow highlights in his blond hair. His blue jeans hugged his long muscular legs.

As if he sensed her presence, he looked up and his slow smile greeted her. A shy, uncertain smile lifted the corners of her mouth. She wanted to run up and throw her arms around him, but her equilibrium was way off.

In a blink of an eye, the nurse had let go, and Jack had his arm around her, holding her tight.

His concerned gaze scanned her face and then dropped toward her bandage. "I'm sorry. I forgot about your neck. Did I hurt you?"

"No." Her head bobbled again. "They've got me pretty doped up." She leaned her good side into his chest, and his arm slipped around her with the lightest of touch.

"Oh, Jack. It's so good to see you." Even though her words were a bit slurred, she continued talking. "I've missed you so much. I'm so sorry for the way I've been acting lately. Can you ever forgive me?"

Softly he smiled. "It's not you who needs to ask for forgiveness. It's me. I'm sorry." His breath brushed against her ear as he spoke, sending chills scurrying through her body.

"It's okay. I—"

"We'll talk later." Jack cut off her words. "When we don't have an audience."

Her head bounced like a bobble head doll when she turned.

Several ladies were gawking at them with big grins on their faces. An elderly lady dressed in a hospital volunteer uniform hustled up to them and handed

Jasmine's parka to Jack. He held it while she put it on.

"Do you want to wait here," he pointed to a chair. "while I go get the pickup and bring it to the door?"

"No. I can make it. If you help me."

He braced her to himself and led her toward the door.

She clung to him, knowing her ribbon knees wouldn't hold her up. "Where's Chloe?"

"She went back to her shop. She thought we needed to talk. And I agreed. I hope you don't mind." Hope dripped from his words. His familiar yellowish hazel eyes threatened to melt her into a liquid puddle right there. How she'd missed seeing his gorgeous face, his friendly smile, and just Jack himself.

Her lips curled upward. "No. Not at all. But can we get something to eat first? I'm hungry. Then I have something I want to tell you."

Oh, Lord. Give me the courage to go through with this, she silently pleaded.

Chapter Eighteen

Jack scooped Jasmine up in to his arms and sat her on the seat in his pickup, then closed the door. As he walked around to his side of the truck, he prayed. *Lord, I need your wisdom in this situation. Give me the right words to say. Thank You.* He opened the driver's side door and slid in.

Jasmine perched her head against the headrest.

"What do you feel like doing? Grabbing something and taking it back to your house or eating out someplace?"

"How about going to The Village Inn?"

"You sure you're up to it?"

"With the meds they gave me, I feel *really* good." She giggled.

"Okay then. Village Inn it is."

Inside the eating establishment, a hostess seated them in a booth in the corner. Their waitress came up and handed them each a menu. "Can I bring you something to drink?"

Jack looked at Jasmine.

"I'll have hot chocolate, please."

"Coffee. Decaf, please."

The waitress nodded and scurried off.

Jack picked up his menu and scanned it, not really seeing anything. What would he say to her? He'd never been at a loss for words before.

"I already know what I want." The way Jasmine said it made Jack peer over his menu at her. From the strange look on her face, her implications went further than the food. But just what she was implying exactly, he didn't know.

He lowered his menu. "Me, too." His response had nothing to do with food either.

Jasmine looked as awkward as he felt. Their relationship had definitely changed.

Jack fidgeted with his menu and gazed around the room. He wasn't used to the discomfort between them. Numerous times they'd argued over the years, but only one time had been as bad or as serious as this one. That heated argument had nearly severed their relationship. He refused to dwell in the past. Reining in his thoughts, he focused on the present.

He resisted the urge to plow his fingers through his hair. Once they placed their order, he would have to force himself to say some things that would hopefully put her at ease but break his heart.

The waitress returned with their hot beverages, some iced water, napkins, and silverware. After setting them down, she looked at Jasmine. "Are you ready to order, ma'am?"

"Yes. I'll have a cheeseburger with Swiss cheese and extra pickles. And onion rings instead of French fries, please."

"And you, sir?"

"I'll have the same, except hold the pickles."

The waitress gathered their menus and left.

While Jack wondered how to start the conversation, without thinking, he grabbed his steaming coffee and took a big gulp. The hot liquid burned all the way down his throat. "Whew, that's hot." He worked his tongue in and out like a snake, snatched up his water, and took a big swig.

"You okay?"

"Yeah. I'm fine." He wiped his mouth with a napkin and forced a smile onto his face.

Jasmine stared at him with those sexy blue-green

eyes and reticent smile. "I really am sorry... for everything." She laid her hand on top of his and gave it a squeeze.

Jack couldn't believe how her simple gesture sent his blood pressure soaring. He fought to keep the emotional turmoil going on inside from showing up on his face, not wanting to scare her off again.

The last three weeks had been some of the worst of his life. He'd never felt so empty and so alone. Every time the phone had rung, he'd rushed to it, hoping it was Jasmine. Numerous times, out of habit, he had started to call her, but then he remembered their parting words, so he hung up.

Because he never wanted to feel that much pain again, he would give her all the space she needed and keep their relationship strictly on a friendship level.

Give me the strength I need to say this, Lord. He cleared his throat. "I'm sorry, too. Let's just go back to the way things were before." Before the kiss that had rocked his whole world. Before the kiss that sealed his love for her forever. "Let's just put all of this behind us, okay?" He nodded his head once. "Friends?" He offered his hand to her and forced what he hoped was a smile on to his face.

While he waited for her to shake his hand, he added. "Now, you said earlier you had something you wanted to tell me. What was it?"

Friends! Jasmine's mind screamed. She was just about to tell Jack how much she loved him, but he said he wanted to go back to the way things were. As friends. How could she have been so stupid? Did she really think he had picked her up so he could confess his undying love for her after the horrible way she'd treated him? Her heart shattered into a million pieces, along with her dream of marrying the man she loved and living happily ever after.

Those kind of endings only happened in romance novels. And her life was everything but a romance story.

Talk about a stab to the heart. This one was a doozy.

Surely this wasn't the Lord's way of showing her that Jack wasn't the man He had intended for her. That thought broke her heart. *C'mon, girl. Pull yourself together.* Mustering up all the strength she could manage, she drew in a deep breath and plastered a smile on her face and shook his proffered hand. "Friends," she said, ignoring the sparks shooting up her arm from his touch.

The waitress brought their food and set it in front of them. "Can I get you anything else?"

Yes, Jack's heart, please.

"No, thank you," they said in unison.

Jasmine picked up her fork and stared at it. Her appetite had vanished.

"Jazz?"

She looked up at him. His beautiful eyes held the same concern she'd seen in them so many times before. The urge to blurt out how much she loved him overwhelmed her. But fear of his rejection propelled her to stuff down the impulse. "Yeah?" She forced lightness into her tone and hated every single second of it.

"What's going on in that pretty little head of yours?"

"Why?" She stirred her hot chocolate and took a sip.

Jack leaned forward and ran his thumb over her upper lip. "You've got whipped cream right here."

A strange look crossed Jack's face.

Jasmine's stomach flip-flopped.

He yanked his hand away as if he'd just run it over a razor blade instead of her lips and scraped the cream onto his napkin. "Now tell me what's bothering you."

Tired of doing stupid things she would regret later and knowing there was no way she would tell him what she'd been thinking, her mind scrambled for a response. "I need to go home and rest."

"Are you hurting?"

"Just tired." She set her fork down.

"Let me get the ticket, and then we'll leave." He scanned the room.

Seeing his still full plate, she refused be selfish and not let Jack eat because she was upset. She pressed her hand on his arm. "Wait. Let's just go ahead and eat first. I'll be fine."

Unconvinced, Jack studied her face. "Are you sure?"

"I'm sure. How's your ulcer?" she asked while squirting catsup on her burger.

"It's getting better," he replied as he layered the lettuce and tomato onto his cheeseburger. "The acid-reducers are finally starting to help." He looked up from his plate. "You look tired. We can take this to your house and eat there if you'd like."

"No. Let's stay. And yes, I'm sure." *And I'm sure I'm in love with you. But after your speech about being friends, I can't tell you that.*

"Okay." Jack bowed his head.

Jasmine joined him.

"Father, we ask Your blessing on this food, and we thank You for Your provision. Thank You for keeping Jasmine safe today. And thank You for restoring our friendship. Amen."

Friendship. That one word now burrowed into her like an unwanted rodent. She picked up an onion ring and bit into it. Nothing had any flavor, but she continued forcing herself to eat.

A young couple headed their way, walking arm-in-arm, smiling and gazing at each other as if they were the only two people in the restaurant. She picked up her water and took a sip. She knew she had blown her chances of ever being with Jack like that. It was probably for the best, but she still envied the happy looking couple. Jasmine shrugged off her glum mood, set her glass down, and stared at it.

"Tell me about the mountain lion. Chloe said you saw it on a rock ledge." He took a bite of his cheeseburger and chewed.

Jasmine blotted her mouth with a paper napkin and placed it next to her plate. "It was weird. I had this feeling someone or something was watching me. When I got my binoculars out, I spotted it."

"What did you do?"

"I backed down the mountain as slow as possible."

"Then what?"

What was this—interrogation day or fifty questions? "When I got back to the house, Bougé was growling and staring out the window. I saw something move and thought it was the mountain lion, but it wasn't, it was—" She pulled her eyes to Jack's, wondering just how much she should tell him.

"It was what?" Jack set his half-eaten onion ring back onto his plate and brushed the crumbs from his fingers.

"Oh, never mind. I'm sure it was just my mind playing tricks on me."

Jack's brows rose. He covered her hand with his. His touch nearly sent her over the edge.

"Tell me what you *think* you saw?"

Grateful for the distraction his touch induced, she answered. "Maybe I was just being paranoid."

"Was Bougé being paranoid, too?"

She scanned his handsome face. Every time he wore that gold shirt, it made the yellow in his hazel eyes, stand out. How she longed to get lost in them, forever

"Please, tell me, Jasmine." He brushed his thumb over her hand.

Her insides quivered. Not able to handle the intimate gesture, she slipped her hand out from underneath his and rested it next to her plate. "I thought I saw a man slip behind the blue-spruce tree outside my living room window."

"What?" Jack boomed.

Jasmine darted a quick look around the restaurant. People gawked in their direction, frowning.

"Why didn't you call me?" His jaw muscles flexed.

Jasmine's eyelids lowered, and she concentrated on the silver speckles in the blue table top. She picked up her paper napkin and twisted it into a tight wad.

Jack reached over and grasped her hand.

Stop touching me! I can't stand it! She wanted to yell at him. Instead, without looking at him, she answered his question. "I didn't want to bother you. Besides, after the way we left things, I thought you—" She tugged her hand free again and grabbed her napkin, rubbing the stiff paper between her fingers. "I thought you didn't want to see me anymore, especially after the way I had treated you. When you didn't call or anything, I assumed our friendship no longer existed."

Concern lines etched across his face. Jack tilted her chin up with his finger. "Hey."

Afraid her feelings would give her away, she refused to let him get a glimpse into her eyes. Tattle-tale eyes that would reveal her very soul and with what depth she loved him.

He dropped his finger. "Jasmine."

She chanced a half-glance at him.

"I didn't call because I didn't think you wanted me to. I'm sorry. We were both being stubborn. But that's in the past. Let's just forget it and go on from here. Okay?"

She nodded her agreement, but her heart would never forget that moment, and neither would her lips. She could still remember how his soft satisfying kiss made her mouth and body tingle. *Get a grip, Jasmine! Stop it.* Drawing in a deep breath, she licked her lips.

She'd come this far. She might as well tell him the rest. "There's more, Jack. Last Tuesday, I went to Chloe's shop to drop off some of my stuff, and some man had followed me to my car." She noticed Jack's jaw muscle working back and forth and the veins in his neck expanding.

She hurried on before she lost her nerve. "At the time, I didn't think anything about it because he got into the car next to mine. But Sunday, when I saw him again, he was leaning against his car, wearing the same dark sunglasses he had on the first time I noticed him." Jasmine watched Jack's reaction.

His body tensed, but his eyes held concern, giving her the courage to keep going.

"The last couple of weeks, I saw the same black car parked next to mine at the grocery store, then at Shanell's, my parents', and at—" She shuddered, remembering how it had been parked by her house too. She stared out the window, seeing nothing. "Actually, everywhere I went the last couple of weeks, it's been there."

Jack squeezed her fingers. She glanced down at their clasped hands, wondering why she didn't feel the need to yank hers away this time.

He rubbed his thumb over the back of her hand. The soothing gesture only escalated her desire for more.

Jasmine looked at him, tenderly.

"Jazz, we've never had secrets between us. I know there's something you're not telling me."

Just how much should she tell him? The thought of going home and being alone propelled her to reveal all. "Today—"

"Can I get you anything else?" The waitress interrupted, then glanced at Jasmine's plate. "Is something wrong with your food, ma'am?"

She slid her hand from Jack's. "No, no it's fine. I just wasn't as hungry as I thought I was."

"Oh, okay." The waitress turned toward Jack. "Would you like some more coffee, sir?"

"Yes, please." He smiled. But Jasmine noticed the strain in his lips.

"Okay, I'll be right back." She turned and walked away.

"What happened today?" Jack took a drink of his coffee and set it down, never taking his eyes off of her.

"Today, I saw that car parked near my house. I can't help but wonder if this man is same man that's been peeping into women's windows here. The Steamboat Springs' Peeping Tom Chloe told you about." *Or RodeoCowboy.* But she wouldn't mention him. Right now she just didn't feel like listening to another lecture on Internet catastrophes.

"Go on." His voice sounded strained. Something she rarely heard from the calm and in control Jackson Warren.

"I've gotten several more of those strange phone calls. I thought I'd gotten over the fear. But I'm scared, Jack." Her eyes locked on his as she gathered up all the courage she could muster before she rushed on to say, "I'm going to see if Granddad will let me move into his lake house right away. I need to get away from here." *And fast.*

Jack felt the color drain from his face. His protective instincts once again went on full alert. The situation with Jasmine was getting out of hand. Until he figured out what to do, he didn't want her out of his sight. Some nut was trailing her. And that same nut might possibly follow her to Louisiana too. Then she'd be a sitting duck out there all alone. *God, show me what to do here.*

The waitress topped off his coffee and asked if they wanted any dessert. They both declined, so she placed the check on the table and left. Jack took a long drink of his coffee and then set it down. Leaning forward, he took both of Jasmine's hands in his. "Look, you need time to heal. So, instead of going to your granddad's house right now, why don't you stay at my place for awhile?"

Her eyes shot open, and her chin almost hit the table.

He tapped her mouth closed with his finger. "It wouldn't be *that* bad." He chuckled. "Besides, if you stay with me, I can keep an eye on you."

"I can't do that. What would people say? I don't want to be known as *that* kind of girl. It isn't right. I'm surprised you even asked. Besides, what would I do with Bougé? Willbee would mistake her for one of his meals."

"Don't worry. I'll take care of everything. As far as your reputation goes, what's worse, having some strange man following you with who knows what on his mind, or people thinking we're—" He stopped and shrugged. "If it will make you feel any better, I could have Rena come and stay. That way no one would think anything of it and your reputation would stay intact. What do you say?" He studied her face.

"Your sister has better things to do with her time than babysit me. Staying at your place is not an option. It wouldn't be wise for either one of us."

Jasmine had a point. His fantasy of having her lying on the angora rug with his ring on her finger flashed through his mind. Perhaps having her in his house all the time wasn't such a good idea after all.

He was going to suggest she stay at Chloe's or Shanell's, but he wasn't sure that was any safer. Especially if the guy followed her there.

Jack looked over in time to see Jasmine tilt her head and grimace. She sucked in a sharp breath and touched her neck.

"I need to get you home." Jack slid out of the chair and helped her to her feet. After paying the check, he led her to his pickup and helped her inside.

On the way to her house, he glanced her way. "Don't worry, Jazz. I'll figure something out."

The look of pure trust she gave him warmed his heart

and did funny things to his insides.

He wouldn't let her down.

The first thing he needed to do was to get in touch with Stan and let him know about the man following Jasmine.

Deep in his gut, Jack knew without a doubt that that someone was Simon and not the stalking Peeping Tom he'd read about.

What would Jasmine's reaction be when she found out the person scaring her was a man she trusted?

CHAPTER NINETEEN

Jack turned his pickup into Jasmine's driveway and surveyed the area for a black car but didn't see one anywhere.

Seeing Jasmine sound asleep, his heart gave a tumble. She'd been through a lot this last month.

After he unlocked Jasmine's front door, he went back to his pickup, scooped her in his arms, carried her into the house, and settled her on the sofa.

Careful not to awaken her, he removed her snow boots and covered her with a blanket.

How peaceful and beautiful she looked. Her dark eyelashes were long and thick, and her small, straight nose sported a sprinkle of freckles. Her slightly parted lips lured him under their spell until his heart rate increased. He remembered kissing those lips. He could still feel their satiny moistness wreaking havoc with his mouth as if he had kissed them only moments ago, instead of weeks.

Jasmine stirred.

Not wanting to wake her or have her catch him staring at her, he spun around and made a thorough check of the house, turning off all the ringers and making sure all the windows and doors were locked before he headed outside to search for tracks.

As he traipsed around Jasmine's yard, the bright afternoon sun beamed down on him, keeping the usual February nip out of the air.

His focus zoomed in on fresh snowshoe prints behind the tree in her yard. He followed them across the street, down the block and up to the edge of the trees. Whoever had followed Jasmine had followed her up into the woods.

His gut twisted like a contortionist. She could have been—. He stopped his mind from going there.

Jack followed the tracks back toward the house, right up to her living room window. A mixture of anger and fear rippled through him.

The need to check on Jasmine pressed in on him. Once he made sure she was okay, he slipped outside again and headed toward his pickup. He grabbed his cell phone off the seat and punched in Stan's number. Nerves strung as tight as a circus high-wire, he drummed his fingers on the steering wheel. "C'mon, Stan."

Just when he was about ready to hang up, he heard, "Top Notch Investigators, Stan speaking."

"Stan. This is Jack." He slid out of his pickup and paced back and forth.

"Hey, buddy. What's up?"

Jack explained the tracks in the snow and about Jasmine being followed by some man in a black car with dark windows.

"You think it's Simon?"

"Yeah, I do. Did you find out anything more about him yet?"

"I was going to call you later on tonight after I talked to Mick. I wanted to know for sure before I said anything to you."

"Said anything to me about what?" Jack stopped pacing.

"Well, I kind of want to wait until I know for sure."

Jack didn't like the cautiousness in Stan's tone. That meant it wasn't good news. "Tell me, Stan, please. I need to know so I can protect her," he said, bracing himself for the news.

"There's no person using the nickname Simonrapport in California as far as we can tell. However, there is a Simon using that nickname in Arizona. And from what we're able to ascertain, I think it's the same man. If it is, he's bad news."

This information didn't really surprise Jack. Deep in his spirit he already knew that, but to actually have his suspicions confirmed made him even more uneasy.

"There's more."

"What's that?" Jack tugged at his lip.

"The guy's wanted in three states for assault. Colorado is one of them. But that's not the worst of it. Simon's not near as bad as that RodeoCowboy dude. In fact, he's a saint compared to him. RodeoCowboy uses several aliases, and he's so bad that he's on America's Most Wanted list for kidnapping his victims and torturing them. Every one of his victims he found on the Internet."

Jack leaned against the pickup for support.

"The same goes for Simon. But I hate saying anything more until I know for sure if it's the same guy or not, but the M.O.'s the same. All of Simon's victims reported meeting him online too. Shortly after, they received strange phone calls, and then they noticed someone following them."

Jack didn't think his gut could pinch any tighter, but it just had. He scoped out the perimeter around Jasmine's place.

"Well, let's just hope it's not the same guy. It's hard to track down nicknames off the Internet, but I should know more by tonight or at least by the end of this week."

"Thanks, Stan. Hey, how do you deal with something like this? Should I call the police or what?"

"Right now, just make sure Jasmine isn't alone until I find out from Mick if it's the same guy or not. If we're lucky, it won't be."

"Man, I feel so helpless." Jack ran his fingers through his hair.

"I know, buddy. But, don't get too worked up. Just keep an eye on her. And Jack?"

"Yeah."

"Don't go playing Superman on me. These guys are dangerous. If you see anything suspicious, call the police right away."

"I will. And there is no way Jasmine's going to be alone. Even if I have to drag her kicking and screaming, she's either coming to my house, or I'm staying at hers. Now I've just got to convince her. That's the hard part. You know how stubborn she can be."

Stan chuckled. "I sure do."

"Well, let me know as soon as you find out anything. Talk to you later." Jack snapped his cell phone shut and scrubbed the back of his head. Jasmine was in more danger than he had originally realized.

Two more calls, then he hurried back inside. He sat down in the overstuffed chair on the other side of the end table.

Clasping his hands, he leaned his elbows on his knees. *Lord, send your angels to surround Jasmine and watch over her. And, Lord, prepare Jasmine's heart to accept our help.* His lips curled in a wry grin. *You sure have Your job cut out for You there, Lord.*

◦◦◦◦◦

Jasmine batted her eyes open and looked around the living room. With his legs spread and arms across his chest, Jack stared out her window. She took the opportunity to study him.

What a hunk.

His broad shoulders and muscular legs made him look like he should be in a Superman movie. His long eyelashes and straight nose gave him a regal look. And his perfectly shaped mouth…

An acute sense of loss filled her. Would she ever be able to taste those lips again?

Jack turned his head, locking gazes with her. He walked over and knelt down in front of her. "How you doing, sweetie?" His endearment and tender voice melted her insides like butter in a hot skillet.

She lightly touched her wound. "My neck's pretty sore. I need to get up and take some ibuprofen."

"Stay there. I'll get them."

Jasmine waved her hand. "No, no. I need to get up and use the restroom. Thanks anyway."

He stood, tossed the purple blanket onto the back of the sofa, and helped her up. His touch placed her senses on full alert as shockwaves pulsed throughout her body. Ever since they'd kissed, whether she wanted to or not, she saw Jack differently; she saw Jack for the man he was instead of the kid she grew up with. Summoning her inner strength, she pulled away from him and walked to the bathroom.

What a mess! Jasmine gaped at herself in the mirror. Her mascara-smudged eyes reminded her of a raccoon, and her dark brown hair resembled an angered porcupine. She refused to go back to the living room looking like something the cat had drug in.

With the water as hot as she could stand it, she wet a washcloth and positioned it over her face. Heat penetrated her skin and eyes, refreshing her. Once she had the mascara scrubbed off, she corralled her hair into some semblance of order. Satisfied with the transformation, she opened the medicine cabinet, grabbed a couple of Advil, tossed them down with a glass of water, and then headed into the living room.

Jack strode toward her. "You need help?"

"No, I'm fine. Thank you. How long was I asleep anyway?"

Jack checked his watch. "About three hours."

"Three hours! Have you been here all that time?"

"Yeah."

"Why didn't you wake me?"

"Now why would I do that? You needed rest."

"I have to admit, it did feel pretty good." She

stretched but stopped when pain gushed into her neck.

"Did you take anything for the pain yet?"

"Yes."

"Good. Listen, we need to talk." He motioned toward the loveseat. "I made you a cup of Irish Crème coffee." Before she had a chance to even open her mouth and thank him, he whizzed into the kitchen.

Jasmine made her way to the loveseat and sat as close to the arm rest as she possibly could.

"Here you go." He handed her the coffee and sat down.

His nearness caused every cell in her body to stand up and take notice. The tingling sensation drove her crazy. She couldn't even be in the same room with him anymore without having an overwhelming desire to be in his arms and have him passionately kiss her like before. But that wasn't ever going to happen again, and that very idea tormented her.

Being here with Jack, but *not* being here with Jack, was going to drive her certifiably insane.

She made a mental note to call her granddad. Even if he didn't want to sell the cabin, perhaps she could convince him to at least let her rent it until she found a place of her own.

Thoughts of warm sunshine all year around, swimming in the lake whenever she wanted, and bright flowers caused a twitch at the corners of her mouth.

"What are you smiling about?"

"I was just thinking about Granddad's lake house. I can't wait to call him and find out if he'll let me buy it, or maybe even rent it, so I can move right away." The idea of living in Louisiana made her heart feel lighter than she'd felt in years. Only the thought of leaving Jack behind caused a mountain of dread. She faced Jack. "Now what did you want to talk to me about?"

While Jack was thankful he and her granddad had already discussed how the man would deter Jasmine from buying his place, he now had the unpleasant task of telling Jasmine some news she would be furious to hear.

Jack pulled her hands into his and nervously rubbed his thumbs over the back of her hands. "There's no easy way for me to say this, so I'm just going to come right and say it." He took a deep breath to steady the words. "While you were sleeping I walked around outside. It wasn't your imagination. Someone was outside your window."

Her olive skin paled. He wanted to draw her into his arms and comfort her, but that would be a mistake.

"Jasmine, this is getting serious. Whoever it was also followed you up into the trees. And after everything that's been happening lately, it's just not safe for you to be out here alone. We talked earlier about you coming to stay with me. Knowing how you feel about that, the only other solution I could think of was to call your sisters to see if they would take turns spending the night with you here, and I agreed to come and stay with you during the day." *And the police will be driving around the neighborhood on a regular basis.*

Jasmine yanked her hands from his and shot off the loveseat. "Jack!" She glared at him. "How dare you do this without discussing it with me first? I don't want—"

In an instant he was standing in front of her and cupping her upper arms.

"Listen to me, Jasmine." He knew he sounded gruff, but was powerless to stop it. "Don't you think I know how you feel about having Chloe over here? I know she takes charge when she's around, but don't you understand?" He searched her eyes. "I can't bear the thought of anything happening to you."

The anger disappeared from her eyes. They turned tender and contemplative. "Jack," she spoke, softly. "I know you care, and I appreciate it. I just wish you would have discussed this with me first. After all, this is my life we're talking about here."

"You're probably right, I should have. But I knew you'd say no. I'm worried about you, Jazz. Don't you understand? I—" He couldn't believe he'd almost slipped and said he loved her. That would have been an enormous mistake.

Earlier at the restaurant when he suggested they remain friends, she hadn't refuted it, so he had to guard his tongue and his heart from making any more stupid mistakes. If friendship was all she offered, he'd take it. As the last three weeks had painfully taught him, it would be better than having nothing at all.

Jasmine touched his arm.

Electrical currents charged through him.

"You what, Jack?" Her velvety tone sent a deeper longing further into his heart. He wanted to wrap her in his arms and never let her go.

He held her gaze, battling the urge to kiss her. Overwhelmed with desire, he forced himself to look away. "I'm sorry I didn't talk to you first."

"Oh." Disappointment flashed through her eyes. "Listen, Jack. I know you're worried. But do you really think all this precaution is necessary?"

If she only knew how necessary it really was; that her very life depended on it. "Trust me. It's necessary." The second the words left his mouth, a feeling of foreboding shrouded him. *God, have mercy on Jasmine.*

CHAPTER TWENTY

I can't take another day of this. They're driving me nuts. I can't even go to the bathroom without someone following me. Jasmine knew she was exaggerating, but not by much. Ever since she agreed to have someone stay with her, her sisters stuck to her like duct tape. And this morning when the famous screenwriter picked up his order, Jack had refused to leave her side.

They were only trying to protect her, but eight days of overbearing cosseting took its toll on her sanity. Tonight was the first time someone wasn't in the same room with her. Not yet anyway. Drama queen came to mind when she sighed. But hey, she was entitled.

Shanell sat downstairs watching some reality show on television that she insisted she couldn't miss.

Jasmine refused to watch the detestable program.

Upstairs in her bedroom, dressed in her flannel pajamas, she lowered herself into the sinking softness of her purple, down-filled comforter. She fluffed several pillows against the headboard, scooted her body around to a comfortable position, then picked up her laptop.

While Windows booted up, she bit into her Snickers bar, savoring the rich chocolaty nougat, thick caramel, and crunchy peanuts.

Double-clicking the dial up icon, she waited while it connected, then brought up her instant chat messenger and typed.

Good evening, Simon.

Send

She stared at the screen, tapping her fingernail on her teeth. That sweet musical chime sound brought a tingle of excitement mixed with a small amount of apprehension. Surely her uneasiness was a result of Jack's comments earlier about Simon being her stalker. When she'd opened her mouth to defend him, Jack had interrupted her, stating she'd never had any phone calls or had anyone following her until she'd met Simon. As much as she hated to admit it, Jack did have a point.

Wait. What was she thinking? Jack didn't know Simon like she did. Simon lived in California, and she had been talking to him online when she received those creepy phone calls. Plus when she'd gone to the store and other places, she had just finished talking to him then too.

Did you stop to think that he could take his laptop with him and communicate with you from anywhere in the world?

Jasmine sucked in her lower lip. She refused to believe it was her dear friend Simon. It was probably RodeoCowboy or Steamboat's Peeping Tom.

Whoever it was, she didn't want to think about it anymore. So, she focused her attention on Simon's message.

Good evening, sweetie. How are you doing? I was hoping to see you online tonight. I hadn't heard from you for over a week. Hope all is well there. The sun is setting here, displaying a wonderful array of pink and golden hues across the sky. Yellow lights are dancing on top of the ripples in the ocean. The temperature here is a cool sixty-five degrees. Well, that's cool for us native Californians anyway. <grin>

Her sigh bordered on annoyance. Two weeks ago if Simon had called her sweetie, she would have welcomed it. But now, her heart belonged to someone who wanted to remain friends. *Oh, Jack, how I wish you loved me as much as I love you.* Somehow she had to stop wallowing in the fantasy land of what could never be. For now, she'd just enjoy Simon's friendship.

Placing her fingers on her keyboard, she typed.

You know me well. Thank you for letting me 'see' your view. Oh, if only it were sixty-five degrees here. Well, I can always dream can't I? I'm SO jealous. I wish I were sitting near the lake at my granddad's cabin right now. It's beautiful this time of year in Louisiana. I'm planning on moving out there soon. By the way, the reason you haven't heard from me was I saw a mountain lion in the woods near my house. When I tried getting away, a branch jammed into my neck.

Send.

Jasmine grabbed her water bottle off her nightstand and took a long swig. Snatching up her Snickers, she peeled back the wrapper, bit off a big chunk, and licked the stringy caramel off her lip.

Bougé meowed and jumped up on the bed. "Hi baby, how's my girl?" She snuggled her cat against her chest and planted a kiss on top her head. Musical chimes rang. "Sorry." She situated Bougé next to her hip and patted her back, then read Simon's message.

Please tell me you're okay!

Jasmine smiled, touched by his thoughtfulness. How could such a considerate man possibly be her stalker?

*I'm doing pretty well now. Thank you for asking. So far, this year's not been a very good one. In January I got a concussion. And this month I got stitches in my neck. I'm hoping March will be better. hehe. It's so strange. These kinds of things usually happen to my sister, but this year they seem to be happening to me. Meeting you is the only nice thing that's happened to me so far this year. *smiling**

And Jack's kisses. But she batted away the tender memories.

Send.

I'm relieved to hear you're doing better. I'm glad you feel that way about meeting me because I feel the same *way about you. You have enriched my life in many ways. <grin> Someday I'd like to meet you in person. If the opportunity ever arises, we could meet in a public place. If it would make you feel safer, you could even bring someone with you. Just think about it, okay?*

Whoa! Simon wanted to meet her? A deep nagging pit settled into her already fidgety stomach. *Stop it, girl. You're letting Jack's words spook you.* She took another bite of her candy bar and continued to read his message.

So, you had an encounter with a mountain lion? I bet that was some experience. Tell me all about it and don't leave out one detail. The only wild animals I've ever seen are some of my friends. <Just kidding> I love seeing wild animals—at the San Diego Zoo, that is. I'm not sure what I'd do if I ever came across one that wasn't safely tucked behind bars. I know it isn't very macho, but I'd probably run like a criminal who's being pursued by the police.

For some unexplained reason, his analogy made her insides squirm.

Her phone rang. Before she could even move her laptop, Shanell hollered, "Jasmine, Jack's on the phone."

"Okay. I'll get it up here," she yelled. Her insides fluttered with the brush of hummingbird wings. Having him around all day long the last few days had been difficult and at the same time amazing.

She enjoyed watching him work. Whenever deep in thought, Jack rubbed his chin. And the way he hunkered over his drafting board reminded her of the Charlie Brown cartoon character Schroeder playing the piano. Each time she walked by Jack and got a whiff of his fresh, clean soap smell, she ached to be closer to him. Even now she longed to hear his voice, and it had only been a couple of hours since he'd gone home.

She rushed her message to Simon.

I'm sorry, but I have to go. I'm wanted on the phone. Will you be online later? If so, I'll tell you all about my experience in the wilds then. Gotta run. Bye.

Send.

She closed the lid on her computer and snatched the phone off her nightstand. Covering the mouthpiece with her hand, she hollered, "I got it. You can hang up now, Shanell."

"Hey, what are you up to?" Jack asked, smiling.

Willbee nudged his nose into Jack's hand until he rubbed the dog behind his ears.

"Umm. Not much. What are you doing?" Her evasiveness gave Jack the impression she was talking to Simon again. If only she would listen to reason where that psychotic creep was concerned.

Then there was RodeoCowboy. That man made him even more nervous than Simon did. For three nights, Jack had tried to do the same thing with RodeoCowboy as he had with Simon, but RodeoCowboy never responded to any of 'Kailee's" messages.

How he wished Stan would have found out more by now, but he hadn't. Frustrated, Jack ran his hand through his wet hair.

"I just called to make sure you're doing all right. Have you changed your dressing and made sure your wound isn't red?"

"Yes, I did, *Chloe*," she answered mockingly and then giggled.

He smiled into the phone. "Okay, okay. Give me a break. I just care. And so does Chloe."

"I know. I don't mean to sound ungrateful. Chloe has a big heart, and she means well, it's just sometimes she can be so suffocating. Oh, before I forget, tomorrow's Valentine's Day, so I thought it would be a great time to invite my family over for dinner. I'm making Tacoritos. If you don't have any plans, I'd love for you to stay and eat with us."

"Sure. There's no way I'm missing out on your Tacoritos. Are you sure you're up to it?"

"Jack. Nothing major is wrong with me. Just a sore neck. Besides, I want to do this. I know it doesn't even begin to pay back what everyone has done for me, but it's a start."

"No one expects you to payback anything. And as far as nothing major being wrong with you... Well, that's debatable." Jack chuckled.

"Hey."

"Just teasing. Seriously though, Dan said your injury could have been fatal." Just saying the word fatal left him feeling cold and empty inside. Life without Jasmine... He cringed.

"Who's Dan?"

"Dr. Dan Hayden. He's a client of mine."

"You talk to your clients about me?"

He heard the small intake of breath and the exasperation in her voice.

"No. But I did this time because he asked me why I wasn't working out of my office. I told him my girlfriend had hurt herself, and after I explained what had happened, he said the branch could have hit a major artery and that you were one lucky lady. I let him know luck had nothing to do with it, that it was God's grace." He rubbed his mouth and chin, hoping Jasmine hadn't caught his 'girlfriend' slip. They were just starting to get back to their easy bantering and camaraderie. He'd hate it if anything spoiled their relationship again.

Silence on the other end made him wonder. The leather on his recliner squeaked underneath him with the shifting of his weight. "Jasmine? You still there?"

"Yeah. I'm here."

"What's wrong?"

"I was just thinking," she said through a sigh.

"About what?"

"About God's grace. Ugh. Hang on a second, Jack. My other line is beeping."

Jack stared at the roaring blaze in his living room fireplace and thought about how much fun he'd had this past week. Jasmine had been her relaxed, bubbly self again. The black car hadn't been around, and she hadn't received any more phone calls. Too bad her good mood hadn't stemmed from their spending time together. Taking a couple of sips of his coffee, he set it on a nearby leather coaster.

"Sorry, that was Chloe calling to check up on me."

Jack detected the sisterly love in her tone along with a hint of irritation.

"Well, listen, I should probably let you go."

"Oh, okay." She sounded disappointed.

"I'll see you bright and early tomorrow morning."

"I can't wait."

Jack warmed at her words. "Night, Jazz."

"Night, Jackson."

Jackson? Usually when she called him that she was mad at him. But this time he didn't detect any anger in her voice. Only a softness he had never heard before. He waited for a dial tone. Hearing none, he lowered his voice, "Goodnight, Jazz." He leaned back in his recliner, draping an arm behind his head.

"Goodnight, Jack," her raspy whisper sent a tremor of delight shimmering through him.

"I'd better go now," he said, not really wanting to.

"Me, too."

He waited. But again, neither one of them hung up.

"Jasmine?"

"Yeah?"

"I love you." His voice sounded husky even to him. He ran his hand over his face. He'd meant to say it lightheartedly even though they were the truest words he had ever spoken, and the most deadly too. Pressing his fingers against his forehead, he braced himself for her rebuke.

"I love you too, Jack."

Was he imagining it, or did her voice sound as smooth as velvet just now? A flicker of hope ignited within him. "I'm glad you're feeling better," he said, wanting to keep her on the line.

"Thanks for taking such wonderful care of me. I don't deserve you."

He heard her sniffle.

"Jack, don't ever forget me."

"Forget you?" He bolted upright. "What do you mean? Where did that come from?"

"I was just thinking. Pretty soon I'll be moving to Louisiana, and you'll be here. And we won't be able to see each other as often anymore."

Heaviness pressed against his chest.

"Don't worry. You aren't getting rid of me that easy. I'll make sure we see each other often." *More often than you think.*

"I don't want to get rid of you at all," she replied in a broken whisper. "I gotta go, Jack. Bye."

The dial tone droned in his ear.

He blinked, completely confused.

Why did she hang up on him and why did he hear tears in her voice? Did he dare hope she loved him more than she let on? More than just a friend? He closed his eyes and leaned his head back. "Father, this roller-coaster ride is driving me crazy. I love Jasmine so much it hurts. But I'm getting mixed signals here. Am I her friend, or does she love me as a man? How will I know? And what do I do now, Lord?"

Faith is the substance of things hoped for and the evidence of things not seen. Trust me, Son. Trust me.

Jack clung to the Lord's words. They were his last shred of hope.

CHAPTER TWENTY-ONE

The next morning Jack sat in Jasmine's sunroom staring at a design he was working on. Jasmine had just finished watering all the plants and flowers. The scent of wet, clean potting soil cascaded through the air. Clear morning sun filtered through the skylights, and fountain water filled the normally dry room with moisture.

A high-powered chain saw couldn't cut through the strained awkwardness hanging between them. Obviously, telling her he loved her the night before had been a huge mistake.

Closing his eyes, he rubbed the back of his neck. What a way to spend Valentine's Day.

They needed to talk. And talk now before the awkwardness stretched any further.

He stood and walked up behind her.

Jasmine didn't move.

She sat on her stool with her back straight and her feet hooked on the crossbar below, staring out the window. Sunlight glistened on her brown hair, bringing out her natural reddish-gold highlights.

She seemed a million miles away.

Jack hated to interrupt her reverie, but had no choice. "Jasmine."

"Yeah," she responded without looking at him.

"I have a lot of work to do today." He moved his hand to her shoulder, ignoring the longing surging through his fingertips. "Do you mind if we go to the office for a couple of hours this morning? There's an extra drafting table there where you could work on your sketch if you'd like."

"No. I don't mind at all." Her focus never wavered from the window.

He dropped his hand to his side and examined her sketch.

A man and a woman were sitting on a moonlit beach, wrapped in each other's arms and staring into each other's eyes as if they were the only two people in the world. Amazing how Jasmine had captured the couple's love-filled emotions.

He leaned closer. The two people resembled him and Jasmine. Too bad it wasn't them.

No longer able to handle the melancholy-laced atmosphere, he racked his brains, trying to figure out how to break its gloomy spell. When he glanced down at the floor, he did a double take. He had on one brown shoe and one black one. "I guess I was more tired than I thought," he said with a nervous chuckle.

In slow motion, Jasmine swiveled around and glanced up at him with a puzzled look.

He pointed at his feet. Her attention slid to the floor. He tapped his right foot to the side and back again, and then did the same with his left foot.

Jasmine's mouth formed a lazy grin.

That's when he noticed it. "Looks like I wasn't the only one."

Jasmine frowned. "What do you mean?"

He tugged on the shoulder of his shirt and then pointed to her wrong-side-out turtleneck. She titled her head toward her shoulder. With a humorless titter and a cheeky grin, she rose. "I'll be back."

Jack watched her walk away, admiring the view as she headed out of the room. With her turtleneck tucked into her snug blue jeans, it revealed her tiny waist and shapely hips. When she stepped out of sight, he rolled up his papers, stuck them in a tube, and then strode to the bottom of the stairs to wait for her.

"Okay, how's that?" she asked. Her eyes locked on his as she descended the steps.

Just as she reached the second-to-last step, her foot caught on one of them, propelling her forward. Before Jack had a chance to react, his back slammed against the hardwood floor, and Jasmine's knee landed in his belly.

Air whooshed from his lungs.

Her face collided with his, and she ended up with her body sprawled all over his and her face in the crook of his neck.

Jasmine's moan vibrated against his chest.

Even as he struggled to pull air into his lungs, her nearness sent his pulse shifting into overdrive, and her warm breath on his neck shimmied through his spine. He knew he should move, but his emotions had left him paralyzed.

She shifted her body next to his side and looked at him.

Jack forgot all about breathing for a moment until his lungs gasped for air. He closed his eyes and concentrated on drawing in several deep breaths.

When he opened his eyes, their gazes connected.

If his tattletale eyes unmasked his love for her, then so be it. He refused to hide it any longer.

The dreamy look he saw in hers sucked him in like a whirlpool. Against his ribs, he could feel Jasmine's heartbeat increase. Her eyes roamed toward his mouth.

Tossing all caution to the wind, he parted his lips, beckoning hers to join them.

Jasmine's awareness turned into a question.

Jack sent her a silent message of encouragement and permission before his lids demurely lowered.

With the lightest of touches, her soft lips became one with his, making this the sweetest kiss he had ever experienced. His body trembled when her fingers wisped through his hair. He slid his arms around her and snuggled her body against his. Their kiss deepened, intensifying his longing. Just when he couldn't stand it any longer, Jasmine stopped.

Their breath mingled as she brushed her lips against his. "Oh, Jack," she said in a breathless whisper before possessing his lips again.

His heart matched the tune of her breathy whisper. He had dreamed of this day for such a long time.

When Jasmine ended the kiss, he loosened his hold, and held his breath, wondering if she'd jump up and run. Instead, she draped her arm over his chest and tucked her head under his chin. His chest rose and fell as he drew in slow unsure breaths.

Jasmine scented perfume floated under his nose, sending his already skyrocketing senses into orbit. Not wanting to spoil the moment or have it end, he waited for her to make the next move. When she trailed her hand over his cheek and down his neck, it was all the encouragement he needed. He slid his hand down her arm and held her tight.

A sniffle.

A wet spot penetrated his shirt.

She was crying.

Oh, dear God, please, please don't let Jasmine regret our blissful moment again. I can't bear another rejection.

"Jasmine?" he whispered hoarsely.

"Yes," she rasped, not moving.

"Why are you crying?" His voice was soft.

"I can't be your friend anymore." She sounded like the helpless little girl he had helped so many years ago.

Quick as a heartbeat, Jack shifted their weight until Jasmine was on her back. With his hand cupping her waist, he leaned on his elbow and gazed down at her. "What do you mean you can't be my friend anymore?" He searched her face for the answer and all air vanished from the room.

"Because." She paused. Her eyes locked with his. "I'm in love with you."

Jack pinched his eyes shut, and his lips stretched as far as they could, forming a huge smile. Warmth spread through him and joy unlike any he'd ever known before possessed him. *Thank you, Lord.*

"I want more than friendship. I want you." Then, without warning, she pushed herself up, hurried to the window, and wrapped her arms around her waist.

Jack leapt up, and in two long strides stood behind her. He cupped her upper arms and turned her around to face him.

Her downcast eyes unsettled him.

Placing his index finger under her chin, he urged her face upward. "Look at me, Jasmine."

"No." She shook her head. "You said the other day that you wanted us to go back to the way things were. I can't, Jack. I just can't." Tears spilled over her lashes and trailed down her cheeks.

"Sweetheart. Look at me."

Slowly, her eyelids rose. Her uncertainty tenderized his heart even more.

"I only said that because I thought that's what *you* wanted. Don't you know how long I've waited to hear those words from you?" he asked with a reassuring smile. "Or how long and hard I've prayed that one day you would love me more than just a friend? Ah, Jazzy," he moaned, crushing her into his arms and pressing her head against his chest. He kissed the top of her head. In a deep guttural tone he continued. "I love you so much it hurts. I have for years."

"But—" She wiggled in his arms, but Jack tightened his grip. Now that he had her, he never wanted to let her go.

Jasmine tilted her head back and looked up at him with tears clinging to her lashes. "Both times... when we kissed, I got the impression you regretted it."

"Regretted it!" His eyes flew open. He moved her back an inch or two and his eyes roamed over hers. "You've got to be kidding me. Each time, I felt like I had taken advantage of your weakened state and that you only kissed me because I made you feel secure. I hated seeing how uncomfortable I'd made you, so I went along with you and acted like it was no big deal. But trust me. It was a big deal to me." He cupped her face and secured her gaze. "Don't you know how much I love you?"

Jasmine took a step back.

His body tensed.

She pressed her lips together, tilted her head, and shook it a couple of times. "Um, uh uh." She dipped her chin and flashed him a saucy smile. "Maybe you'd better show me."

He yanked her tight against him and claimed her mouth with a promising, lingering kiss.

A moment of time suspended as their hearts and mouths became one. When his rapid pulse matched hers, he knew he had to put some distance between them before they got carried away. Summoning a mountain of restraint to himself, he broke the connection and whispered breathlessly against her ear. "We'd better go."

On the way to Jack's office, Jasmine snuggled next to him with her arm settled around his shoulder. The falling snow reminded her of powdered soap flakes. As far as she could see, which wasn't too far because of the heavy snowfall, everything had a good two-foot snow covering. The snowplows weren't even able to keep up with it, and the tree branches hung low under its weight. Normally a sight like this depressed her, but nothing, including the weather, could ruin her good mood today. Jack loved her, and she loved him. And she had never been so happy in her life.

"Don't forget to stop by the shelter. I need to drop the brownies and cookies off."

"On my way there now." He squeezed her hand.

Minutes later, Helen Mace greeted Jasmine with a bright smile. Or did it just appear brighter because everything seemed brighter today? "I brought the women and children some more goodies." She looked at the stack of containers she and Jack held.

"That's so sweet of you, Jasmine. I don't know what we'd do without your generous donations." Her smile slipped and a frown along with a weighty sigh replaced it. "Unfortunately, more and more women and children are flocking in here."

Jasmine's heart ached for these abused women. So much so, that even though she worked on saving enough money to buy Granddad's cabin, the last time she'd been here she'd given a sizeable donation, which put her purchasing the cabin further into the future. But she didn't care. These women needed her help now.

She and Jack placed the baked goods on Helen's desk. When she turned back, Jack's shoulders were slumped over the desk as he filled out a check. He tore it out of his checkbook and handed it to Helen.

"Mr. Warren." Helen eyes bulged and filled with tears. "This is so generous of you." She shook her head in awe, and when Jasmine got a glimpse of the check amount, her heart swelled with pride.

"I don't know what to say except thank you." Helen gave Jack a hug and then hugged Jasmine. "Thank you, Jasmine. For everything." She released her.

"If you or the shelter ever need anything, call me. Anytime. I mean it." And Jasmine could tell by the look on Jack's face he meant it too.

Helen nodded, obviously too choked up to speak.

"We'd better go." Jack cupped her elbow and led her out the door.

"Jack, that was so sweet of you," Jasmine said on the way to the truck.

"It's the least I could do." Jack looked down at her, love flowed from his eyes. "I'm so proud of you, sweetheart. You might be stuck in the house, but you use that time to help others." He reached down and when his cold lips touched hers, she felt nothing but warmth.

Fifteen minutes later, they pulled up to the log office building where a man using a snowblower was working at clearing off the sidewalks.

Jack tilted her head up with his finger and brushed a light kiss on her lips. "I love you," he said tenderly, then kissed her again.

"I love you too," she replied against his lips. Her mouth still tingled from their last kiss. Good thing this kiss was short and that she was sitting down, or she'd have to be carried into the building because the last one had turned her legs into ribbons.

They greeted everyone inside and Jack led her to his office where he showed her which drafting table she could use. Even the rugged log walls loaded with pictures and photographs of wildlife mostly in snowy mountain areas didn't bother her today. Many times, she had teased Jack that he should replace them with sailboats and beach scenes. But he only laughed, saying somehow he didn't think sailboats and beaches went very well with rustic logwood. He was probably right.

She sat down and tried to work, but her mind wouldn't stop reliving their shared kisses and declarations of love. Forty-five minutes later, Jasmine still hadn't touched her sketch. With Jack in the same room, she didn't want to work. She wanted to spend her time staring at him.

And stare at him she had. In fact, many times he had looked up from his drafting table and caught her doing just that. He'd smile and mouth I love you. Each time, her insides flipped with love. She needed to pull herself together before she ran over to him and kissed him until neither one could stand. "Would you like some more coffee?"

He picked up his cup and peered inside. "No, I'm good. But thanks for asking."

She slid off the stool. "Okay. I'll be right back."

"Oh, no, you don't." Jack motioned with his finger for her to come to him.

She tilted her head, her brows knit together.

"You can't leave here without giving me a kiss first."

"Well, if you insist." She giggled. Sashaying over to him, she cupped his face. Her lips played across his, and his cinnamon breath became hers. He pulled her closer, but she pressed her hands against his chest and pushed back. "Hey now, enough. I haven't even recovered from the last ones yet," she whispered, her cheeks flamed with the admission.

"Me either," he rasped, capturing her hands.

She tugged her hands free. "I'll be back." She kissed his cheek, and as fast as her rubbery knees would carry her, she hustled toward the coffee room.

While she waited for her hot water to heat in the microwave, she looked around. A white tablecloth, patterned with a light sprinkle of indigo flowers, covered the long table. In the center sat a beautiful silk flower arrangement with a dark navy candle. Sapphire padding covered the chairs, and the walls were white with a hint of blue. Jack said it was a relaxing color and that he wanted his employees to sit in a nice atmosphere and be comfortable while on their breaks. Always thinking of others. That was Jack. *My Jack.* No sweeter words had ever brushed across her soul.

Jasmine was impressed with how his business had taken off over the last few years. The quality of workmanship and his fabulous designs drew people from all over. The continual ringing of the telephone had attested to that fact. Jack spent more time answering calls than designing.

The microwave timer dinged. Jasmine removed her cup and ripped open a packet of hot cocoa mix. While stirring, she peeked inside the cupboard. A small jar of marshmallow cream set on the shelf with a note. *Jasmine, I knew I had to come here today and I didn't want you deprived.*

She shook her head. Her heart could scarcely contain the enormous love she felt for this sweet and thoughtful man.

She glanced at the clock. 11:47. Catching sight of the calendar next to it, she noted today's date. Valentine's Day.

After looking up the number for the flower shop and their favorite Chinese food place, she picked up the break room phone and punched line four. Satisfied after making three successful, albeit scheming phone calls, she quietly clapped her hands and smiled.

On the way back to Jack's office, her feet sank into the lush carpet. Just outside his door, she froze when she heard Jack say, "Yeah, me too. I never thought I'd be leaving Steamboat either. I'm really going to miss this place. But Jasmine hates the cold, so…"

Her heart splintered at the sad and wistful sound of Jack's voice. Careful not to spill her drink, she hurried into the restroom where she set her beverage down on the granite vanity top and stared at herself in the mirror. Tears pooled in her eyes. She blinked them away and forced herself not to cry. Jack planned on moving from the town he adored because of her.

Reality hit her full force.

When she finally stopped resisting and gave in to her love for Jack, she hadn't thought that far ahead. She would have to stay here, or he would have to move.

Well, she would never allow Jack to leave his beloved Steamboat. And as selfish as it sounded, she wasn't sure she could handle living here the rest of her life either.

All her life, even before she had gotten stranded in the wilderness and things had so drastically changed for her, she had dreamt of moving to Louisiana. And while Jack seemed willing to move, she loved him too much to allow that to happen. Judging from the regretful sound of his voice, without a doubt her fears of what happened between Lori and Steve would become a reality for them too. The only difference was, she would never try to take her own life.

Gathering massive amounts of courage, Jasmine determined to not dwell on any of that now. She picked up her drink and headed toward Jack's office. Mary had just come back from the post office as she rounded the corner.

"Is it still snowing outside, Mary?" she nearly whispered. She pointed toward Jack's office and then placed her forefinger over her lips.

Mary eyed her suspiciously, then understanding covered her face. "I bet we have four inches of fresh snow already." She followed Jasmine's example, keeping her voice low.

"That's nice."

Mary dipped her head and peered over her glasses. "Okay, what's wrong? You *never* think it's nice when we get more snow."

Jasmine chuckled quietly. "I know, I know." She darted a quick look toward Jack's office again and leaned closer to Mary. "I'm having Chinese food and two dozen red roses delivered here." She glanced at the office wall clock. "In the next ten minutes or so Kimberly's driver will be delivering the bronzed bald eagle fountain I ordered last year for Jack. Would you please let me know when they arrive? And don't let Jack hear you when you do, okay?"

Understanding lit the woman's eyes, and a motherly smile filled her face. "Oh, how sweet. Yes, I can do that." She winked.

"Thank you, Mary. By the way, I'd like you to join us for lunch."

"That's very sweet of you, dear, but I already have a luncheon date."

Jasmine waggled her eyebrows. "How many years have you been married, Mary? Does your husband know about this hot date of yours?"

Mary tsked her, pressed her lips together, and looked upward. "You know good and well it's with Joseph, you big tease. We've been married thirty-six years today."

"Wow, that's six years longer than my parents. Congratulations. And Happy Anniversary." She hugged the kind, matronly woman who cared about everyone and everything. Just like someone else she knew. Jack.

Jasmine picked up her cup and headed toward Jack's office. Making sure she said it loud enough for him to hear, she threw the words over her shoulder, "Tell Joseph I said Happy Anniversary if I don't see him, okay?"

"I will, dear."

With that, Jasmine stepped into Jack's office just in time to see him hang up the phone. He looked up and smiled. Holding up his index finger, he looked down and jotted something on a yellow legal pad.

Jasmine sipped her hot chocolate and watched the heavy snow falling outside the window. A few minutes later, Jack stood and walked over to her. He took her drink from her and set it on his desk, wrapped her in a hug and whispered in her ear, "I have a surprise for you."

She had one for him too, but he wasn't going to like his surprise. Of that she was certain.

CHAPTER TWENTY-TWO

"Where're we going, Jack?" Jasmine asked him for the third time.

"Just be patient." He turned his pickup into the ranch where they normally rented horses all summer.

Jasmine turned questioning eyes on him.

"I have to drop off some plans for the McGuires."

Jack pulled up in front of the stables, put the truck in neutral, and set the emergency brake. "Stay put. I'll be right back." He was out the door in a flash and followed the plowed pathway into the barn.

The blowing heater filled the pickup cab, making it warm and toasty. Jasmine's thoughts tumbled back to Jack's comments about having a surprise for her. If his surprise included telling her about his moving away from Steamboat, she didn't want to hear it. Much to her relief, he didn't get a chance to tell her because Mary had knocked on his office door and when he saw the five-foot bald eagle water fountain Jasmine had bought for him, he never mentioned his surprise. Instead, for several seconds Jasmine got the pleasure of watching him stand there with his mouth draped open. Then he grabbed her and kissed her right in front of everyone.

With nothing else to do while waiting for Jack, Jasmine stared out the truck window, watching the swirling snow flurries that reminded her of the aftermath of a downy pillow fight. As much as she hated to admit it, she found the sight beautiful. Because it was snowing, the temperatures had risen to thirty-five degrees instead of twenty below. And judging by the looks of the white, low-hanging clouds, it wasn't stopping any time soon.

She just hoped and prayed her dinner plans wouldn't be ruined because of it. But then again, her family had gotten together in worse conditions than these.

Jack opened the truck door, and huge snowflakes rushed inside.

"Sorry, sweetheart, but this is going to take longer than I thought. Look, there's no sense in you sitting out here. Why don't you come in with me?"

Jasmine hesitated, then nodded. She slid her hands into her gloves, snatched up her matching hat, and pulled it onto her head. Jack put his hands around her waist and lowered her to the ground. His cold, moist lips touched hers as he stole a quick kiss. Hand-in-hand they walked into the barn. But instead of going to the stable's office, they headed toward the stalls.

"What are you doing?" Jasmine asked, looking around and then back at him.

His smile held a secret. He stopped in front of the first stall. Love glowed in his eyes as he gazed down at her. "I hope you won't be too disappointed this year, but I didn't get you any plants for your sunroom." He opened the top part of the stall door. "I got you this instead." He moved off to the side. "Happy Valentine's Day, Sweetheart."

Jasmine peered inside. Her mouth and eyes widened.

Her favorite dapple-gray gelding walked up to her sporting a huge, red ribbon bow around his neck.

"Mine?" she choked. "Mr. Dapper is mine?" She scanned Jack's face to make sure it wasn't a joke.

Jack nodded.

She threw her arms around him and pulled him close, smothering his face with alternating kisses and thank yous.

"You're welcome." A deep chuckle rumbled out of him.

Jasmine spun around, opened the bottom half of the

stall door and cooed greetings to Mr. Dapper as she neared him. Removing her glove, she ran her hand over his silky nose and kissed the horse.

"I finally talked Janet into parting with him. She knew how much you loved him and that you would treat him very well. Plus, she couldn't ride him anymore with her arthritis getting so bad, so she decided to let me buy him. And just so you know, I'll be taking care of his room and board no matter where we live."

Jasmine's joy dissipated, and her heart sank. Not wanting to respond to Jack's comment about where they lived, she hoped and prayed that he wouldn't say anything else about moving. Besides, he hadn't even asked her to marry him yet.

Knowing she had a lot of decisions to make, she needed time alone to think. The decision was made. A trip to her granddad's lake house would help clear her mind.

But with Jack, Chloe, and Shanell hanging around her twenty-four-seven, she needed to figure out a plan of escape.

A niggling pit gnawed at her stomach. That had been happening a lot lately and yet nothing bad had happened or anything. Well, unless she counted the strange black car and the phone calls, which she now just blew off as a prankster getting his jollies out of trying to scare her. Besides, for more than a week now, the black car hadn't been seen anywhere. Convinced she'd be safe, she made up her mind to head out to Louisiana at the first opportunity.

⚬⚬⚬

"What do you mean she's gone? Gone where?" Jack asked, stepping inside Jasmine's front room.

Shanell burst out crying. "I don't know. Oh, Jack, I'm so worried. For the last three days I've been sleeping in the guestroom. I guess I should have slept on the sofa, and then maybe I would have heard her leave. I've always been a sound sleeper. Mom says a horserace could be held in my room and I wouldn't know it."

Although he wanted to strangle her, he pulled Shanell into a hug and patted her back. "It's not your fault. It'll be all right. We'll find her," he said with more conviction than he felt. His gut started to burn.

"Thanks, Jack." Shanell moved away and wrapped her arms around her waist.

"Did she say where she was going?"

She shook her head. "All I know is, wherever she went, she plans on being gone quite awhile."

"How do you know that?"

"Because. She took Bougé with her. And... She left this for you." She extended a purple envelope toward him.

Jack took it from her, ripped it open and pulled out the lavender paper.

My Dearest Jack. If you're reading this letter, you know I've gone away. Please don't be angry. I need time alone to think and to pray and to figure things out. I'm sure you know where I've gone. But please, if you love me—don't follow me. I really need this time to be by myself without any outside distractions. And don't worry about me. I'll be fine. All my love, Jasmine

Jack crumpled the paper and slammed his fist into the palm of his hand. He could kick himself. Yesterday evening he had a gut feeling to call her even though it was after midnight. Stan had telephoned late last night saying a clerk from the car rental agency said that weeks ago, a guy with a slight southern drawl had rented a black sedan with dark windows.

Southern drawl?

Did Simon have a southern drawl?

More than likely RodeoCowboy did.

His gut twisted into knots, and a deep pit settled there when a sickening thought bombarded his mind. What if whoever had been following Jasmine, followed her to

Louisiana too? *Dear God, no! Lord, please keep her safe.*
He couldn't fall apart now. He'd be no good to Jasmine.
He pulled himself together, so he could think with a clear
head.

"Do you know if Jasmine drove to your granddad's
place, or did she take a plane?"

"Her car's gone, but I can't answer that for sure. I'll
call the airport and find out."

"You do that. I'm going to make some calls on my
cell phone."

"If you're planning on calling Jasmine—" Her face
paled. "She forgot to take her cell phone, and there's no
telephone at the lake house."

"She didn't take her phone? What was she thinking?"
His face heated with anger and overwhelming concern.
"Whatever possessed her to do such a stupid thing?"

Looking haggard and stressed, Shanell shook her
head, shrugging. "I don't think she meant to leave without
her phone. It was sitting on the dumbwaiter near the
door." She straddled a bar stool in front of the kitchen
counter and pulled the phone book in front of her. The
sound of pages turning grated on Jack's stretched nerves.
"I'll be outside," he called over his shoulder. As he
headed down the hall and out the door, he punched in
Stan's number.

"Stan, this is Jack. Jasmine's headed to Louisiana."
He heard Stan groan. "I don't know if she flew down
there or drove. All I know is she went alone. Can you call
Mick and see if he's still following that jerk?" Jack's
heart pumped so hard he thought it would burst from the
stress.

"I'll call him now. Hang tight. I'll get right back to
you."

Jack paced the long porch. "Jasmine, how could you
do this? You knew someone was watching you. Just
because you hadn't gotten any phone calls or seen anyone

following you, that didn't mean a thing." Puffs of white rose from his warm breath. "That lousy creep knew I was here all day and you were never alone at night," he muttered. "Of course he wouldn't show up then."

But what if the slime ball who was stalking Jasmine wasn't Simon?

What if they were trailing the wrong guy?

What if it was the Peeping Tom?

Or RodeoCowboy? That thought made Jack cringe. If the FBI hadn't been able to track down RodeoCowboy, what made him think Stan and his men could?

Confused didn't begin to describe how he felt right now. For awhile, he was certain Jasmine's harasser was Simon, but now, he wasn't so sure.

An idea struck him. He rushed inside and into the kitchen.

Shanell hung up the wall phone.

"Did Jasmine take her laptop?"

"I don't know. It's been up in her room."

Jack took the stairs two at a time. He scanned her bedroom but didn't see her laptop anywhere. Down the stairs he flew and into the sunroom. There it sat on the table.

He opened the computer and went through all the necessary steps until he brought up the instant messenger.

Jack clicked on Simonrapport's nickname and looked in the history archives. At 11:33 PM, Valentine's Day, she'd sent Simon a message saying she was heading to her granddad's place 'to get away'.

Shivers of apprehension shimmied through his body.

Jack dropped his head back and closed his eyes. With a deep groan he cried out, "God, keep her safe."

He clicked on RodeoCowboy and pulled up the history archives. What he read there turned his blood to ice.

That creep knew where she lived.

He even mentioned Colorado and its mountains and had threatened her with evil if she ignored him.

That man is one sick puppy. A sick puppy who could very well be following Jasmine.

Jack slammed the laptop lid shut. "Shanell!" he hollered on his way to the living room.

"What?" She met him halfway, her eyes wide with fright.

"Did you find out if she booked a flight?"

Her eyes pooled. "Her plane left at 4:40 this morning."

Jack groaned. He pulled his hand over his face.

"I even tried finding a flight for you, but everything is booked up solid for two days. They said you could try getting on standby, but there were no guarantees."

"You tried all the airlines then? Even a private plane?"

She nodded. "There's nothing." Her bottom lip quivered.

Jack's cell phone rang. He popped it open. "This is, Jack."

"Jack. You'd better get out there. Mick followed the guy in the black sedan to the airport and found out he got on the same plane as Jasmine. Mick tried to get a ticket, but there weren't any available seats. The soonest available departure is in two days."

"I know." Jack shoved his hand through his hair.

"There's more, Jack. Some guy wearing a black cowboy hat is following her too."

Every nerve in his body stood at attention. "Should I call the Louisiana police and have them meet her plane?"

"They won't do it, Jack. Not without probable cause."

"You've got to be kidding me! Following her isn't probable cause enough?"

"Afraid not."

"I thought Simon and RodeoCowboy were wanted men."

"They are, but we don't know for sure if either of those two men following Jasmine are them or not. The M.O. fits, but we aren't certain."

Jack couldn't believe what he was hearing. "I'm driving down there."

"Want me to go with you?"

"I can't ask you to do that."

"You didn't. I offered. Besides, it will take a good twenty-four hours to get there, and you can't drive that long by yourself. Listen, I'll run by my house and let my wife know, and then I'll meet you out at your house in a few. You're bringing Willbee, right?"

"Definitely." *And a gun too*, he thought. "See you after bit. Thanks, Stan. I appreciate this."

"No problem."

Jack quickly tapped End on his touchpad phone. "Shanell, I'm going to pick up Willbee and some clothes and head out to your granddad's lake house."

"Be careful, Jack. I'll call the church prayer chain." She touched his arm. "Thank you."

He nodded, then whirled around and darted toward the door.

"Jack," Shanell hollered after him. He stopped and spun around. "Please, don't let him hurt my sister." She sniffled and ran her fingertips under her wet eyes.

⚬∕⚬

After enduring a restless four-hour long flight, excitement buzzed through Jasmine as her plane landed. She clutched Bougé's carrier and watched the wheel with various colors and sized suitcases go by. She juggled her shoulder bag and Bougé's carrier around before she snatched up her unmistakable purple suitcase and released the handle. She pulled the large luggage behind her and headed toward the car rental shop.

While standing in the long line, Bougé started growling low and deep. Jasmine raised the carrier to eye level and peered inside. "It's okay, baby. I know you're tired of being cooped up in there." Her cat didn't even look at her. Her glassy red eyes were fixed on something directly behind them.

Jasmine followed Bougé's line of vision to a nice looking man in blue jeans and a teal button-down shirt. He didn't look at all menacing. Behind him was a tall bow-legged cowboy who looked and grinned at her as if he knew her. But his smile was anything but friendly, more of a leer. She quickly looked away.

Bougé growled again.

"Something sure has your cat upset."

Or someone, Jasmine thought as her focus jerked back to the man in the teal shirt now directly behind her. He smiled, revealing bright, even teeth and one deep dimple on his left cheek. His silky-timbre voice was smooth and easy. For some strange reason, the man seemed vaguely familiar to her. Which was completely bizarre because she'd never seen this man before in her life.

"Yes, she is." She sent him a nervous smile. Something about the man made her uneasy; however, these days everything made her edgy. Perhaps it was his strikingly handsome face, tanned skin, gray eyes, and sandy-blond hair. That gorgeous combination would make any girl jittery.

"You here on business, or do you live here?" he asked while perusing her face.

A low, menacing growl emanated from Bougé again. "Neither." Jasmine peered into the cat carrier. Bougé had her back pressed against the corner of the small cage. Her hair stuck straight up, her ears pressed flat against her head, and her eyes glistened with anger. The only other time she'd seen her cat act this way was the day she had spotted the man outside her window. Jasmine insides gave a quick quiver.

The line moved forward. She reached for the handle on her luggage.

"Here, let me get that for you," the man offered.

"Oh no, that's okay. I can get it, but thanks anyway." *Just leave me alone, will you?*

"I insist." He gently removed her fingers from the handle. Bougé hissed and spat several times, making him let go.

This man appeared as sweet as taffy, but something just didn't feel right about him. Knowing Bougé was a great judge of character, Jasmine glanced down at his brief case. Maybe he was a no-good, pushy salesman like that man who had forced his way inside her house a few years back. Bougé had attacked him the minute he had stepped inside her door. He'd fled in a hurry. She pushed those thoughts away as the ticket agent called her forward.

After renting an SUV, Jasmine grabbed her luggage, readjusted her shoulder carry-on bag, and picked up Bougé. She darted a quick glance behind her. The strange expression on the man's face made her skin prickle. The tall, ruggedly handsome cowboy tipped his hat at her, and the smirk on his face made her cringe.

Unease settled deep inside her. Jasmine hustled out the exit. She shook her head at being so silly. It was probably just her imagination again anyway. Nice looking guys like that weren't psycho killers.

The car rental employee opened the trunk and helped her load her suitcase. After thanking him, she quickly slid behind the wheel and darted a glance over her shoulder. The guy from in line stared after her, and the tall cowboy stood in front of a rented pickup with his legs straddled and his arms crossed over his chest glaring at her.

That was creepy.

Was it just her imagination, or were these two men following her?

With a quick tug of the stick shift, making sure the way was clear, Jasmine pressed the gas pedal to the floor and hurried toward the exit. Checking both ways for traffic, she turned and headed down the road. Before leaving the city, she made a quick stop at a grocery store near the edge of town.

An hour later, she saw a large green sign, *Lake Boomingtown 1 mile.* Jasmine could hardly contain her excitement when she turned off the exit. The familiar sound of tires crunching on the white-shell road cover and the canopy of large oak trees looming above her made her instantly feel at home. In a strange sort of way it kind of reminded her of driving through the Eisenhower Tunnel in Colorado.

Shafts of light feathered through the bare branches.

She shifted in her seat and pressed the gas. Excitement and anticipation made her insides feel giddy, reminding her of when she was a little girl heading to Grandma's house at Christmastime. No snow, only beautiful sandy beaches and thousands of sparkling Christmas lights.

The lake came into view. Sunshine glistened across the still water. Docks with boats tied to them, and board walks leading to various types and sizes of houses, lined the private beach. On the other side of the lake, cows grazed contentedly on the golden meadow.

Anxious to get to the cabin, she turned south and then east until she pulled up to her granddad's place.

Jasmine threw the car in park, released her seat belt, and swung the door open. Thick, humid air filled her lungs, and attached itself to her clothing, making them tacky. Even though the man on the radio said it was sixty-two degrees, the humidity made it feel cooler, but she didn't care, it was still much warmer than Steamboat.

Jasmine grabbed her sweater and quickly slid into it.

Mesmerized by the fact she was really here, she stood and slowly scanned the area. No bright flowers or leafy trees greeted her. A hint of sadness flitted over her, but only for an instant. She closed her eyes and visualized how the place would look in a few weeks with white magnolia bushes and gardenias in full bloom. She could almost smell their sweetness. A myriad of azaleas in several shades of pink and a variety of colored roses fringed the driveway. The image took her breath away. She opened her eyes and waved away a pesky mosquito. Long needle pines, oak trees, and weeping willows filled the woods around the lake house.

Jasmine's tennis shoes crunched along the shell covering as she strolled over to the large L-shaped oak tree facing the lake. It was if God had made a built-in seat out of the colossal tree just for her and Granddad. Many times they had sat there, talking about flowers, life, family, but most of all, about their wonderful Heavenly Father. Jasmine lovingly ran her fingers over the rough bark. Granddad had a way of making her feel as if God were sitting right there with them.

She turned her attention toward Granddad's house—a replica of a miniature ante-bellum mansion, with a partially screened-in porch.

Bougé's frustrated meow broke through her walk down memory lane. Jasmine reined in her reverie and opened the backdoor of the four-wheel drive to remove the carrier. "Sorry, baby," she crooned and hurried up the cabin steps. She opened the screen door and set the carrier down on the hardwood floor. Lifting the edge of the frog statue, she removed the key and unlocked the door.

She wished she could have asked her Granddad first if it was okay to come here, but she didn't dare because she couldn't risk him saying anything to anyone. Besides, he'd told the family anytime any one of them wanted to use the place, they could.

She picked up Bougé's carrier and set it down inside the house.

The dank place smelled musty and closed up. A touch of melancholy washed over her as she looked around the open, spacious living room and kitchen. On the east end were two bedrooms with a loft above them. Wooden staircases spiraled upward on each end of the loft. Jasmine smiled. Her granddad had built two so her sisters wouldn't fight over who got to climb up to the loft first.

Bougé meowed. "Just a minute, sweetie." Jasmine rushed outside and loaded her arms with kitty stuff and hurried back inside. After getting her cat's litter box and food ready, she opened the carrier door.

Bougé darted out and jumped onto the kitchen window. With her ears pinned tight against her head, she growled low and long. Jasmine hurried over to where Bougé was perched and leaned over the sink, peering both ways. She saw nothing out of the ordinary. Perhaps Bougé growled because of the unfamiliar surroundings? Or maybe, Mrs. Jenkins, the nosy widow neighbor who reminded Jasmine of those sweet little old ladies in the movie *Arsenic and Old Lace*, was nearby spying on her. It wouldn't be the first time.

Bougé's growl became more aggressive.

Something moved outside the window.

Apprehension wiggled its way up Jasmine's spine.

More movement.

The broken sunlight filtering through the trees made it difficult to decipher what was there.

Something darted in front of them.

Jasmine screamed.

Bougé hissed.

Jasmine jerked away from the window.

Bougé arched her backed and her hackles rose.

"It's okay, baby." She rubbed the soft fur on her cat's head, hoping to sooth her own nerves as well. Knowing Bougé only acted like this when something wasn't right, the cat's continued aggressive growling made Jasmine skittish. *Get a grip, girl.*

She slowly leaned toward the window and peered right. A deer yanked her head up and stared at Jasmine before darting off into the thick wooded area.

Whew. She could breathe easy now.

Poor Bougé though. With her back legs crouched, she crept toward the window. Maybe having other animals this close to her terrain bothered her.

Jasmine decided to go unload everything out of the vehicle while Bougé explored the place. Piece by piece she brought it into the house.

When the last of the perishable items were put away, Jasmine made a mental note to drive down to Roger's house and let the grounds keeper know she was here. It would have been so much easier to call him, but she was in such a hurry to get away, that she forgot to grab her cell phone off of the dumbwaiter. Oh well. She needed the solitude this place offered anyway, so she could pray about her future.

She opened a small bottle of orange juice and took a long gulp. Resting her elbows on the black and white granite counter, she leaned over and peered around the room. Bamboo blinds covered the floor-to-ceiling, wall-to-wall windows. The circular, black and white toile sectional couch and white swivel rockers were situated so one could look out over the lake. Grandma had insisted every room have a rocker. "Kind of a Louisiana thing," she'd always said.

Memories of her grandma made Jasmine both happy and sad.

Shortly after her grandmother died, Jasmine had shopped for new furniture. Her eyes had been drawn to a blue and white toile loveseat and sofa. And now she knew why. Except for the color, it was a perfect match for the one here.

The one place she called home.

The one place she was truly happy.

And the one place she loved the most.

In fact, she loved it so much that when she found out Granddad was thinking about selling the lake house, she begged him to let her buy it.

Sadness pinged down on her like heavy raindrops. Being in this wonderful cabin again, her desire to live here grew. But Granddad was one of those people who took his time making decisions, and apparently this was one of those times.

She looked around the place that made her feel more at home than anywhere else and thought about Jack. Could there really be a future for them together? Jasmine scraped her teeth across the top of her thumbnail. Could she really stay in Steamboat, knowing how much she hated it and how much physical and emotional pain it caused her? Granted, she wouldn't be alone every night anymore, but she would still have pain all winter long.

Could loving Jack make enough difference for her to stay?

Love hadn't been enough for Lori and Steve.

Her mother always said love was enough, but Jasmine wasn't convinced it could be. After all, Lori and Steve had been madly, deeply, and totally in love with each when they married.

Like she and Jack were.

But look at Lori and Steve now.

The image of Lori's limp body flashed through her mind. She squeezed her eyes to erase it from her mind.

The walls suddenly closed in on her.

Jasmine dashed toward the door.

CHAPTER TWENTY-THREE

Down at the wharf, Jasmine lowered herself onto the wooden dock and dangled her feet over the water. A fishy smell hung in the air. Thick humidity plastered her short tendrils of hair against the back of her neck.

Leaning back, she placed her hands behind her, tilted her head toward heaven, and stared at the eternal blue sky. The sound of water lapping against the hollow barrels underneath her had a lulling effect, reminding Jasmine just how much this place epitomized peace to her. Would her lifelong dream and goal of owning this place ever come true?

Then she thought of Jack. She already missed him something fierce. How could she live without him?

"Lord, what do I do? I love Jack, and I can't imagine living without him. But I can't stand living in Steamboat Springs. I know most people would die to live in a place like that, but it isn't for me anymore. I'm sick and tired of the long winters and the pain that comes along with it." She rubbed her fingertips relishing the fact they didn't hurt or feel numb here.

"Oh, Jesus. You can't believe how nice it is to not have pain or numbness. Or to be chilled to the bone. Here, it's warm and toasty, and I can go outside anytime I want. If I lived here, I wouldn't have to sit around for months and months on end, staring at four walls, watching them close in on me more and more with each passing winter.

"Here I could actually plant a garden and be a blessing to people again. Plus, there's such a sense of freedom here. A freedom of knowing I can take care of myself instead of depending on someone else. I don't feel smothered or stupid or that suffocating guilt. Or like I'm not as good as they are." Her chest rose and fell. "I'm tired of feeling like a failure and a huge disappointment back—" She stopped before saying 'home'. Steamboat was not home to her.

Her eyes roamed the surrounding lake.

This place was home.

"Lord, You of all people know how much this place means to me. And how for years I've dreamt of moving here. I can't imagine giving up this dream. And there's no way I'm asking Jack to give up what he loves either. And if I tell him I'm willing to stay in Steamboat, I feel like I'd be settling for a life I don't want. And I don't want either of us to have any regrets. I'm so afraid we'll end up resenting each other. Or even worse, hating each other."

Trust in the Lord with all your heart and lean not unto your own understanding. In all your ways, acknowledge Him, and He will direct your paths.

Her mouth quirked to one side. "I haven't been very good at trusting You in this area, have I, Lord? I guess it's because I'm afraid You'll make me stay in Steamboat and I'll feel trapped and smothered. And feel even more worthless than I do now. I know I sound like a stuck record, but it really does seem like the only time I'm truly happy," she sat up and waved her arms as if to show God the vastness of this place, "is when I'm here."

Memories of carefree, happy-go-lucky times scrolled through her mind. No wonder she adored this place so much. It was a place where she felt whole—instead of like a cripple.

A place where she could be free to live again.

To be herself again.

To use her creative abilities to bless others again without pain and without fear of failure.

This place not only represented peace and acceptance to her, but love.

Like the continual waves lapping on the shore, understanding washed over and over her as the Holy Spirit revealed that love wasn't a place, but love was all about sacrifice. Love represented God. A Father who loved her so much, He sacrificed his only Son, Jesus, by sending Him to die for her.

Love was about family and friends who cared enough about her that they sacrificed their lives and their time to stay with her and to help her when she needed it the most. That wasn't smothering and cosseting, it was love.

Another wave of understanding splashed over her. That was why she had felt guilty for so long. Not being able to help her sisters and Jack and other people like she used too, she felt like she had failed not only them but herself.

She felt useless.

But most of all, she felt unlovable.

And yet she really wasn't.

Her family and Jack loved her unconditionally even though she had changed drastically since her accident. In spite of her lack of being able to do the things she loved and the things that gave her value and worth, her family and Jack had never given up on her or stopped loving her.

That realization rose in Jasmine like the dawning of a beautiful new day. The people who truly loved her and she truly loved were back home in Steamboat Springs, Colorado.

Home.

She pulled her legs up and wrapped her arms around them. Closing her eyes, she rested her chin on her knees. Had she actually just thought of Steamboat as her home? Astonishment surged through her.

Any place can be home where there is love.

"Oh, Lord, I see it now. Forgive me, Father, for being so blind and bull-headed. For only thinking about what I wanted and being so self-absorbed. I feel terrible about how I've been. I had made up my mind a long time ago this was the only place I would ever be happy, or I ever felt truly loved. But that's not true. I mistook happiness and good times for love."

She pressed her eyes together and opened them. "I desperately wanted to be on my own, so I could prove to myself and to them I was capable of doing things myself and live without them. But I can't, Lord. I don't want to. I need them. I love them. Forgive me for being so selfish, and thank You for showing me that my heart is back in Steamboat with Jack and my family." Joy poured through every inch of her soul, her spirit, and her body.

"Oh, God, I've been such a fool. You're right. I thought of Granddad and all of us being together here sharing picnics, going water skiing, taking the pirot out, taking long walks on the beach, and hiking through the trees. The magnificent sunsets, singing around the campfire eating hot dogs and s'mores." Happy tears trickled down her face.

"Lord, I'm in love with the memories. Yes, this place is beautiful, and yes, I hate being cold. But, Lord, even though my wrist hurts and my fingers get numb, You've helped me all these years to do my work and do it well in spite of an aching wrist and numb fingers. Thank You for revealing that to me. And for showing me that without love, this place is just another place, and not a home."

She realized just how true that revelation was when she thought back to when she first walked into the cabin earlier.

Her loving grandmother hadn't been there to greet her or to give her a big hug.

The place smelled musty, not yeasty with a hint of cinnamon and spices. Or like Southern fried chicken or catfish or crawfish.

And there was no Granddad or mom or dad or sisters or Jack to fill the place with laughter and with love. A smile of contentment coveted Jasmine's face. How truly blessed she was to have her family. To have her eyes opened to the fact that what good would dreams and goals be without loved ones around to share them with. "Oh, thank You, Lord Jesus, for opening my eyes. I feel like the blind man in John 9:25, 'I was blind, but now I see.'

"I, too, see. I now know that I can fulfill my dreams anywhere. Besides, it's not like I can't come here often. After all, hopefully someday I'll still own it. And as far as my fear about what happened between Lori and Steve... Well, I cast that burden onto You right now, along with the guilt I've carried over how I surely must have contributed to Lori almost taking her life because it was my pain pills she'd taken, and every other encumbering weight I've lamented over the past several years."

Movement in the water caught her eye. A large fish swam under the dock. "And I'm *not* going to go fishing and reel those cares back in." She chuckled. "They're Yours. I refuse to allow anything to stop me from being with Jack."

With a new resolve, Jasmine jumped up and sprinted toward the house. She hadn't expected her answer to come so soon. On her jaunt back, she remembered she still hadn't let her granddad's overseer know she was here.

Hunger pains gripped her stomach until it hurt. She decided to eat a quick bite before she headed down to Roger's.

As she neared the house, a persistent sense of foreboding aroused her spirit. Something didn't feel right. She looked around. Nothing seemed amiss. Perhaps the excitement of her revelation was making her antsy. That had to be it. She jogged the rest of the way. When she opened the front door, her hair stood on end, same as it had the day she encountered the mountain lion. She looked around, searching for Bougé.

"Bougé?" she hollered, glancing around the room as she headed toward the bedroom on the bottom floor. "Bougé. Come here, baby." She peeked into the bedroom and frowned. Her cat was lying sprawled on the bed in a weird position. "Bougé!" Fear shot through her.

She bolted toward her pet. "Bougé? What's wrong, baby?"

"I'll tell you what's wrong with her."

Jasmine whirled at the voice.

Her eyes went wide as fear jammed into every inch of her being.

The man with the sandy-blond hair and gray eyes from the airport was standing behind her bedroom door.

She screamed and bolted for the door.

He stepped in front of her, caught her by the arms, and yanked her hands behind her back.

"W—who are you, and what do you want?" She gasped in pain from his tight grip.

"Jasmine, I'm hurt," he said near her ear, making her cringe.

"How—how do you know my name?" Fear snaked its way up her spine.

"Because I know you, and you know me." That velvety timbre voice sounded familiar.

"From the airport?" she choked out.

"No, my dear Jazzy. From online."

His words slammed against her heart. Jasmine's world tilted and spun like the earth's axle. "S—Simon?"

"One and the same," he replied cheerfully.

Jasmine moaned. Jack's suspicions had been right all along. Why hadn't she listened to him?

She leaned her head back and looked up at him. "What are you doing here? How did you know I was here?" She sent him a confused look. "How did you find me?"

"Well, let me tell you, sweetheart." He smiled.

Sweetheart. Coming from him it reminded her of a fork scraping across a china plate.

"But first, I have to do something." He led her inside the walk-in closet and picked up some shackles.

"W—what are you going to do with those?" Her body started shaking, and her heart pounded so fast she feared it wouldn't be able to handle the pressure before bursting.

"I can't have you running away now, can I, Jazzy?" he said through a tight smile. His too-smooth voice frightened her, and she wanted to scream, *Don't call me Jazzy.*

Lord, keep me safe.

"I won't run away. I promise," she stammered, forcing down the lump of fear clogging her throat.

"Well, I can't take that chance now, can I? I've waited too long to have you all to myself."

He shoved her on the bed and jerked her into a sitting position. Jasmine winced from the pain and swallowed hard. She darted a glance toward Bougé, who still remained motionless. "What have you done to my cat? And how did you get past her?"

"Well, thanks to your information. I came prepared."

"My information?" She gulped.

"In one of our conversations you mentioned that your cat attacked strangers. So, I bought some ether and wore leather gloves. Pretty clever, huh?" He chuckled.

The sound grated against Jasmine's taut nerves. Thank God Bougé was only sleeping. But oh how she wished her cat would wake up and attack Simon. Jasmine would have a chance to escape then. Simon. She still couldn't believe this intruder was him.

How could she have been so stupid? Jack had warned her, but did she listen? No-o-o-o. She assured him she'd be careful not to give out any personal information. But Jack knew better.

Simon pulled out a pair of handcuffs from his back pocket.

Bile burned Jasmine's esophagus. *Maybe I'm dreaming.* He jerked her hands and slapped the cuffs on. No such luck. This definitely wasn't a dream.

Jasmine leapt to her feet and plowed headlong into the door. She had to get away while she had somewhat of a chance.

Simon grabbed a handful of her hair and with great strength forced her back onto the bed.

She fought back the tears threatening to fill her eyes.

She didn't want to appear any weaker than she already did.

Her efforts to fight him off were quickly squelched. Her strength paled against his.

"You sure were right, Jazzy."

"Don't call me that!" The venomous words flew from her mouth.

Simon's eyes blazed, then softened.

Jasmine tamped down the rising panic that threatened to take over.

"That's your nickname, isn't it? I'm only calling you what you said to call you." His sugary sweet voice made her skin crawl.

He leaned down and started putting the shackles around her ankles. She desperately wanted to kick him or hit him over the head with her fists, but knowing she wasn't strong enough to knock him out, she feared what he might do to her if she tried it.

Snap. Snap. The noise of the clamps echoed in her ears, and the rattling of the chains matched the jangling going on inside her.

He rose and ran a finger over her cheek.

The gesture repulsed her and made her want to vomit. She drew back.

"Now, now, my sweet Jasmine. That's no way to

treat me after all we've shared together."

"All we've shared together?" She frowned, wondering what he meant.

"Yes, sweetheart. You told me all about yourself and your family."

Her mind raced through their conversations. *Oh no.* Simon was right. And to think she'd been so smug when she'd told Jack about how discreet and cautious she would be. She forced back the tears stinging the backs of her eyes.

"How did you find me? I never told you my last name." Jasmine frowned.

"There are all kinds of things you can do with a computer if you know how."

He sat on the bed next to her and grabbed her cuffed hand. She cringed and tried to jerk her hand free, but Simon tightened his grip.

Pain sliced through her bad wrist.

She winced.

Simon lightened his hold.

"It wasn't hard to put two-and-two together." Like a slimy serpent, a smug smile slowly slithered upward on his face making Jasmine's skin crawl right along with it. "You told me you owned your own business, created greeting cards, and your nickname is Jazzy. I ran a search and found Jazzy Creations. From there it was a cinch."

Disgusted with herself and him, she looked away.

He reached over, squeezed her jaw hard, and forced her to look at him. "I could hardly wait to meet the woman who filled my every thought and dreams." Lust filled his eyes and words.

Swallowing became difficult.

A hint of sadness flickered through her. What happened to that sweet, sensitive man she'd met online? The one she'd defended and loved visiting with. It couldn't be the man sitting next to her. This man was insane.

"We were fated by God to be together." He parted his lips and leaned toward her.

Jasmine twisted her head to the side.

His mouth landed on her cheek.

Ewww. She swiped at the spot with her fingers, wanting to disinfect her face to rid it of his vile touch.

He clutched her chin so tightly she thought her jaw would snap. "Don't ever do that again! You belong to me now. If I want a kiss, I'll take one." Anger blazed in his eyes like fire from hell.

Jasmine cowered.

Her insides shook harder.

"If you fight me or try to get away, I'll take what I want, when I want." His eyes raked over her body.

Still holding on to her chin, he forced his mouth onto hers, and smashed his lips against hers until she tasted blood. Whether it was his or hers, she couldn't tell.

Jasmine gulped several times as her stomach lurched.

She wanted to shove him away and fight back. But with her hands cuffed and her feet shackled, she didn't dare. His words filled her with dread, threatening to render her unconscious. She fought against the darkness with everything inside her.

God help me, Jasmine begged.

Trust Me.

Rescue me from this crazy man, please.

Only believe.

Lord, I'm trying, but help my unbelief.

A measure of peace settled in her. Tears of relief spilled over her lids.

Simon stood and yanked her up into his arms.

She stiffened. But because of his threat, she didn't fight him.

"Please don't cry." He leaned back and looked at her.

Her focus dropped to the floor. Gently, he wiped the

tears off of her cheeks. "I only want to spend time with you." His tone turned sharp. "Look at me!"

Startled by the contrast in his voice, she turned wide eyes up at him and then frowned. The softness in his eyes didn't fit the sharpness in his tone. *My, God, have mercy. This man is insane.*

"This was the only way I could think to make it happen. When I asked you to think about meeting me in person, you never got back to me." His sad countenance reminded her of a lost little boy. "Neither did the other women."

Other women? What other women? Spots danced before her eyes.

"They refused to meet me too. I never meant to hurt them," he continued, oblivious to the turmoil going on inside her. "I wanted to come to your door, but that guy and your sisters were always there. By the way, it's amazing. You really are identical in every way."

Her eyes widened.

Air.

She needed air.

She blinked several times.

He had been to her house?

Was he the one stalking her?

This time she couldn't fight the blackness. Her knees buckled.

CHAPTER TWENTY-FOUR

Jack pulled off the highway and into a rest stop area. After letting Willbee out to do his business, Stan slid in behind the steering wheel, and they headed back onto the interstate.

"Thanks, Stan, for coming along." Jack gave Stan's shoulder a quick squeeze.

"Anytime, buddy. Besides, it's payback time." Stan held his hand up to ward off Jack's retort. "I know I'm not supposed to say anything about you anonymously making my daughter's dream to study in Paris come true, but I've always wanted to have an opportunity to bless you back in a special way." The gratefulness in Stan's voice touched Jack. "I just didn't figure on it being this way, Jack. Sorry."

Shanell and her big mouth. Jack had wanted his monetary gift to remain anonymous. "Okay, so now we're even."

Jack positioned his head against the headrest and closed his eyes. "I failed Jasmine, Stan. No matter how late it was, I should have called and told her what you said. Then she wouldn't have gone—"

"Jack." Stan cut him off.

He turned his head toward his friend.

Stan glanced at him and then back at the road. "You can't keep beating yourself up over this. Nor can you protect Jasmine from everything. As hard as it is, buddy, you're going to have to give her over to God and trust Him to take care of her. And you did warn her, but she didn't listen. Sorry, but we both know Jasmine can be pretty stubborn."

Through a dry chuckle, Jack agreed, "That she can be." He ran his hand through his hair. "Thanks, Stan. You're right. Jasmine's note said she needed to get away and pray about the future." Jack looked out the window into the empty darkness. "Something keeps her from committing to a relationship with me. I used to think it was because she wanted to move to Louisiana, but now I think it's more. A lot more." He turned slightly in his seat and looked at Stan. "Did I tell you that I bought her granddad's cabin?"

Stan's attention jerked toward Jack along with the steering wheel. He quickly corrected the vehicle. "You did what? She's going to be madder than a wounded grizzly and bounce you right out of her life when she finds out. Whatever possessed you to do such a thing?"

Jack chuckled.

Stan kept glancing between the road and Jack, looking at him like he'd lost his marbles.

"Her birthday's in May. Once I told her granddad I wanted to give it to Jasmine for her birthday, he decided he would go ahead and sell the place to me. He said the thought of Jasmine happily married, living in the house he and his wife had shared, gave him great joy. And that he could finally let it go. I didn't correct him about us being married because I had every intention of one day asking her. In fact, I'm going to ask her to marry me and let her know she doesn't have to live in Steamboat anymore."

"Well, that's a nice gesture, buddy. But you better pray it doesn't backfire on you. You know how Jasmine jumps to conclusions and how she feels about that cabin."

"I know. I just have to trust I did the right thing. I wanted to be the one to give her what she wants most in life—her granddad's lake house." *If only it was me she wanted most in life.*

Knowing Jasmine was at the lake house now, and possibly Simon or RodeoCowboy too, all excitement over his gift fizzled. He stared out the window and prayed.

Only a few farm lights dotted the darkness, making the drive seem as endless as the empty fields.

What was Jasmine doing now? Was she safe? His gut twisted thinking about Simon hurting her. "Dear God, keep Jasmine safe."

Stan squeezed his shoulder. "Try and get some rest, buddy. The Lord will keep her safe."

"Thanks." Jack pushed the illumination button on his watch. 8:49. Hopefully, they would get to their destination by sunrise.

Father, Stan's right. I can't always be there for Jasmine, but You can. I relinquish all holds on her and give her into Your hands. Send Your angels to watch over her and protect her.

Jack's gut wrenched again at the thought of any harm coming to her. Swallowing hard against the lump in his throat, he continued, *And please don't let anything happen to Jasmine. I need her.*

Jasmine heard a voice in the distance. "Come on, sweetheart, wake up." A light tap on her cheeks and she slowly opened her eyes. Her heart lunged to her throat. Simon was holding her on his lap. She jerked her focus down at her fully clothed body, and relief poured over her.

She struggled to get off his lap, but Simon clutched her tighter. The last thing she remembered was him saying those awful things to her. His words echoed through her mind. She squeezed her eyes shut to blot out the memory. But the reality of what had taken place crashed into her like a tidal wave smashing against the jagged rocks. Her stomach churned. He knew everything about her—where she lived, her sisters, the name of her company, her cat, and Jack.

Oh, Jack. You were so right. What a fool I've been.

You tried telling me that it was Simon following me, but I didn't listen. Lord, you tried warning me too. Your Spirit jangled inside me every time I talked to Simon. All that time I passed it off as a chocolate high, or nerves over a new adventure, or something else. Because deep down I didn't want to deal with the fact it might have something to do with Simon, so I excused it away. I wanted my own way. And look where that got me. Dear God, why didn't I listen to You and Jack? I'm so sorry. Forgive me. Help me, Jesus. She groaned.

"Are you okay, sweetheart?

She wanted to scream out loud, *Stop calling me sweetheart!* But she didn't dare.

"Answer me, please." His one dimpled smile turned her stomach. "After hearing your sweet voice on the telephone, I couldn't wait to hear it in person."

Jasmine frowned. Phone? They'd never talked before.

"Every time I called, I reminded you we'd be together one day, and here we are, just like I said."

Jasmine's blood flow slowed. Her mouth felt like sandpaper. She swallowed against the lump in her throat and squeaked, "You? You were the one calling me?"

Simon ran the back of his hand over her cheek. Jasmine recoiled at his touch. He jerked her chin with a roughness she'd never experienced before. "Look at me! Don't pretend you didn't know it was me. I knew you were just playing hard to get." A lustful look filled his eyes. His eyes once again roamed over her body. "It only made me want you all the more." He licked his lips then glanced at hers.

As one thought chased the other, fear clawed her mind at his revealing words. Not only had he been her stalker, but he was the one who'd been calling her too. All that time, had she just imagined a slight southern accent because somehow, psychologically, she wanted it to be

RodeoCowboy?

Never before had she felt so stupid or so betrayed. "I didn't know it was you." She shook her head. "I trusted you. How could you do that to me?"

"Do what?" He tilted his head sideways and innocence clothed his face.

Was this guy psychotic? Didn't he know how much he had frightened her? Was he playing some kind of sick game? She searched his face for the answer. Was that innocent look a ploy? She didn't know what to say or do.

"What do you mean?" His velvet voice sounded sincere, but Jasmine knew this guy was certifiably nuts.

"Y-your phone calls s-scared me half to-to death," she stuttered.

"Oh, baby." He pressed her head against his chest and held it there.

Jasmine stiffened, and her nauseated stomach churned from repulsion.

He caressed her hair while crooning, "I'm sorry I frightened you. I thought you knew it was me." Suddenly Jasmine felt sharp pain in her head as Simon clutched a handful of her hair and yanked her head back. "Wait!"

Jasmine blinked up at him and her breathing came in short gasps as he tightened his hold.

"Just who did you think it was? Are other men pursuing you besides that Jack person?"

Her pulse hammered against her ears.

"H—how do know Jack's name?"

"Right when you passed out, you said 'Jack'." His face scrunched with disdain. "Plus, when I told you about my friend Kailee, you told me about your friend Jack. Remember?"

Boy, did she remember. Me and my big mouth. How many other things had she told him without thinking? Well, Jack was no longer just her friend. For fear of what he would do to her, she didn't feed Simon that piece of information.

He yanked her head again.

Jasmine cringed against the fresh onslaught of pain. Her mind flashed to the women at the shelter. To think they had gone through something similar or worse made her determined to do even more for them if she survived this ordeal.

"You still haven't answered me," he snarled. "I want to know who else you've been talking to."

The evil look in his eyes caused Jasmine's tongue to freeze. Her lips moved, but no words came out.

He tossed her off of his lap and onto the bed and then shot to his feet. He balled his fists at his sides. "Tell me now, or I'll—" He reared his fisted hand back.

Jasmine squeezed her eyes shut and braced herself for the forthcoming blow. Tears stung her eyes and slipped out. *Oh, Jack, why didn't I listen to you?*

Simon jerked her off the bed and pulled her into his arms. He rubbed her back in circles. "I'm sorry, sweetheart. Please don't cry. I can't stand to see women cry."

In spite of the anguish Simon inflicted on her, she grieved the loss of a dear friend. The man she had trusted online. The very man she had grown to care about. This man, the same one she had defended, wasn't the sweet person she knew. He was mentally unstable.

Fear twisted around her throat, cutting off her air. She struggled to draw breath, wondering what he would do with her now, and if he planned on killing her or something even worse.

Her knees wobbled.

Not again. Please, Lord, don't let me pass out. The room tilted. Her eyes slid shut, but she managed to remain conscious. She had to stay awake and alert if she was going to figure a way out of this mess.

Simon, however, apparently thought she had

succumbed to fainting again. He swept her into his arms, carried her into the living room, and laid her on the sofa.

Not wanting him to know she was conscious, she kept her eyes closed, hoping and praying he'd leave her alone.

Simon's personality resembled that of Dr. Jekyll and Mr. Hyde's, nice one minute and completely neurotic the next. The sound of shells crunching under tires captured Jasmine's attention. A surge of hope shot through her. Perhaps Roger had noticed her vehicle. Fervently, she prayed it was him. She'd even settle for Mrs. Jenkins, the nosy old neighbor lady. While she wouldn't come to the door, if she noticed something amiss, she would contact Roger.

Without thinking of the consequences of her actions, Jasmine planted her feet on the floor and scuttled toward the door. The rattling of the chains across the wood floor reverberated off the walls. Simon grabbed a handful of her hair, slammed her back against his chest, and pressed a sharp knife blade against her throat.

Her body went numb from fright.

"If you yell or make any noise at all, I'll make a nice jagged scar on your sleek little throat." His tone was smooth, as if he'd just offered her a beautiful diamond necklace instead.

Jasmine shuddered and willed her knees to hold her up. Tears slipped over her eyelids and landed on his hand.

Simon spun her around and rubbed her back with one hand, cooing, "Ah, baby, don't cry."

What? she silently screamed, her face scrunched. Did he really expect her to calm down with a knife at her throat and now pressed against her back? Her frayed nerves felt as if they would unravel at any moment. *Dear God, have mercy on me.*

"All you have to do is cooperate, and I promise I

won't hurt you."

Yeah, like she could trust anything he said. His promises were like the devil's. All lies.

He pulled her head back, and before she had a chance to move, he pressed his mouth hard against hers.

The intense pain nearly sent her to her knees. Simon tried forcing her to respond by tugging on her lower lip and pushing her upper lip with his top lip. But she refused to give in.

After several tries, he smiled and whispered, "I'm a patient man. I'll wait a lifetime for you to come willingly to me if I have to. You're worth the wait. I love you."

Jasmine wanted to barf at his words. If only she could, then maybe, just maybe she could purge away his appalling declaration, unwanted kisses, and advances. Simon had a long wait ahead of him. It would be a hot day in Iceland before she ever willingly kissed him.

A knock sounded at the door.

Simon slammed his hand over her mouth.

She held her breath hoping and praying whoever it was wouldn't leave.

"I don't think this is the right place, Mary Beth. Buckley said he'd have a sign that said, Warner Family Reunion. I don't see it anywhere."

"Well, maybe you could ask someone where it is. Knock on the door again, Melvin."

Another knock.

Please, God don't let them leave.

She tried to move her foot to rattle the chain, but couldn't. Simon had his foot firmly placed on the chainlinks to keep them from moving.

The screen door squeaked open.

The door knob rattled.

Jasmine's pulse quickened, pounding in her ears like a jackhammer.

Seconds passed, but they felt like hours to her.

"No one's home, Mary Beth. The place is locked up tight. C'mon, let's go."

No! Don't go! Jasmine tried to yank her body free so she could bolt to the door, but couldn't. She tried to scream. To do anything to get the people's attention, but Simon's grip was so tight she couldn't even budge. And with his hand covering part of her nose, breathing was fast becoming difficult.

Footsteps heading away from the cabin door and down the porch stairs shot down any hopes she had of getting away from this maniac. Tears stung the back of her eyes, but Jasmine refused to cry. The very thought of Simon trying to comfort her again made her shudder with repulsion. That alone was all the incentive she needed to keep the tears from gushing out.

The rest of the day passed by in a blur of Dr. Jekyll and Mr. Hyde moments. All day long Simon's moods had been unpredictable, and she never knew what would set him off.

As the evening drew near, a vile and distasteful idea slashed through her mind. Several times, Simon could have forced himself on her, but he hadn't. Was he waiting until it was time for bed? *Oh, Dear God, help me. Please don't let him rob my innocence.*

Simon moving around in the kitchen drew Jasmine's attention that direction. Ire rose inside her. Who did Simon think he was making himself at home in her granddad's kitchen? The only man she ever wanted to see there was Jack. *Oh, Jack. I miss you, and I love you.* She cringed as a feeling of foreboding crashed in around her. What if she never saw Jack again?

I have to escape. But how, Lord? Every time she moved, the two-foot chain on the shackles rattled, and the noise summoned Simon to her side. If only there was some way she could muffle them so she could sneak out.

Through the slats in the window, a moonless night on

the lake was all she saw. A plan sprouted in her mind. She sucked in her lower lip and kneaded it with her teeth.

I'll do it.

"Simon?"

Like a doting husband, he rushed to her side.

"Yes, sweetheart? What do you need?"

She recoiled at the endearment but kept from showing it. "I need to use the restroom."

"Oh. Okay." He effortlessly hoisted her into his arms and carried her to the bathroom door. His nearness made her stomach want to hurl again, but she knew better than to fight him. Once there, he carefully set her down.

"I'll be right outside the door. I know it's difficult to walk with those things on, so I'll carry you back to the couch when you're done." Mr. Hyde's smile curdled her insides.

"I'll be a few minutes." She blushed.

"That's fine. I'm not going anywhere."

His sinister smile sent a shiver slithering up and down her spine, but she smiled in spite of it. For this to work, he had to trust her.

"Are you cold?" Dr. Jekyll sounded genuinely concerned.

"No. Excuse me, please. I have to go."

Simon backed away from the door.

Jasmine scuttled through it, closed it, and quietly turned the lock. *Why didn't I think of this earlier?* Then she realized it was probably a good thing she hadn't. In the dark she knew her way around the woods, but Simon didn't. She also knew of an excellent hiding place. She glanced down at the length of chain on her feet. Yep. She'd be able to climb.

Careful to not make any noise, she held her breath as she wrapped a towel around the chain, then flushed the toilet. Her heart rammed her ribs as she eased the large bathroom window open and popped the screen out.

"You almost done?" Simon boomed outside the door.

Panic threatened to seize her, but she wasn't about to quit now. "Almost." She turned the water on in the sink. "It's hard to wash your hands with cuffs on." She yelled over the running water.

"Okay. If you need me, I'll be right here."

Don't hold your breath. I need you like I need the bitter cold. "Thanks." She sat on the low window ledge and grabbed the chains, making sure they didn't hit anything. She jumped out the window and took off, shuffling along the forest floor.

She rushed through the woods as fast as she could. The towel snagged on a broken branch and she almost crashed to the ground. She stopped and with exorbitant speed removed the cloth, tossing it far from her. The shackles made it difficult to run, but fear propelled her forward.

Simon's voice echoed behind her, penetrating the darkness. Relieved that she knew her way, she continued trudging through the forest.

Simon's angry voice grew louder.

Mr. Hyde was in hot pursuit.

Her chest burned from the exertion.

Almost to the hiding spot, she silently cried. *God, help me.* Finally she reached the massive oak tree. Finding the first cut out groove, she maneuvered her way up the tree until she reached the hidden playhouse her granddad had built for her and her sisters. Only a handful of people knew of its whereabouts. Her granddad had built it so that it blended in like a chameleon with its surroundings. Even in the winter when the branches were bare, its whereabouts remained concealed.

"If I catch you, Jasmine, you'll be sorry," Mr. Hyde snarled from somewhere nearby.

Jasmine covered her mouth, taking in small panting breaths. *Oh, Granddad, thank you so much for building this place where no one could see it. God, please conceal me from Simon.*

"If you give up now and come back to me, I won't hurt you. I promise." Dr. Jekyll's sugary sweet voice took over, making the lie even more bitter. Did he think she was stupid? Who knew what he'd do to her? She shuddered at the thought of finding out.

Jasmine peeked through the tiny window. The dim glow of his flashlight headed away from the tree.

She heard him hollering at a distance. "If you don't come to me now, I'm going to go torture that cat of yours."

A heavy dose of fear rushed through her body, tormenting her soul. *Bougé!* She closed her eyes. "Oh, God," she whispered. "Please show me what to do." She covered her mouth to muffle her sobs. "You know I can't let him hurt my precious baby."

CHAPTER TWENTY-FIVE

Jack hid his SUV at the bottom of the lane. With it still somewhat dark outside, he hoped to have the element of surprise on his side. He snapped Willbee's leash onto the dog's collar, and he and Stan quietly lumbered their way toward the cabin thankful for the small amount of light before sunrise.

As they neared the lake house, Willbee let out a low growl.

"Quiet," Jack whispered sternly.

Willbee immediately obeyed, but the dog kept glancing back and forth between Jack and the woods.

The woods blocked their view of the cabin and the cabin of them. Jack knew right where the key was, and he planned to use that knowledge to his advantage.

"Stan, I think we need to go up front and around back. Which one do you want?" Jack whispered as he pulled a 45-hand gun out of his shoulder holster.

"You be careful with that thing, Jack. This guy isn't playing with a full deck."

Jack tapped Stan's gun and raised his brows as if to ask the same question of his friend.

"You forget, Jack, I'm highly trained in stressful situations. I was a police officer for a several years before I went to school and became a detective. I know how to use one of these things." Stan's whole countenance turned serious. "Listen to me. Don't try to play the hero. Use your head and not your heart. If you don't, you could get Jasmine kil—"

Jack knew what he almost said. Killed. His gut wrenched. He drew in an unsteady breath and nodded.

"Lord, help us to rescue Jasmine. Protect us and keep us safe, in Jesus name."

"Amen," Stan added.

"Heel," Jack commanded Willbee. The two of them cautiously walked around the cabin. With the blinds shut, Jack couldn't see inside. Still, every nerve in his body went on full alert. He heard Bougé growling and eased his way that direction.

Her growling became louder. He was getting closer.

The bathroom window stood wide open.

Jack rushed back to Stan and caught him just before he went inside. "The bathroom window is open. I'm going to slip inside and check it out. I'll meet you inside," he whispered.

Stan nodded.

Jack tied Willbee's leash around the porch rail.

His adrenaline kicked in as he made his way to the back of the cabin. Quietly, carefully he climbed inside the bathroom. He peered around the door and scanned the large room beyond. No sign of Jasmine or Simon. The only rooms left were the upstairs loft and main floor bedrooms. Jack's heart sank. *Dear God, don't let me be too late.*

He met Stan in the middle of the cabin. Jack pointed toward the loft. Stan went up one spiral staircase, and Jack climbed the other.

No sign of them there either.

Stan signaled for Jack to take the master bedroom and he'd take the guest room. With his heart in his throat, Jack cocked the gun and clasped both hands around his weapon.

At Stan's nod, Jack burst through the door and spun his aim around the room, checking behind the door and then the closet.

The instant he opened the closet door, Bougé darted out and made a B-line toward the bathroom.

Jack caught her just as she lunged toward the open window.

"It's okay, girl," he crooned while laying the gun down on the sink. "You're trying to tell me she's outside, aren't you?"

When Jack shut the window, Bougé escaped from his grasp and raced from the bathroom, growling and hissing. Jack snatched up his gun and Jasmine's hairbrush off the vanity and rushed after the cat.

"It's okay, Bougé." At the sound of Jack's voice, Bougé quit growling but never took her eyes off of Stan.

"They're not in here. Let's go." Jack headed toward the front door.

Jack's mind whirled with the ramifications of why she wasn't in the house. "Dear God, have mercy."

Once outside, Jack unlatched Willbee's lease and held Jasmine's hairbrush under his dog's nose. "Search, Willbee. Search."

Willbee darted behind the house. Jack and Stan took off after him, dodging tree branches as they followed the dog's strong lead.

His dog stopped at a large oak. Standing on his hind feet, the retriever glanced at Jack and then up the tree.

Through the morning's gray haze, Jack's eyes trailed up the tree trunk. He recognized this tree. It was the tree house Jasmine's granddad had built. "Stay, Willbee." He turned to Stan. "I'm going up."

Stan stared at Jack as if he were nuts.

"There's a hidden tree house up there," he whispered in case Simon was holding Jasmine hostage there. Jack felt for a cut out groove in the tree trunk and worked his way upward. Glancing down, he barely saw Stan and Willbee. When he reached the last step, he grabbed his gun and cocked it. Jasmine wouldn't tell Simon about the tree house, but he didn't want to take a chance in case he had followed her up here.

Jack slipped through the canopy of tree branches until he reached the hidden door.

Gun aimed as he crouched in the branches, he kicked the door open.

Jasmine screamed.

Huddled in the corner, with shackles on her feet and cuffs on her hands, Jasmine stared at him wide-eyed. Jack quickly surveyed the room and behind the door, then rushed to Jasmine and knelt down.

"Jack. Where? How?"

He crushed her into his arms and held her trembling form.

When he found his voice, he rasped. "Thank God, you're safe." He held her tighter.

"I'm s-s-so c—cold."

Jack removed his coat and wrapped it around her. Pulling her close, he willed heat from his body into hers.

"Oh, Jack. You were so right about Simon. I should have listened to you. Y—you t—tried to warn me." She burst out crying. "I've never been s—s—so scared in my life. It was awful." Her body convulsed.

Jack hated to ask her now, but he had to. "Where is Simon?"

"I—I don't know." She pulled back and looked at him. Her eyes smoldered with fear. "He threatened to kill Bougé if I didn't come back to him." She twitched her head back and forth in devastation. "But I couldn't. I just couldn't take any more. My poor Bougé. My poor baby." Sobs wracked her words. Jack pulled her closer and held her tight.

"Bougé's fine. He didn't hurt her, and you're safe now." He pulled her into his arms again, wanting to never let her go but knowing he must. "We need to help you out of here and get you warmed up."

She slunk away and turned fear-filled eyes on him. "I can't leave. What if he's hiding and—" She closed her eyes and shuddered.

"I'll find him."

"No!" She clutched the front of his shirt. "Don't leave me, Jack. Please, don't leave me," she begged, through chattering teeth.

Jack's heart wrenched. It was then he caught sight of fingertip-like bruises on her jaw and a split on her upper lip. What had Simon done to her? He glanced at the shackles and cuffs and wondered what kind of monster this jerk was. Anger trampled through him like a charging bull. Simon would pay for what he'd done to Jasmine. Jack would see to it personally.

"Don't worry, sweetheart. I'll take care of you." With that, he swung her into his arms and headed out of the tree house door. Steadying her from behind, they made their way down the tree.

⁓ᏧᎧ⁓

"I have to go." Jack cupped Jasmine's face. "I'm the one who trained Willbee. Roger and the police will stay here with you. You'll be safe with them." He pulled the blanket tighter around her and tucked her head against his chest. With each beat of his heart, her nerves settled another notch.

Roger and the police had bombarded her with questions until her mind was fried. The only positive thing about this whole mess... Jack was here.

"We won't let anything happen to you," Roger tried to reassure her. "I'm sorry I was gone all day yesterday and didn't get back until way after dark, or I would have come sooner."

A young police officer walked up and handed Jack a set of keys and an article of clothing Jasmine recognized as Simon's jacket. The sight of it made her shudder.

Jack inserted a key into the cuffs. The iron pressed against the tender spot in her once broken wrist. She flinched and yelped.

Because Simon had yanked her around so much, her wrist throbbed until she could hardly stand the pain. She even wondered if Simon had fractured it.

Jack finished removing the cuffs, and with the gentlest of touch, he turned her hands and examined them. Black and blue bruises lined her wrists. "Oh, baby." He drew her into his arms and pressed a kiss on top of her head. "I'm so sorry I didn't get here sooner."

Jasmine pulled back enough to look up at him. "It's not your fault. It's mine. None of this would have happened if I would have listened to you in the first place."

"Let's not talk about that now. We need to get all of these things off of you." Jack bent and removed the shackles from her ankles.

Jasmine ran her fingertips over her wrists. It felt so good to have those heavy things off.

"Jack, we need to head out." Stan sent Jasmine an apologetic look. Before Jack had a chance to respond, a police officer, who appeared to be in his mid-forties, asked Jasmine, "Can you give us a description of the perpetrator?"

After she described Simon, Jack let go of her hand. "Listen, sweetheart, I have to go now." He paused. "Don't leave again." He winked.

Even though he only meant his words in a teasing manner, they still stung.

She stared at Jack's hiking boots. "Trust me, Jack. I learned my lesson on that one."

Jack gave her a brief hug before placing Simon's jacket under his dog's nose. "Search, Willbee, search."

Willbee darted into the wooded area with Jack, Stan, and two officers in hot pursuit after him. Jasmine watched until they were out of sight. Apprehension mixed with love slashed her already tattered emotions.

How far did this guy go anyway? Drained emotionally and physically, Jack forced himself to keep up with Willbee.

All of a sudden Willbee froze and emitted a low growl.

Jack stilled in his tracks.

Simon had to be nearby.

Images of Jasmine shackled like some vile prisoner, huddled in the corner of the tree house, hugging her knees played through Jack's mind. He couldn't wait to get his hands on Simon and make him pay for what he'd done to her.

Vengeance is mine, saith the Lord, I will repay.

Willbee barked and took off at a mad dash.

"Willbee!" Jack hollered, chasing after him.

A shot rang out.

"No! Willbee!" Jack willed his feet to move faster.

He ran through the trees like a wild phantom, his stomach burning like an out of control wild fire. The instant he spotted Willbee, the tension in his body eased a bit.

Willbee had Simon pinned down and his jaws were clamped around Simon's throat.

"Get this dog off me," Simon wheezed, kicking.

Jack snatched up the gun lying next to Simon. "Heel, Willbee." The dog obeyed. Jack pointed the gun at Simon. Hate for this man coiled around Jack until his fingers itched to pull the trigger. Never in his life had he wanted to hurt a man as badly as he wanted to hurt Simon.

Again he heard, *Vengeance is mine, saith the Lord, I will repay.*

"Please, please, don't shoot." Simon's whiny voice turned Jack's stomach.

Fear twisted through Simon's eyes.

It was the same fear he'd witnessed in Jasmine so many times over the last couple of months.

Simon jerked his head sideways, and like the coward he was, he cringed away from what he clearly knew was coming.

It took every ounce of willpower Jack possessed not to pull the trigger. He stared at the pathetic form lying in front of him and something in him let go. He refused to stoop to the scumbag's level. "Get him out of here," Jack ground out through clenched teeth as he handed Simon's gun to Stan.

"That's working with your head and not your heart," Stan praised him.

Yet he deserved no praise. He had wanted to do bodily harm to another being. In his book, that made him just as bad as Simon.

The officers apprehended Simon and read him his rights.

Severe pain spiked Jack's arm. He rolled his arm and looked at his bicep. Blood soaked his shirt.

Jasmine paced back and forth in the front yard of the cabin near the oak tree with the L-shaped branch. Too wired to sit inside, she opted to stay outside in the warm sunshine where she could keep watch for Jack's return.

For the fiftieth time, she glanced in the direction Jack and the others had headed.

All of sudden a loud bang rent the air.

Jasmine's heart leapt into her throat. She knew the sound of a gun when she heard one, and that was definitely a gunshot.

"Jack!" She darted toward the sound of the blast, but a police officer apprehended her. "Let me go!" She twisted and squirmed, trying to break free, but the cop held onto her.

"Miss Moore. I'm sorry, but I can't let you go. You need to wait here."

As much as she didn't want to, she knew the man

was right, and this time she wouldn't be foolish, she would heed the sound advice she was given. If only she'd done that earlier when Jack had warned her, then none of this would be happening, and Jack wouldn't be out there risking his life because of her. She sent up a long, silent prayer for him and for everyone else.

The wait was grueling.

Finally, movement in the trees snagged her attention.

Simon rounded the corner of the cabin, and even though two police officers escorted him, a tunnel of fear shimmied up her spine at the sight of him, making her shudder. The instant her eyes landed on Jack, she bolted toward him and threw her arms around him.

He winced.

Pulling back, she looked him over and noticed the blood on his sleeve.

"Jack! You're hurt." A sudden take-charge strength rose up inside her. "Roger, I'm taking Jack to the hospital. Stan, would you please get my vehicle from around back and look after Bougé and Willbee while we're gone?" she asked while helping Jack sit on the oak tree's L-shaped branch.

"Ma'am, we need to ask you a few more questions," Mark, the policeman, stated.

Without looking at him, she retorted, "They'll have to wait. I have more important things to do right now."

"Jasmine, let Stan take me. You've been through enough." Jack trailed his finger over the tender bruises on her face where Simon had grabbed her.

"No!" She brushed his hand away. Jack's eyebrows spiked into an upside down V. "*I'm* taking you, and that's final."

"Jasmine?" Dr. Jekyll said from behind her.

She spun around and glared at Simon. "What?" she snapped.

"I'm sorry. Really I am. I love you. All I wanted was

to be with you."

"Love?" she spat, storming over to him. "You don't know the meaning of the word. When you love someone, you don't treat them like you did me. You cherish them, and you're there for them when they need you. You're willing to sacrifice your own wants and desires just to be with them. But, you—you take what you want by force. That's *not* love." She shook her head and turned on her heel, calling over her shoulder, "Get him outta here."

Everyone, including Jack, was gawking at her.

"Let's get you to the hospital," she told Jack just as Stan pulled up with her vehicle.

She reached down and helped Jack to his feet.

After settling him in the passenger's seat, she trotted to the driver's side and slid behind the wheel. She started the vehicle and headed toward the hospital. They had driven as far as the main road before she finally corralled enough courage to say what was on her mind. "Jack."

"Yeah."

"I'm sorry for everything I've put you through. I really was shocked to find out Simon was the one who'd been stalking me and making all those phone calls. I truly believed it was either RodeoCowboy or the Peeping Tom." She looked both ways, then pulled onto the highway. "He lied to me about everything." She spoke barely above a whisper. She glanced at Jack. "I should have listened to you—and trusted you. I'm sorry."

Jack smiled weakly at her. "It's over. You don't need to apologize."

"Yes, I do. In fact, I owe you another apology too. Ever since that day I got lost hiking, I've wanted to move more than ever before, to get away from everyone. I resented the way you and my sisters were babying me. I felt smothered and inadequate. Like you all felt you were superior to me and didn't think I was capable of doing anything for myself because I was stupid or something. I couldn't wait to leave to prove you guys wrong."

"We don't think you're stupid and we never meant to—"

Jasmine cut him off. "I know, I know. It wasn't you guys. It was me." She kept her eyes on the road and didn't look at him. "I'm sorry, Jack. I understand it now. You weren't smothering me. Everyone was showing me just how much they really loved me." She wiped her wet eyes. "I can't believe how stupid and blind I've been. I wanted to be independent so bad. But no one is really independent. We all need each other."

Jack nodded his agreement.

"I'm so blessed to have each and every one of you in my life." She turned her focus on to Jack, whose head lay sideways against the headrest. "I love you, Jack."

Eyes half-mast, he whispered, "I love you too."

She turned her eyes back toward the road. "Thank God, He opened my eyes to the truth before it was too late."

As she drove, she relayed everything the Lord had shown her. When she finished, she looked over at him. Seeing his peaked face and closed eyes, Jasmine shoved the gas pedal to the floor. "Hang on, my love. We're almost there."

CHAPTER TWENTY-SIX

Only a few patches of snow remained in Steamboat Springs. Buds dotted the trees, and the lawns and meadows were lush and green with the sweet signs of Spring. Jasmine couldn't believe it had been three months since her nightmarish encounters with Simon. When she'd arrived home from Louisiana, she'd been too scared to stay by herself, so she'd moved in with Shanell until she felt safe enough to go home.

That time was now. Especially since Stan informed her and Jack several days ago that the FBI had captured RodeoCowboy in Florida, and this morning's paper said the Steamboat Springs Peeping Tom had been captured. Those facts, along with the one that she hadn't had any reoccurring nightmares, let her know it was time for her to completely trust God and go home. Something she both dreaded and looked forward to. She hated leaving Shanell.

Jasmine glanced around her sister's Victorian-style house. Staying here had been like one big slumber party. The two of them giggled like teenagers, played with makeup, watched old movies, and ate junk food. But most of the time, Jasmine prayed and studied the Word.

The phone rang. Jasmine answered it. "Shanell Moore's residence, Jasmine speaking."

"Happy Birthday!"

"Thanks, Lori." It was good to hear her friend's voice again even though the two of them had spoken several times since Jasmine had gotten back from her ordeal with Simon. "Aren't you at work?"

"Yes, I am. But I had to take a break and wish my friend happy birthday." Jasmine heard the smile in Lori's voice. "Plus, I just had to tell you something. You're not going to believe this one."

"What did Steve pull this time?" The last time they had talked, Lori told her about Steve's latest deceptive schemes. Everyone was worse than the last.

"He's decided to divorce his third wife. And get this. He said he's never stopped loving me and that he wants me back. Can you believe it?" Lori snorted, and Jasmine's own grunt joined her friend's. "You want to hear something really pathetic? Even after everything that man has put me through, I still love him." The sadness in Lori's voice made Jasmine wish she were here, so she could give her friend a hug. "But love isn't enough, Jazz. I've learned that the hard way. So, be careful. If you see any sign of deception in Jack. Run!"

How many times had she thought that very same thing. That love wasn't enough.

"I'm sorry, Jazz. I don't mean to put a damper on your relationship with Jack, but just be careful, okay?"

Call waiting beeped in Jasmine's ear. "Hang on a sec, Lori. I need to answer the other line."

"Wait. I'll let you go. I need to get busy anyway. I have a meeting in a few minutes, so I'll just talk to you later. Happy Birthday."

"Thanks, Lori. Talk to you later. Bye."

Jasmine pushed the flash button and opened her mouth to speak but didn't get a chance.

"Happy Birthday, Sweetheart." Jack's deep voice wrapped around her like a caress. Daily she thanked God for healing him of his gunshot wound.

"Thank you, Jack. What are you up to?"

"Just checking to see if you changed your mind about letting me take you home."

Unlike before, she no longer resented his coddling. In fact, now she welcomed it. "No. But thanks. I need to do this on my own. I'm not afraid anymore. Especially after reading this morning's paper. Did you see where they caught the Peeping Tom?"

"No. I've been too busy. I haven't read the paper for weeks now. I'm so glad they found the guy. I'll sure sleep a lot better knowing you're safe and that he's sitting in jail where he belongs." There was a long pause on Jack's end and then a heavy sigh. "You sure you don't want me to go with you when you go home? I'd sure feel a lot better if you'd let me."

"I'm sure. Besides, I really do need to do this on my own."

"Okay. Even though I don't like it, I understand. Just thought I'd double check. I'll see you tonight then. Be ready, okay?"

"I will. I love you, Jack."

"Love you, too, sweetheart."

Jasmine disconnected the call, then dialed her granddad's number.

"Hey, Gramps."

"Hey, how's my favorite granddaughter?"

Jasmine giggled. "You say that to all three of your granddaughters."

Her granddad's low chuckle brought a smile to her face.

"I wanted to ask you something, Granddad."

"What's that, honey?"

"Have you decided if you're gonna sell the cabin? I finally have enough money saved to buy it if you do." How long she had waited to say those words, and yet she didn't feel near as excited as she thought she would saying them.

Silence.

"Granddad?"

He cleared his throat. "Umm, Jasmine, can we talk about this tomorrow? I'm kind of busy right now."

Something in his tone didn't settle quite right with

her. "Uh, okay." She flicked her thumbnail. "Well, I guess I'll talk to you later then. I love you, Granddad."

"I love you too, honey. Oh, and Happy Birthday."

"Thanks, Granddad. Bye." Jasmine's heart sunk to her toes as she hung up. Even though she didn't plan on moving to Louisiana, she still wanted to buy the lake house so she could visit it often—especially during the most frigid times of the year.

But maybe her granddad had decided not to sell the cabin after all and just didn't want to tell her. She quirked her mouth to one side. Well, she would have to wait until tomorrow to find out. Once her granddad said not right now, he meant not right now.

To keep her promise to Shanell, she punched in her sister's business number. "Shanell's Fine Cuisine, how may I help you?"

"Hey, Happy Birthday, sis!"

"Back at ya." They both giggled.

"Listen, I promised to let you know when I was getting ready to head out the door."

"You sure you're up for it?" The note of worry didn't bypass Jasmine.

"Yeah." Jasmine sighed.

"Uh-oh. What's wrong?"

Jasmine stared out the window. "Well, I just talked to Granddad about buying the cabin. He sounded strange and said he didn't want to talk about it now. What if he's decided not to sell it to me? I don't plan on moving there anymore, but it's still my dream to own it and spend time there." She shook her head at the thought of it slipping from her when it was so close. "I don't understand why he's putting me off."

"Because Jack bought it several months ago so you wouldn't."

Jasmine heard Shanell gasp.

Her skin prickled. "What? What do you mean Jack

bought it so I wouldn't?" Her words came out gruff and hard.

Shanell groaned. "Oh, no. Me and my big mouth. I'm so sorry, Jazz. I wasn't supposed to say anything. Jack didn't want you to know."

"I can't believe this! I gotta go." Stunned over what she'd just heard, Jasmine slammed the phone down. It was awful. Unthinkable really. Jack knew how badly she wanted that cabin. He knew it, and he'd gone behind her back anyway.

Madder than a swarm of angry hornets, with her suitcases already loaded in her SUV, Jasmine stormed over to the front door, snatched up Bougé's carrier, and out the door she flew.

How could he? She trusted him. Lori was right. Men truly couldn't be trusted. They're rescuing you one minute and stabbing you in the back the next.

She remembered overhearing Jack one time telling Chloe he'd do anything to keep Jasmine here. Well, when he said anything, he literally meant anything. How could he do this to her after she'd finally given her heart to him and decided she would rather stay in Steamboat Springs and be with him than live at her granddad's cabin without him? The man was no different than Steve.

Ignoring her ringing cell phone, Jasmine placed Bougé's carrier on the front seat, started her car, jammed it into gear, and headed for home. When Jack showed up at her house tonight, she'd be ready all right. But not the way he expected her to be.

Jasmine rushed Bougé into her house, fed and watered her, and as fast as she could, she jumped into her car and peeled out of her driveway.

Instead of the usual wall of snow lining Rabbit Ears Pass, only traces of winter remained amongst the tall pine and aspen trees. Green grass peeked through what little snow remained. Jasmine glanced at the bright, sunny sky.

Normally a drive like this cheered her up, but not today. Every time she hit a cell phone reception area, the incessant ringing of her phone drove her nuts.

Between being angry and hurt, she didn't want to speak to anyone. She refused to answer it, so she finally shut it off.

How could Jack and her granddad do this to her, knowing how much that place meant to her?

Lori's warning about if she saw any kind of deception in Jack she needed to run, kept flittering through her mind no matter how hard she tried for it not to.

On her way through Kremmling, she stopped at a rustic little coffee place and ordered a hot chocolate, topped with whipped cream and a drizzle of chocolate syrup and a blueberry scone. After getting her order, Jasmine straddled a wooden bar stool and set her stuff on the wooden slab. It reminded her of Jack's breakfast nook. Jack. Humpft. Fresh anger rose inside her. She broke off a piece of scone, shoved it into her mouth, and chomped down hard. The rich buttery flavor filled her mouth. She only wished she could enjoy it like she usually did, but she was just too frustrated to.

Maybe shopping at the Factory outlet stores in Summit County would calm her down. She gathered her stuff and got back into her vehicle. In forty-five minutes she'd be cruising through all the stores, starting in Silverthorne first.

She wanted to buy some more gifts for her sisters anyway. Hopefully their birthday was going better than hers.

Jack paced Jasmine's porch and glanced at his watch again. 5:35. "Where are you, Jasmine? Don't tell me you ran away again. I thought you trusted me by now." His words disappeared in the breeze. He stuck his hands in his pants pocket and continued pacing.

Earlier, when Shanell called and told him what she'd done, he had to force himself not to tell the woman off. But he didn't because he was the one who made the mistake of telling her about buying the cabin in the first place, knowing she had a tendency to blab. Not on purpose mind you. It just seemed to blurt out of her.

As soon as he'd hung up with Shanell, he'd darted out of his office and driven like a madman to Jasmine's house, only to find her not there.

All day long he kept calling. He left message after message, begging her to trust him and give him a chance to explain. It hurt to know she still didn't trust him. Did she really think he would steal her dream?

"Where is she?" Jack glanced at his watch again. 5:42. He reached for his cell phone and tried calling her again.

"Hi, it's me, Jasmine. Well, it's not really me, but my voice message. Anyway, please leave a message after that annoying little beep we all love so much. Thanks. Have a great day."

A great day? That was stretching it.

He ended the call and slowly shook his head. Stan had warned him that his plan could backfire. Boy, was he right. Did it ever.

All Jack could do now was pray for a miracle. He was going to need one.

CHAPTER TWENTY-SEVEN

At ten minutes till six, Jasmine pulled into her driveway. Seeing Jack's silver Porsche revived her anger, and she couldn't wait to give him a piece of her mind. She'd never trust him again. And to think she would have stayed here just to be with him. What a fool she'd been. What he did was downright inexcusable. Appalling. Despicable.

She had barely shut the engine off before Jack yanked her door open.

"Where have you been? I've been trying to reach you all day. Didn't you get my messages?"

"I got them," she replied coolly. "Could you please move so I can get out?"

Even though she could tell he was stunned, he stepped back to let her out. "Jasmine, it's not what you think."

She whirled on him. "You know what I think? I think you men are all alike. Lori warned me men were selfish. That they couldn't be trusted and only thought of themselves. That they would stop at nothing to get what they wanted. She was right. But no-o-o. I thought I could trust you. That you were different. I even convinced myself we wouldn't end up like Lori and Steve."

"Lori and Steve? What do they have to do with this?"

"Everything," she retorted. "Steve robbed the two things that meant the most to Lori. His love, and working for the largest publishing house in New York. A dream she spent her whole life pursuing, and Steve knew that before they got married.

"He even made all these promises to her before they

walked down the aisle, that he would do whatever it took to support her dream. Yeah right," Jasmine snorted. "Lori never knew it, until it was too late, that Steve hated living in New York. But rather than tell her, he figured the best thing to do was to get her fired. So, he had an affair with her boss, and talked her into firing Lori so they could be together without Lori in the way.

"Once he got her fired, Steve dropped her boss like a hot coal. Lori never knew about the affair, until her job called her, asking her if she would like to come back, and that her ex-boss had gotten the axe because they found out she'd had an affair with not only Lori's husband, but another office gal's husband as well. That was the first Lori had heard about the affair. She was at my house at the time, visiting. I can still see her face when she got the news."

Jasmine closed her eyes, trying to blot the memory of Lori lying on Jasmine's couch in her living room, with an empty bottle of her prescription pain pills lying next to Lori's hand. To this day, Jasmine still blamed herself. She'd only been in the bathroom a few minutes. But that was all the time Lori needed to down Jasmine's pills.

"I shudder to think what would have happened if she would have been alone. She was so devastated she took a whole bottle of pills." Jasmine couldn't bring herself to tell him they were her pills.

"Wait. What? Lori tried to kill herself?" Shock rippled across his face. "When was this? Where was I?"

She swallowed back the memory that still tormented her. Every time Jasmine thought about what Steve did to Lori, and what Lori's misery had led her to do, her stomach twisted with agony. And her anger escalated. If only she would have listened to Lori's warnings. All of this could have been avoided, if she had. And now, she too was left with the ugly truth of what dire lengths men would go through to get what they wanted.

Her own fears were fast becoming a reality.

She never answered Jack's questions. Instead, she paced back and forth, watching the ground, waving her hands in the air. "I knew if I allowed myself to fall in love with you that this would happen. And I was right."

"What do you mean?"

She stopped in front of him and shot him a look filled with disdain. "You took the one thing that meant the world to me too." Two actually, his love being one of them. But she was too angry to give him any more ammunition with which to hurt her.

"How could you even compare me with Steve? I'm nothing like him." He sounded angry. Well, she was angry too.

"Did or did you not buy my granddad's cabin just to keep me here?"

Pain, hurt, and disappointment marched across his face. "Do you really think that's why I bought the cabin?"

"Yes. I do. Shanell said you bought it so I wouldn't." She plunked her hands on her hips. "What else am I supposed to think?"

He ran his hand through his hair. "You're wrong, Jasmine. But if that's how you really feel about me, and you have no more faith in me than that, then I need to go." He paused, anger flashed from his eyes. "Here. I have no use for this." Jack wrapped her hand around a card-size purple envelope. "Now you have everything you need. Or want." He let go with a tight smile. "Happy Birthday."

He turned, and strode to his vehicle, got in, and drove away.

Jasmine watched him leave. Somehow she thought she would feel better after telling him off, but she didn't. In a huff, she went inside and closed the door. Tossing the envelope on the end table, she plopped down on the loveseat.

Even though she was livid with Jack for buying her granddad's cabin, and he'd barely just left, she already missed him.

She missed his presence.

His smile.

And the way her heart lit up whenever he was near.

How would she live without him?

Lori said love wasn't enough. But Jasmine wasn't so sure she agreed with Lori anymore. In fact, she wasn't sure about a lot of things.

Jasmine knew without a doubt that if Steve hadn't cheated on all three of his wives, Lori would take him back in a heartbeat because she still loved him.

And Jasmine admitted, if she had just a little less willpower, she wouldn't hesitate to take Jack back either.

Didn't the Bible say, love covers a multitude of sins, and love doesn't take into account a wrong suffered?

But had Jack wronged her, or had she wronged him?

He did say she was wrong, and it wouldn't be the first time. And she hadn't given him a chance to explain himself.

Surely she hadn't allowed her fears to overrule her better judgment again, had she? With a sigh, she realized that her swift temper and unwillingness to look at life from anyone's perspective other than her own might once again have led her down a less-than-helpful path. Hadn't she learned anything at the lake?

Yes. Yes, she had. She had learned her dreams and goals weren't more important than her loved ones. Than Jack.

And she had learned that heeding the opinion of those who love you often was better than going off your own direction to prove everybody else wrong.

"Dear God, what have I done? How could I have been so cruel in hurting him like that? And after all he's done for me. He's not selfish like Steve. Steve would have never driven all the way to Louisiana to risk his life for Lori. And yet Jack did. In fact, Jack is always putting me first. What an ugly thing fear and anger are, Lord. They keep you from those you love." Jasmine put her head in her hands and wept. "Help me, Lord. Please help me to let go of this ugliness inside of me—especially toward Jack. And the fear of being hurt, the fear of being smothered, and the anger that tears everything that's good in my life apart." Then she grew quiet and listened for His still small voice to speak to her, something she had done a lot more of since her ordeal with Simon.

Faith is the substance of things hoped for and the evidence of things not seen.

His Word hit her with the force of a sledgehammer. She swiped at her tears as a fresh revelation washed over her. "I see it, Lord. I didn't have any faith in Jack or in You. I've always wanted some sort of guarantee that what happened to Lori and Steve wouldn't happen to Jack and me, and I've acted irrational because of that fear. Once again, all I thought about was what I was going through and how it would affect me. I never once thought about how this was affecting Jack or even stopped long enough to consider any of this from his point of view. All I saw was mine. Forgive me, Father, for being so selfish. What do I do now?"

Go to him.

"Go to him? Will he want anything to do with me after the horrible way I've treated him?"

The just shall live by faith.

"You're right, Lord. This is a step of faith, and I'm going to take it." She snatched up her keys and flew out the door. She drove so fast she pulled up in Jack's driveway nearly right behind him. Unsure of the reception she'd receive, she strode up to him just as he climbed out of his vehicle.

He stared at her with no expression whatsoever.

"I'm so sorry, Jack." She touched his arm as she beat back the emotions crowding in over her. "I am. I'm so sorry for everything. Can you ever forgive me for the horrible things I said?"

Jack picked up her hand and let it drop. "I really thought we had a future together. But without trust, there is nothing to build a relationship on." His gaze dropped, and when it came up, it was empty. Devoid of love. "It's over, Jasmine. You need to leave now."

Before he brushed past her and headed toward his house, she caught a glimpse of pain dashing through his eyes.

Jasmine stared at his back, and tears trickled down her cheeks.

He stopped, turned, and looked back at her. "Enjoy your cabin." He whirled and walked off again.

She swiped under her eyes, frowning. "What do you mean, 'enjoy your cabin'? You own it. Remember?" she hollered after him.

Jack halted. Cocking his head, he reeled around, and eyed her with a scowl. "Didn't you open the card I gave you?"

"No." She shook her head and chewed on her thumbnail. Her focus dropped toward her feet. "I felt so bad for the way I treated you, I tossed it on the end table and started praying."

Within seconds, Jack was standing in front of her.

She looked up at him, embarrassed and chastened. "You're right. I *was* comparing you to Steve, and I had no right to do that. I didn't have any faith in you or God. But now I see how wrong I was." She stared at his polished cowboy boots. "I never meant to hurt you or to misjudge you like that. It's just that I was so afraid of losing you and ending up like them that—" She shrugged. "Without realizing it until now, I was protecting myself from getting hurt by running you off. I'm sorry, Jack. For everything."

"So, let me get this straight... you haven't opened the envelope that I gave you?" His look held disbelief along with a tinge of excitement.

After all she had just shared with him, that was all he could say? "I said I didn't. What's that got to do with anything?" Jasmine couldn't keep her frustration from coming through her voice.

Before she even knew what was happening, Jack scooped her into his arms and swung her around. "Ah, baby. You do trust me." His mouth found hers.

Jasmine buried herself in the passion of his heated kiss. It seemed like forever ago since their last kiss. As his lips continued to embrace hers, he slowly lowered her until her feet touched the ground, which she barely noticed because his enchanting kiss had her floating on a cloud of elation.

When he released her mouth, she instantly felt the loss, and her senses returned to earth. "Did—did I miss something?" Her voice was hoarse.

"C'mon," he rasped through short breaths. He grabbed her hand and led her to his vehicle. "Slide in."

Still reeling, she obeyed. The feel of his pillowy soft lips and the taste of his cinnamon gum still lingered on her lips.

Jack lowered his large frame into his Porsche, the one he used only for special occasions, and his body filled most of the car's interior. His nearness wreaked havoc with her already heightened senses. He fired up the engine and tore out of his driveway.

Jack rushed through all four gears, then slipped his arm around her, pulling her as close as he could without pulling her onto the console that separated them. She, however, gave no regard to that annoying hump and snuggled her head against his shoulder. Where he was taking her, she had no idea, but she didn't care either. She was in Jack's arms, and she never wanted to leave them again.

When Jack pulled in her driveway, her brows knit together. Wherever she had thought they were going, this wasn't it.

He shut off the engine, hopped out of his car, and ran around to her side of the vehicle. "What are you doing?" she asked as he swung open her door.

"Come on." He tugged her out and led her to the door like a little boy leading his daddy to a surprise. "Give me your key."

"Jack, my keys are in my car. I didn't have a chance to grab them."

O Jack mouthed, then chuckled.

"Have you forgotten that you have a key?"

"Oh, yeah." A sheepish smile curled his lips. Jack was clearly up to something. He had never been scatterbrained a day in his life. He pulled the key ring out of his pocket and opened her door. Once inside, he went to the end table and picked up the card.

"Here, open this." His face glowed .

Jasmine ran her finger under the envelope seal and slid the card out. Something fell to the floor.

Jack picked it up. "Read the card first."

Attached to the card with a purple ribbon was a dainty gold chain with a diamond heart set in an elegant key. "Oh, Jack, it's beautiful." She gave him a quick peck on the cheek and read the card.

Jack nodded at the card. "Out loud."

"To my dearest, Jazzy." Her heart filled with happiness. "Happy Birthday. This necklace is a reminder that you hold the key to my heart. My love belongs to you, now and forever. Now, open envelope number two. I want to give you another key."

She held the necklace up and sighed. "It's so beautiful, Jack." Tears slipped down her cheeks.

Jack brushed them away with his thumb. He leaned down and fastened his lips to hers in a sweet caress. "Just like you." His husky voice whispered against her lips. He cleared his throat and handed her the second envelope, along with a key.

She noticed a purple bold number two inscribed on the front. Clutching the key, she ripped open the envelope, pulled out its contents and gasped. In her hand she held the deed to her granddad's cabin—in her name.

"Oh, no." The date on the deed, blurred through her tears. "January first," she whispered. "You did this months ago." Shame washed over her until she couldn't even look at him.

He took both of her hands in his. "I wanted this to be a fresh start for you—for us." The low timbre of his soft voice sent shudders rippling through her. He exhaled, then reached in his pocket. "This wasn't the setting I had planned, but—" He handed her an envelope with a purple three on it.

After laying the key and deed on the table, she opened it with unsteady fingers.

In the envelope, neatly tucked on a piece of purple tissue, set an antique ring. And not just any antique. "Grandmother's engagement ring." Her words came out in a broken whisper. More tears spilled over her eyelids. "How did you know I always wanted this?"

"Because I know you." His soft voice flowed with love. Jack took her hand in his and read the words on the card, "Now that you hold the key to my heart and the key to your granddad's cabin, allow me the privilege of claiming and holding the key to *your* heart forever." He got down on one knee. "Jasmine, will you marry me?"

Jasmine stared into his tender, hazel, love-filled eyes. The joy in her heart burst with overflowing love.

"Wait. Before you answer..." Jack rose, holding her gaze and her hands captive. "I know how much you hate the cold, so I've expanded my business to Lake Boomingtown, and I bought your granddad's cabin in hopes we could live there—together. That is, if you'll have me."

"Oh, Jack."

His unselfish gesture sent a new wave of shame over every fiber of her being. Not only had Jack bought the cabin for her, but he had expanded his business there too. She turned away in utter humiliation.

Jack coaxed her around and tilted her head to look at him. "Jasmine?" Confusion and fear shrouded his face. "Did I do something wrong?"

"Wrong. Oh, no, no." She shook her head. "It's just—after the way I treated you... Oh Jack, I don't deserve you." She sniffed.

He pulled her into his arms. She buried her head in his chest as the tears spilled from her eyes.

"Don't you know I love you, Jazz? That's all that matters. The past is just that, the past. It's behind us." He cupped her chin with his finger and gazed into her eyes. "This is the day for new beginnings. The past is gone, over with, done."

She tried to smile but only more tears came. "Thank you. Oh, Jack. I love you so much. I want to marry you more than anything in this world." Her eyes roamed over his handsome face. "We don't have to live at Granddad's cabin. We can stay right here. As long as I'm with you, I don't care where we live." She cupped his face with her hands and pulled his lips toward hers. "I love you," she whispered on a sigh. "I love you so much." She kissed him again, only this time, with all the love she had for him.

When the kiss ended, Jack slipped her grandmother's engagement ring on her finger and kissed her hand. His strong arms slipped around her, pressing her against him. He whispered against her lips, "I love you so much,

Jasmine." He claimed her mouth then. His tender, loving kiss sealed their love and offered her the promise of more to come.

EPILOGUE

Months had passed since Jack had asked Jasmine to marry him. Jasmine thought her heart would burst with happiness. The last of the wedding guests had gone. Jack swung her into his arms, carried her to the massive oak tree, and lowered them both onto the L-shaped limb. Seated on his lap, Jack settled her into him as they faced the lake at her granddad's cabin. No, make that their cabin.

Cuddled together, they stared across Lake Boomingtown at the full moon. Shimmering orange light danced across the water, and love danced across Jasmine's heart.

The August heat warmed her body, but Jack warmed her spirit, soul, and body.

She sighed dreamily.

As far as Jasmine was concerned, life didn't get any better than this. No one could ask for a more romantic setting to spend their wedding night. And in just three short days they would be flying to the Bahamas for two glorious sun-filled weeks.

God had truly blessed her. First, with a magnificent sunrise wedding with all her friends and family, secondly with an all day reception on a rented yacht sailing across Lake Bloomington, and thirdly, with a beautiful honeymoon night in the very place where she had discovered some of the most valuable lessons of her life.

That people can be content living any place where love, faith, and hope abide. And she now had all three.

It was that same deep abiding love that had also led the two of them to a compromise that would satisfy both of their dreams and goals. They had decided to spend their married life between the two places. That way Jack could keep an eye on both businesses, and she would get a break from the dreary winters and the excruciating pain that accompanied them.

Thank you, Lord, for working everything out to everyone's good. But, I especially praise you for Jack.

She turned loving eyes up at her newly wedded husband.

"I love you so very dearly, Mr. Jackson Neil Warren."

"I love you with every inch of my being, Mrs. Jasmine Rose Warren."

Mrs. Warren. Liking the sound of that, she smiled and melted into her husband's embrace. His mouth covered hers, and love poured through his kisses. Jasmine was finally home. And that home was in Jack's arms.

Dear Reader,

While the Internet is the tool that was used in this novel, the story was never intended to bash Internet relationships. I myself have met many wonderful people online. The intent of this story was to show how Jasmine had been forewarned numerous times by not only God, but by Jack and others, as well. Jasmine chalked up their warnings to other things. Even when her gut or her spirit jangled, she truly believed it was nerves about doing something new and exciting, or too much chocolate. Eventually, her own wants and desires overshadowed God's warnings and of those around her, and she nearly paid the ultimate price for ignoring those warnings. Only when it was too late did she wish she had listened to them and that she had prayed for God's will instead of stubbornly pursing her own.

In my own life, I've been guilty of that very same thing and sometimes I still am. Numerous times, when I was about to do or say something, a pit would plunk into my gut, or my spirit would jangle nervously, or God's still small voice would warn me. When I didn't take heed, it almost always came back to haunt me. One of those times, I had a gut feeling not to go to a certain place. I convinced myself I was just being fearful and to go ahead and go because God would take care of me. Well, I should've listened. Our brand-spanking-new truck was wrecked not just once but twice within an hour because I didn't listen. God tried to warn me, but I wanted to go, and I did, disregarding His warning. There have been several other incidences in my life like this as I'm sure there have been in yours. All we can do is learn from those times and try to pay attention and take heed the next time. It is my prayer that this story will serve as a reminder to listen to that still small voice the next time you feel that way about something.

I hope you enjoyed reading Jasmine's story.

Thank you.

God bless you and yours,

Debra Ullrick

Other Books by Debra Ullrick

Groom Wanted

It's a perfect plan-best friends Leah Bowen and Jake Lure will each advertise for mail-order spouses in the papers, and then Jake will help select Leah's future husband, while Leah picks Jake's bride-to-be! Surely the ads will find them what they seek: a wife who'll appreciate Jake's shy charm and a groom who'll take Leah away from the Idaho Territory she detests.

When the responses to the postings pour in, it seems all Leah's and Jake's dreams will soon come true. But the closer they each get to the altar, the less appealing marrying a stranger becomes. Is it too late to turn back- or to turn around and find the happiness they truly seek together, at last?

The Unexpected Bride

After the disaster of his first marriage, Haydon Bowen has no intention of marrying again. Unfortunately, his brother has some intentions of his own, and plans to see to it that Haydon finds happiness once more. So he answers a "groom wanted" advertisement—in Haydon's name—and sends Haydon to meet his new bride at the stagecoach stop!

For beautiful, cultured Rainelle Devonwood, any dangers she may face in the Idaho Territories are preferable to staying with her abusive brother. So even when Rainee learns she's a mistakenly ordered bride, she won't let Haydon drive her away. She's up to the challenge of life on the difficult, demanding frontier...and the great challenge of opening Haydon's heart again.

www.DebraUllrick.com

The Unlikely Wife

The arrival of Michael Bowen's bride, married sight unseen by proxy, sends the rancher reeling. With her trousers, cowboy hat and rifle, she looks like a female outlaw—*not* the genteel lady he corresponded with for months. He's been hoodwinked into marriage with the wrong woman!

Selina Farleigh Bowen loved Michael's letters, even if she couldn't read them herself. A friend read them to her, and wrote her replies—but apparently that "friend" left things out, like Michael's dream of a wife who was nothing like her. Selina won't change who she is, not even for the man she loves. Yet time might show Michael the true value of his unlikely wife.

A Log Cabin Christmas
A New York Times & CBA Bestseller

Experience Christmas through the eyes of adventuresome settlers who relied on log cabins built from trees on their own land to see them through the cruel forces of winter. Discover how rough-hewed shelters become a home in which faith, hope, and love can flourish. Marvel in the blessings of Christmas celebrations without the trappings of modern commercialism where the true meaning of the day shines through. And treasure this exclusive collection of nine Christmas romances penned by some of Christian fiction's best-selling authors.

Also By Debra Ullrick

The Unintended Groom
Colorado Courtship (The Rancher's Sweetheart) Anthology
with Cheryl St. John
Christmas Belles of Georgia
Dixie Hearts
The Bride Wore Coveralls
Déjà vu Bride
Reunited at Christmas
A Dozen Apologies
Catch Me If You Can (2014)